ERLE STANLEY GARDNER

- Cited by the Guinness Book of World Records as the #1 bestselling writer of all time!

- Author of more than 150 clever, authentic, and sophisticated mystery novels!

- Creator of the amazing Perry Mason, the savvy Della Street, and dynamite detective Paul Drake!

- THE ONLY AUTHOR WHO OUTSELLS AGATHA CHRISTIE, HAROLD ROBBINS, BARBARA CARTLAND, AND LOUIS L'AMOUR *COMBINED!*

Why?

Because he writes the best, most fascinating whodunits of all!

You'll want to read every one of them, coming soon from BALLANTINE BOOKS

Also by Erle Stanley Gardner
Published by Ballantine Books:

THE CASE OF THE BEAUTIFUL BEGGAR

THE CASE OF THE LAZY LOVER

THE CASE OF THE FIERY FINGER

THE CASE OF THE SHAPELY SHADOW

THE CASE OF THE HAUNTED HUSBAND

THE CASE OF THE GRINNING GORILLA

THE CASE OF THE VAGABOND VIRGIN

The Case of the Restless Redhead

Erle Stanley Gardner

BALLANTINE BOOKS • NEW YORK

ISBN 0-345-30395-4

This edition published by arrangement with
William Morrow and Company, Inc.

Manufactured in the United States of America

First Ballantine Books Edition: May 1982

FOREWORD

OF ALL PROFESSIONAL MEN, THE DOCTOR OF MEDICINE is called upon to do his work under the most adverse circumstances.

The lawyer may take days to look up an important problem on which he is called to give advice. The engineer figures stresses, strains and gradients with the aid of a slide rule and reference tables. But the doctor is called in the dead of night, aroused from a sound sleep and confronted with an emergency in which immediate action must be taken and highly specialized knowledge applied. The doctor has to carry his knowledge at his finger tips.

The doctor is always haunted by the knowledge that some patient may turn on him, magnifying any unforeseen result, any complication which could not possibly have been anticipated, into the basis of a lawsuit.

It is hardly comforting to think that property which a doctor has acquired through years of effort may be snatched from him overnight by a designing patient who can tearfully appeal to the whims of a susceptible jury.

I have had doctors tell me that when they are driving and come upon the scene of an automobile accident they would like to stop and say, "I am a doctor. May I be of service?" They could then give immediate emergency treatment to the extent of their ability. They tell me they don't dare to do it.

Some of the patients would be grateful, but probably one out of ten of the injured persons would see a heaven-sent opportunity. He would say, "This was not a doctor of my choosing. I didn't call him. He gratuitously injected himself into the picture and started giving treatment without my consent."

It is perhaps only one out of ten injured persons who would take this action, but experience shows that in something like eight or nine times out of ten the injured person would toss into the wastebasket any bill the doctor might send for professional services. He might perhaps be grateful but he would say, "I didn't call this doctor. He just happened to be there. Why should I pay him anything?"

According to simple mathematics, therefore, a doctor treating ten patients would receive not more than ten dollars by way of compensation and would probably find himself faced with at least one lawsuit for malpractice in which the "aggrieved" person would ask for anywhere from one thousand to two hundred thousand dollars.

It doesn't take a trained mathematician to figure those percentages. Reduce them to odds and it's easy to see why so many doctors don't dare to offer help.

I know some doctors who make it a point of professional honor to treat persons who are injured in automobile accidents, but when I asked one of these doctors what percentage of injured persons paid him, he looked at me in surprise and said, "I never even send them a bill. It's a waste of postage."

Now obviously this is not right. There needs to be a stronger bulwark between the reputable, conscientious members of the medical profession and the hazard of legal liabilities.

There are, of course, quacks and incompetents who make mistakes which are not honest mistakes but are the result of negligence, ignorance and incompetence. Those people should be weeded out of the medical profession. Medical associations are getting rid of those people quite rapidly. Another way to get rid of them is to make them pay for their mistakes.

But the honest, competent, conscientious doctor should have some assurance that as long as he is doing a competent job he is not going to be harassed by litigation, subjected to unpleasant notoriety, and forced to spend much of his time in court trying to keep from being penalized.

Obviously this is a field which needs the co-operation of the best legal and medical minds in the country. It is a field where, in all probability, there needs to be some legislative reform and there must be a great deal of clarification as to the rights and liabilities of the various parties.

It is, in short, an important and unfortunately a neglected area of legal medicine.

One of the outstanding authorities among the specialists in this field is my friend, Dr. Louis J. Regan. Dr. Regan is both a doctor and a lawyer. He has an analytical, keenly incisive mind, and a comprehensive knowledge of both his subjects. He is a past-president of the American Academy of Forensic Sciences, is one of the outstanding figures in legal medicine, and is the author of a book entitled *Doctor and Patient and the Law*. He is also the author of *Medical Malpractice*—both published by C. V. Mosby. In addition to these two authoritative books Dr. Regan is the author of more than 150 articles published in American journals. He is a past-president of the Los Angeles County Medical Association and of the Hollywood Academy of Medicine.

Quietly, unostentatiously and diligently he is working for a clarification of the law so that patients will be protected from the negligent, incompetent and unskillful practitioner while the honest, conscientious, capable doctor will in turn be protected from speculative lawsuits brought by chiseling patients in the hope that someone will settle for the "nuisance" value and they can make the down payment on a new car.

This branch of legal medicine calls for highly specialized knowledge both in law and in medicine. It also calls for patience, for understanding, vision and sound judgment.

Dr. Regan has made many valuable contributions in this field.

And so I dedicate this book to my friend:

Louis J. Regan, M.D., LL.B.

Erle Stanley Gardner

CAST OF CHARACTERS

PERRY MASON—The discerning peer among attorneys does it again 1

FRANK NEELY—The obviously self-conscious, young lawyer who is taught the circuitous ways of legal maneuvering by a past master 1

HARRY BOLES—An important star witness who is hopelessly miscast and portrays the part 1

JUDGE DILLARD—Although a stern upholder of the law, he enjoys adroit legal strategy 5

DELLA STREET—Who operates with an acuteness which is part of her woman's intuition 18

EVELYN BAGBY—The restless redhead, with a consuming desire to become an actress, unwittingly plays her most important role 19

IRENE KEITH—Her glowing personality was a bit too overwhelming for the dignity of a drab law office 40

MERVYN ALDRICH—The punctual, broad-shouldered, slim-waisted bridegroom with a crisp, chairman-of-the-board manner 44

PAUL DRAKE—Efficient head of the Drake Detective Agency whose timely hunches usually pay off .. 49

BILL FERRON—Deputy Sheriff, a tenacious stickler for the facts 79

1

SINCE THERE HAD BEEN LESS TRAFFIC THAN PERRY MAson had anticipated, the lawyer parked his car in front of the big gray courthouse at Riverside a full thirty minutes before his noon appointment with Judge Dillard.

There was a chance that the case, which Judge Dillard had explained over the phone might occupy the entire morning and perhaps a part of the afternoon, would have been disposed of sooner than contemplated so that Judge Dillard would be free. Mason, therefore, walked down the wide corridor to the swinging mahogany doors with Judge Dillard's name on them and entered the courtroom.

The trial was in progress. A young attorney, obviously self-conscious, was standing by the defense counsel table, apparently at a loss as to just what to say next.

The witness, seated at ease in the witness chair, waited for the next question.

The jury seemed slightly bored.

Mason eased his long frame into a seat at the rear of the courtroom.

"Now then, Mr. Boles," the young attorney said, "it was dark, wasn't it?"

The witness smiled at the lawyer. "What was dark?"

"Why, the night."

"The night was dark, but the street was lighted."

"What do you mean, it was lighted?"

"There was a light at the corner."

"And that light gave you sufficient illumination?"

"It gave the street sufficient illumination."

"So that you could see?"

"So that I could see."

"Could see what?"

"I saw the defendant, Evelyn Bagby, taking a suitcase out of the back of that automobile. She put the suitcase down on the ground, bent over, opened the suitcase, took out something—"

"Yes, yes," the attorney interrupted impatiently. "You've told us all that before."

"Well, you asked me what I saw. I thought you wanted me to tell you again."

"No, not what you *surmised* the defendant was doing. I want to know what you *saw* her doing."

"I saw her open the compartment at the back of the car. I saw her take out a suitcase. I saw her put it on the ground. I saw her open the suitcase."

"Her back was toward you?"

"Yes."

"Then you couldn't have seen her *open* the suitcase."

"I saw her bend over the suitcase. I saw her hands on the lid of the suitcase. I saw the lid of the suitcase come up. I don't know how else to describe it."

"You couldn't see what she took out?"

"That I couldn't."

The young lawyer lowered his eyes to the counsel table, bent over a file, thumbed aimlessly through notes, apparently trying to think of some question he could ask which wouldn't make his case worse than it already was.

Members of the jury looked at each other, at the clock, let their attention wander around the courtroom.

Judge Dillard caught Mason's eye, looked at the clock and nodded. Mason bowed his head, indicating that his time was entirely at the disposal of the court.

"At that time you didn't know who owned the automobile, did you?" the attorney demanded of the witness.

"No, sir, I did not."

"When did you find out who owned the automobile?"

"After the defendant had left I started wondering—"

"Never mind what you were wondering or what you thought," the lawyer interrupted hastily. "Just tell us when you found out who owned the automobile."

"When the police told me."

"Did you go to the police, or did they come to you?"

"I went to them. I heard about the theft on the radio. As soon as I heard that—"

"Never mind what you heard. Just confine your answer to the question."

"Very well."

The lawyer sat down in the chair at the counsel table, turned to his client, a young woman somewhere in her twenties with red hair and clothes which somehow managed to sag in the wrong places. At one time her suit had been cut along stylish lines, but the cheap material couldn't hold its shape and seemed to be as hopeless as the expression on the young woman's face.

There was a brief, whispered conference.

The attorney once more looked through his notes.

"Any further questions on cross-examination?" Judge Dillard asked kindly.

The young lawyer glanced at the clock, then once more got to his feet.

"How do you *know* it was the defendant?" he asked the witness.

"I saw her."

"What did you see?"

"I saw the way she was dressed. I saw her face."

"Did you get a good look at her face?"

"Good enough."

"What do you mean, good enough?"

"Good enough to recognize her."

"How far were you from her?"

"I've told you over and over, at the time she took these things from the car I was about fifty or seventy-five feet away."

"You never at any time were closer to her than that?"

"Not while she was opening the suitcase. Afterward, however, she turned and walked toward me."

"What was she wearing?"

"As nearly as I can recall she was wearing the clothes she has on at the present time, plus a plaid coat with a fur collar."

"What kind of a coat?"

"A coat similar to that which has been introduced in evidence. To the best of my knowledge it was the same coat that's hanging on the hanger over there."

The witness pointed to a long, full-skirted coat hanging on a wire coat hanger from the edge of the blackboard. A tag on the coat indicated it had been introduced in evidence. The blackboard contained a diagram drawn in chalk, freehand, which had apparently been used to illustrate the testimony of a witness.

"What was the defendant doing when you *first* noticed her."

"Opening the trunk compartment in the back of the car."

"Did she have a key?"

"I don't know.

"You didn't see her fumbling with the lock?"

"The first time I began really to notice her was when she raised the lid of the trunk compartment."

"Then what?"

"Then she took out the suitcase, put it on the ground and bent over it."

"What do you mean by saying she bent over it? Can you describe that action a little better? Suppose you illustrate what you mean."

The witness wearily got up from the chair, bent over, stiff-legged, and extended his arms.

"Like that," he said.

"Her back was toward you?"

"Yes."

"And what did you notice?"

The witness settled himself back in the witness chair. He grinned. "To tell the truth, I noticed her legs."

There was a titter in the courtroom. Even Judge Dillard smiled slightly.

"Good-looking legs?" the young lawyer asked, seeking to relieve the tension.

"Very good-looking legs."

"And then what?"

"I saw her take something out of the suitcase, then she closed the lid of the suitcase, straightened and put the suitcase back in the trunk of the automobile."

The lawyer glanced at the jury, then at the clock, worried his underlip with his teeth, seemed hopelessly undecided.

Judge Dillard came to his rescue. "I feel," he said, "that it is evident the case will go to the jury today and the Court notices that Mr. Mason, an out-of-town lawyer, is waiting with some papers to be signed. It is now fifteen minutes before twelve, but if there is no objection, we will take a recess until two o'clock this afternoon."

The district attorney said wearily, "Could we perhaps conclude the cross-examination of this witness before recess, Your Honor?"

Judge Dillard glanced at the young lawyer.

"If the Court please," the lawyer said, "I feel that I have only one or two more questions to ask this witness, but I would much prefer to confer with my client during the noon hour. The Court will remember that this is an assigned case, and I confess that I—"

"Very well," Judge Dillard said. "The Court will take a recess until two o'clock this afternoon. During this recess the jury will remember the admonition heretofore given by the Court and will not discuss the case among yourselves or permit anyone to discuss it in your presence, nor will you inform or express any opinion until the case is finally submitted to you. Court is adjourned."

Judge Dillard arose and walked to his chambers.

The dozen or so spectators shuffled from the courtroom. The district attorney gathered up papers, dropped them into his brief case. The young lawyer paused for a few words with his client, then a deputy sheriff stepped forward to escort the dejected young woman to the jail.

A brunette with dark, smoldering eyes, tall, lithe, who had occupied an aisle seat, put her hands on the young lawyer's arm. "Oh, Frank," she said in a low, vibrant voice, "you were *wonderful!*"

Mason, walking past the couple on his way to the judge's chambers, saw the young lawyer flush.

Then Mason opened the door to the judge's chambers to find Judge Dillard lighting a cigar.

"Hello, Mason," the judge said. "Sorry to keep you waiting."

"You didn't," Mason said. "I was early. What's the case?"

The judge shook his head. "It bothers me."

"Why?"

"Oh, it's one of those open-and-shut things. I guess the defendant is guilty all right, but you—well, hang it, it bothers you when you're on the bench."

"An assigned case?"

"That's right. I appointed Frank Neely. His father is a businessman here in town, and Frank is a good boy. I've known him for years and known his father nearly all of my life. Frank is a fine young lawyer, but there are some things a man learns only by experience—cross-examination for instance."

"You have doubts about the identification made by the witness on the stand?" Mason asked.

Judge Dillard paused to weigh his answer. "I *always* have doubts about too pat an identification. In the present case there's something irritating in the patronizing manner of that witness.

"As you know, in these assigned cases it's a custom to

appoint the young lawyers and let them get experience that way. The older lawyers are busy. They resent assigned cases. That's the way the younger men get experience. Oh well, you have some papers you want signed in that Dalton case?"

"That's right."

Mason opened his brief case, pulled out a sheaf of papers. Judge Dillard sat at his desk, glanced hurriedly through the papers, affixed his signature.

"How about lunch?" Mason asked.

"I'm sorry, I have a lunch engagement," Judge Dillard said. "I made it several days ago before you called up. I wish I'd known you were coming. How are things in the big city?"

"So-so."

"I see that you still continue your meteoric career, pulling rabbits out of the hat at the last minute. How do you do it?"

Mason grinned. "I don't know. I just reach in the hat. That's my contribution. The rabbit jumps into my hand."

Judge Dillard chuckled. "Lawyers around here think you must keep rabbits up your sleeves."

"Well," Mason said, "I try to believe in my cases and in my clients. That helps."

Judge Dillard glanced at his watch, shook hands. "I certainly wish I were free. You don't get up this way very often."

"Not often," Mason admitted. "They keep me busy in my own bailiwick."

"I follow your cases in the newspapers," Judge Dillard told him, "and get a terrific kick out of them."

Mason thanked him and walked out to find the young lawyer sitting dejectedly at the defendant's counsel table in the deserted courtroom, studying his notes.

He glanced up, caught Mason's eye, nodded somewhat

dubiously, looked away, then impulsively pushed his chair back and came toward Mason.

"Mr. Mason!"

The tall lawyer paused. "Yes?" he asked.

"My name's Neely. Frank Neely. I just wanted to shake hands with you. I didn't have any idea *you* were in court until Judge Dillard mentioned it, and then I recognized you from your photographs. I just wanted to tell you that I've always—well, I've admired you and thought many times of how— Well, I just wanted to shake hands, that's all."

"Thanks," Mason said. "How are you coming with your case?"

"Not very well, I'm afraid."

"What's the trouble?" Mason asked.

"I only wish I knew," Neely told him, "but I just can't seem to get anywhere."

"Perhaps there isn't anywhere to get," Mason told him, laughing.

Neely seemed undecided for a moment, then blurted out, "Mr. Mason, how do you cross-examine a man who has made a positive identification, when you feel that the identification is the result of a mistake, or perhaps that the man is deliberately lying?"

Mason laughed. "That's like asking a mountaineer how he goes about climbing a mountain. It all depends on the mountain. Generally, of course, you start going up and keep going up until you get to the top, but sometimes you go up rock chimneys, sometimes you climb ledges, sometimes you skirt around in order to find a more advantageous place. What's the matter? Do you think this witness is lying?"

"I don't think the defendant is guilty."

"Well, that's a good way to feel," Mason told him reassuringly.

"I—oh I know I have no right to take up your time

and—I—but, Mr. Mason, I feel so futile, so helpless, so utterly at a loss as to what to do next."

"What's the case?" Mason asked.

"This girl, Evelyn Bagby, is a waitress who was on her way to look for work in Los Angeles. She was driving an old model car which broke down. She had to have a part for it and because it's such an ancient wreck it was necessary to send to Los Angeles for a part from a junkyard. Evelyn waited over in Corona in the motel for the part to come. This Irene Keith, whose jewelry was stolen, is a rich girl who was to be bridesmaid at a wedding in Las Vegas. The wedding party was to make a rendezvous in Corona at a cocktail bar and then go over in a wedding procession. You probably read about it. Helene Chaney, the actress, was to be the bride. Irene Keith had several suitcases containing lots of jewelry. Some of it was the wedding presents, some of it her personal jewelry, some of it was Helene's jewelry. Helene was riding with Irene Keith. They'd parked the car and gone to the cocktail bar to wait for the others. When they came out Irene Keith noticed the lid of the trunk compartment was raised. She looked in the suitcases. The jewelry was gone, some forty-thousand dollars' worth. They notified the police. The police felt someone at the motel across the street from the cocktail bar might have seen the car standing there and done a little exploring. Then this man, Harry Boles, heard about the loss on the radio. He came forward and gave the police a description. They checked and found my client, Evelyn Bagby, was staying at the motel. She matched the description given by Boles. Police picked her up, searched her suitcase and found some of the jewelry."

"*Some* of the jewelry?" Mason asked sharply.

Neely nodded. "A diamond bracelet."

"What became of the rest of the stuff?"

"They think she must have hidden it."

"Why would she have hidden part and not all?"

"They haven't advanced any theory on that. They're leaving that up to me to explain."

"Any question about the bracelet being part of the stolen jewelry?" Mason asked.

"No. It's the same."

"Makes it look rather black, doesn't it?" Mason said.

"It does, but she— Mr. Mason, I just don't think she's guilty."

"Why?"

"I don't know. Perhaps it's a hunch."

Mason nodded. "You'll find your hunches are often right."

"I *did* so want to do a good job on this case."

"Naturally," Mason said.

"She hasn't any money, and the Court appointed me as the attorney to defend her. Of course, it's just a routine run-of-the-mill case as far as the Court is concerned, and you know how those things go. They feel that a young lawyer has to get experience before he's any good, and they see that he gets experience by appointing him on these cases where the defendant has no money. I've worked terribly hard on this. I've sat up nights briefing the law. I think I know the law forward, backward and sideways. I've got instructions prepared for the jury, but somehow I feel they aren't going to do any good. I have an idea the jury has already made up its mind."

"When did it make up its mind?" Mason asked.

"Right after Harry Boles took the witness stand and identified the defendant. I could feel the whole thing change."

"Does the defendant have any past record?"

"Apparently not."

Mason said, "Look here, Neely, I drove up to get some papers signed. Come on and have lunch with me and we'll talk it over."

"I—well, I'd sure like to, Mr. Mason, but I—you see,

I—well, I had a luncheon engagement, but you wait, Mr. Mason, I'll break it."

"With the young woman who was waiting in the courtroom?" Mason asked.

Neely flushed, nodded.

"Bring her along," Mason told him.

"Oh, could I, Mr. Mason? She'd be thrilled. She—well, I'm hoping she'll be Mrs. Neely one of these days when I get my practice built up here, and I think I can do that if I get any kind of a break. My dad has lots of friends and we've lived here for years."

"All right," Mason said, "we'll pick her up but we'll try not to talk shop while we're eating."

Neely's face fell. "I thought—I wanted—"

Mason shook his head and smiled. "This is going to be *your* case," he said. "If you come out on top it must be *your* triumph. We'll have lunch and then you'll tell her that you have to be back here by half-past one. That will give us half an hour in the law library. I'll pretend that you're Boles on the stand and I'll cross-examine *you*. Perhaps in that way you can get some ideas."

Neely tried to find words with which to express himself, but could only shake Mason's hand. Finally he said, "You're a lifesaver, Mr. Mason. I think I know law. I had good marks all through law school, but when you get into a courtroom and find yourself confronted with a witness who just grins at you in a patronizing way and won't budge an inch, you feel as though—well, it's like a dream where you're having a fight and keep swinging with all your might and your punches have no more force than if you had feathers for arms."

"I know exactly how you feel," Mason said. "We'll try and explore a few possibilities after lunch."

2

Promptly at one-thirty-five Mason closed the door of the law library, seated Frank Neely in a chair, stood above him and said, "Now you're going to be Harry Boles. I'm going to be you. I'm cross-examining you. So far as possible you'll answer my questions just as Boles has been answering yours."

Neely nodded. There was an air of greater confidence about him.

"And when you get back into court," Mason went on, "you're going to remember certain things. One of them is that you have to hold the interest of a jury. You can't do it by fumbling around with papers. Any time you make a pass at a witness and then quit and start fumbling around with papers you make it appear that you don't know what you're doing, that the witness has the best of you. You're going to keep throwing questions at the witness. Rapid-fire questions. You aren't going to pause for anything. You're just going to keep slamming questions at him. Do you understand?"

Neely nodded lugubriously. "You can't think up questions that fast—I can't. He's said he saw her taking the suitcase out of the car and taking things out of the suitcase. I have to keep asking him if he's certain he saw her and—well, we just go over and over it and he's prejudicing the jury against my client every time he answers. But I can't think of anything else to ask him. What else is there?"

Mason laughed. "We'll see," he said. "Furthermore, you mustn't, under any circumstances, keep going over the same things he's testified to in the same order."

"But I have to do that," Neely said. "He's testified that he saw her. He's identified her and I've got to keep asking him—"

"That's fine," Mason broke in, "but don't ask him in the same order that he's given his testimony. Go at him from a different angle."

"I'm afraid I don't understand."

"Perhaps I can show you what I mean," Mason said. "All right, now you're Boles. You give me the answers that Boles has been giving you. If you don't know what the answers are make up answers that you think will be the most damaging to the defendant. Now can you do that?"

"That," Neely said, "is going to be easy. I've been on the receiving end all morning. I'd like to throw some answers back at you."

"All right," Mason said. "Here we go. You're ready?"

Neely nodded.

"Now," Mason said, pointing his finger at the young lawyer, "you have testified that you saw the defendant taking the suitcase from the back of the automobile, putting it on the ground and bending over it to open it?"

"That's right," Neely said, and then added vindictively, "It was the defendant, all right. I saw her do it."

"Now you indicated the manner in which she had bent over," Mason said, "when I asked you to illustrate to the jury. You bent from the waist, keeping your knees straight."

"That's right. That's the way she bent over."

"You had no reason to notice her particularly at *that* time, did you?"

"How do you mean?"

"She was just a woman taking a suitcase from a car that was parked in front of a motel. There's nothing unusual about that. It happens every night in the year."

"Yes, I suppose so."

"So you *didn't* notice her particularly at *that* time, did you?"

Neely grinned triumphantly. "Oh but I did. You're forgetting that I said my attention was attracted to her legs as she bent over."

"You saw those legs?"

"Yes."

"They attracted your attention?"

"Naturally."

"Good-looking legs?"

"Very."

"When she bent over you saw them?"

"That's right. Her skirts lifted, and I—well, I looked."

"You saw them up far enough to attract your attention?"

"Just about to the knees."

"And you say she took something out of the suitcase?"

"That's right."

"What did she do with it?"

"Put it in her pockets."

"Now was there a pocket in her suit," Mason asked, "or did she put it in the side pocket of that topcoat?"

"In the side pockets of the topcoat that's People's Exhibit C, hanging up there by the blackboard."

"That's fine," Mason said. "So then she must have had the topcoat on at the time and she put the stuff that she took out of the suitcase, whatever it was, in the pockets of the topcoat?"

"That's right, in the pockets on both sides. Then she closed the suitcase and put it back in the car."

"Now then," Mason said, "that's a rather full-skirted topcoat. I'm going to ask the defendant to step forward and put that coat on. Then I'm going to ask her to turn her back to the jury and bend down just as the witness Boles said she did, and we'll see how much of her legs the witness could see."

Neely looked at Mason and his eyes widened in astonishment. "Good Lord," he said, "I never thought of *that!*"

"Neither did Boles," Mason said. "Now I'm going to ask you a couple of other questions in your role of Boles. You say that you saw the defendant at that time. When did you see her *next?*"

"I saw her at a line-up in the police station in Corona."

"That isn't what I asked you," Mason said, shaking his finger in the young man's face. "I asked you when you saw her *next.* I want to know the *very next time* you saw this defendant after this episode when you *think* you saw her at the back of that automobile."

"Why, I—the next time I saw her was in the line-up."

"Are you sure?" Mason asked.

Neely nodded, but there was something about his nod that made it lack emphasis.

Mason laughed. "You seem to be a little dubious, Neely."

"Well, to tell you the truth," Neely said, "I never asked Boles that question in exactly that way."

"Why?"

"Well, because I didn't think it would do me any good. You see, the witness testified that he saw her there at the automobile, and then he testified that he picked her out of a line-up at the police station in Corona."

"But did he say specifically that that was the *next* time he had seen her?"

"No, he didn't," Neely admitted. "He intimated it, but he didn't say so in so many words."

"Keep after him," Mason said. "Find out if, when he went to the police and gave the description, the police didn't pick this girl up and if they *then* didn't go get Boles and ask him to take a surreptitious look at her and see if she was the woman. When he said that she was, then the police put her in a line-up."

"Why that would—that would be almost the same as

perjury because he certainly conveyed the impression that the next time he had seen her was in the line-up."

"Never mind the impression," Mason said. "Bore into him. Give it to him hammer and tongs. Don't let him have any time to think in between questions. The minute he answers one question, fire another one at him."

"I can't think of questions that fast," Neely said. "That's been my trouble this morning. I'd try to think of something to ask him and my mind would go blank."

"Don't let your mind go blank," Mason told him. "Keep throwing questions at him, any questions, Ask him what the weather was. Ask him what kind of tires were on the automobile. Whether they were white sidewall or not. Ask him exactly where the car was parked. How many feet from the corner. How many inches from the curb. Ask him how he happened to be there. Ask him if he was walking, or ask him if he stopped walking. If he had stopped walking to watch the girl, find out when he stopped walking and why. How long he stood there. Ask him how he happened to be there, where he'd been, how long he'd been there, where he was going, what stopped him, when he started walking again. Just keep throwing questions at him and all the time keep watching him like a hawk, using your powers of concentration to remember everything he says and to correlate every answer, looking for a weak spot."

"Gosh, Mr. Mason, do you have to think of all those things at once?"

Mason said, "If you're going to be a trial lawyer, you not only have to think of all those things but in addition you've got to keep watching the jurors out of the corner of your eye. You've got to see what impresses them and what doesn't. You've got to see when they're getting bored, and when they're getting bored you've got to do something spectacular that will arouse their interest. You've got to keep thinking about the record. You've got to keep watching for errors. You've got to keep an eye on the Court. You've got to frame your questions so they're calling for evidence that is legally admissible and not have your questions couched in such phraseology that the other side can object and have the objection sustained. That makes the jury feel you don't know what you're doing."

"But, good Lord, you can't think of all *those* things at once."

"You will," Mason told him, grinning. "You'll get so they're automatic. You'll be able to stand on your feet, throw out a steady stream of questions, and keep thinking of all those things and half a dozen others. Now I've got to go on back to my office. You go in there and tear into that witness."

"Do you think he's lying, Mr. Mason?"

Mason shrugged his shoulders. "He may be lying. He may be telling the truth. He may be telling what he thinks is the truth. I'll tell you one thing though—he didn't see that young woman's legs when she was bending over, not if she had that coat on. That's a long, full-skirted coat. You put it on her shoulders and have her bend over and you won't see any legs."

"I never thought of that," Neely said, "and I should have. I—well, now you've pointed it out it's just as plain as day."

Mason glanced at his watch, reached out and shook hands with Neely. "Go on in there," he said, "and do your stuff. And remember, it's *your* stuff. Don't tell anyone about this little session with me."

3

IN HIS OFFICE MASON GLANCED THROUGH THE SECTION of the morning newspaper devoted to out-of-the-city news.

"Looking for something special?" Della Street, his secretary, asked.

Mason nodded. "Probably there won't be anything in here, but there was a case up in Riverside that interested me. I—oh-oh, here it is."

"What?" Della Street asked.

Mason folded the newspaper and handed it to her to read.

"Well," she said, "a young man by the name of Neely seems to have made a brilliant cross-examination in the case involving Helene Chaney's bridesmaid. The identification witness broke down and became covered with confusion; the defendant, Evelyn Bagby, testified that someone must have planted the article of stolen jewelry in her cabin. The Court instructed the jury that mere possession of stolen property standing alone was not enough to justify a conviction; that there must be some other circumstance; that if they believed the defendant's explanation, they couldn't convict her."

Mason nodded.

"Why are you grinning like a Cheshire cat?" Della Street asked.

"Oh," Mason said, "I happened to look in on the case, for ten or fifteen minutes before the noon adjournment, and I was wondering how it came out."

Della Street looked at him sharply. "You had no other interest?"

"I thought that the young lawyer who was representing the woman was doing a pretty good job."

"That's all?"

"Of course," Mason said.

Her steady eyes surveyed the lawyer with the appraisal born of long experience. She picked up his expense account, said, "I see you had guests for lunch. Who were they?"

"Just a couple of local people," Mason said.

"The income tax department would like a little more information than that," she reminded him.

Mason laughed. "This is personal. Don't charge it. A chap by the name of Frank Neely and the young woman he expected to marry, Estelle Nugent."

Della Street picked up the expense account. "I thought so," she said, and left the office.

A few moments later she returned with a smile. "Well Mr. Good Samaritan, I see you've cast your bread upon the waters and you're now in the garbage-disposal business."

"How come?"

"In the outer office," she said, "is a very starry-eyed young redhead with a figure that is much more important than her clothes would indicate, who gives the name of Evelyn Bagby. She says that she simply *must*, and I quote, thank Mr. Mason personally, unquote. She's redheaded and determined."

Mason frowned. "She wasn't supposed to know that I had anything to do with it."

"Well, she does."

"Bring her in, Della," Mason said. "We'll acknowledge her thanks and then send her on her way. Unless I'm greatly mistaken she's in need of finding work and I'm in need of doing some."

"That pile of mail at your left," Della Street reminded pointedly.

"Yes, yes, I know. I'll get at it some time today. Send her in, Della."

Evelyn Bagby, seeming much taller standing alongside Della Street than when she had been sitting beside her lawyer in court the day before, came striding across the office. Her steady blue eyes rested unwaveringly on Mason's face. Her handclasp was simple, strong and direct as she gripped the lawyer's hand.

"Thanks."

"For what?" Mason asked, smiling down into the frank blue eyes.

"As though you didn't know."

"Do you?"

"Certainly."

"How?"

"Mr. Neely told me."

Mason frowned. "He shouldn't have."

"He told me that he was going to be frank with me. I—well, I was terribly grateful and I was a little curious."

"About what?"

"About the way he went after that witness in the afternoon. He seemed to have an entirely new approach. He'd been floundering around in the morning, and then right after lunch he started in just as full of confidence as though he'd been a veteran. After about four questions he had this man Boles all mixed up. Then Boles started kicking the case all around the courtroom. I asked Neely about it afterward and he told me what had happened."

"Sit down," Mason invited.

She shook her head, said, "You're too busy. I wasn't at all certain you'd see me. I understand a client has to have an appointment in order to get even a foot inside the door. But I wanted you to know that I *did* understand and I *do* appreciate."

"Thanks a lot," Mason said. "Neely said you were looking for work."

She nodded.

"Think you can find some?"

"Sure. I'll get by."

"Do you have any idea how it happened that the witness Boles identified you?"

She shook her head. "He didn't either after Frank Neely finished with him yesterday afternoon, but he sure was going strong in the morning. That's the way with his type. They make a great showing when things are going good, but when the going gets tough they certainly run for cover. That's one thing you learn being on your own and dealing with all sorts and all types. You get so you can classify them pretty fast. The only thing I'm sorry about is that they have my fingerprints on file now, and whenever anybody wants to know anything about me, why there'll be a record reading, 'Arrested but acquitted,' as though somehow the jury had been at fault."

"Did your attorney say anything about the possibility of some compensation to you to make up for all this annoyance, publicity and all of that?"

"Why, no. They acted as though they were doing me a great favor turning me loose. The matron certainly hated to let go of me and give me back the few dollars I had in cash."

Mason said to Della Street, "Get Frank Neely on the phone for me, Della. He's the attorney at Riverside.

"Sit down, Miss Bagby. This will only take a few minutes."

Evelyn Bagby looked at him with thoughtfully speculative eyes while Della Street was putting through the call. She lowered herself into the clients' big chair.

"If you feel that I'm entitled to ask for anything, there's one thing I want and only one thing."

"What's that?" Mason asked.

"You'll laugh when you hear this one," she said, "and probably throw me out of the office."

"Go on," Mason told her. "What is it?"

"I'm not interested in money—that is, I am, but there's something I want more than money."

"What?"

"Don't laugh. I want a screen test."

Mason looked her over with critical appraisal. He slowly nodded his head.

"You might be good," he said, "but don't think that—"

"Oh, I know," she told him, "you're going to tell me that I mustn't think screen tests are easy or that anything will come of them even if I make a good test. Hollywood is overcrowded. It takes luck, brains, ability, good looks, poise, influential contacts, and even then the chances are one in a million."

Mason smiled. "Something like that."

"I know, I've heard it all. I've read it all. It's taken me seven years to get here."

Mason raised his eyebrows.

Della Street interposed, "The Riverside circuits are busy. It will be two or three minutes, Chief."

Mason, without taking his eyes from his visitor, said, "Tell Gertie to keep trying, Della. Why did it take you seven years to get here, Miss Bagby?"

She laughed and said, "Seven years ago I was a girl eighteen years old. I was rather striking. Most redheads have freckles. I didn't. I had pretty good features and a very good figure."

"You still have a good figure."

"Not like it was, Mr. Mason. Seven years of hard work, waiting on tables, knocking around, learning about the world the hard way, have levied a toll. I thought I was all over my ambition, but what you said just now suddenly caused it to flare up."

"What did I say?"

"That I might be entitled to something."

"I was talking about some pecuniary compensation. That's a possibility that may be rather remote under the circumstances but we *might* get enough to give you some get-by money."

"Well," she said, "the figures in this case are prominent in Hollywood. Helene Chaney should have a lot of influence."

"If she wants to use it," Mason said.

"Well, I thought I'd let you know what I had in mind. You see, Mr. Mason, I was very ambitious and very determined at the age of eighteen. I had some money that had come to me on my father's death. My mother died when I was ten, my father when I was seventeen. I was going to Hollywood and make good, and then I met a man named Gladden. I still have one of his cards as a souvenir. Staunton Vester Gladden."

"Who is he?"

"He was the dazzling sun who moved into my young life. He was on intimate terms with all of the great and near-great in Hollywood. He was a dramatic coach. He breathed the atmosphere of the theater. He was the man whose genius had made half a dozen actors and actresses. He called all of the principal figures of Hollywood by their first names. He was—"

"I never heard of him," Mason interrupted.

"Neither did anyone else." She laughed bitterly. "He was a man who was just as stage-struck as I was, only he was just a natural-born confidence man and a perfect heel. Of course I didn't know it at the time. I was a wide-eyed girl of eighteen who thought I knew my way around from what I had gathered from magazines, motion pictures, and the amateurish passes that the small-town guys made at me. I wasn't hep to this high-powered stuff."

"What happened?" Mason asked, interested.

"Oh," she said, "Gladden did the usual. Look, I mustn't take up your time with this."

Mason waved his hand in the direction of the telephone. "We're waiting for a call, Miss Bagby, and you interest me. After all, a lawyer has to know a lot about human nature—and if I'm going to try to get you a screen test I should know something of your background."

"That last does it," she said, smiling. "Well, Gladden laughed at my ambitions. He told me I wouldn't stand a ghost of a chance in Hollywood with my unsophisticated background and girlish dreams. He said I must become a polished young woman. Well, of course, you know the answer. There was only one person who could do the polishing and that was Staunton Vester Gladden. He gave me a ninety-day course. By the time he had finished, I had lost a lot of things. I'd picked up some polish and a lot of wisdom. He had absconded with all of my little inheritance and I was flat broke, disillusioned, and had to take a job as waitress."

"Did you go to the police?"

"Oh sure," she said. "I went to the police. Of course I didn't tell them the *whole* story. I told them the high lights about how he had got control of my money and had skipped out. He played it very skillfully. At first he told me money wouldn't enter into it at all. Then he said he wanted to be my permanent agent. He wanted twenty per cent of my earnings when I hit the big time. He was to be my manager, agent, dramatic coach and all the rest of it.

"He started in very smoothly and easily, laughing at me, then gradually rubbing his eyes as he became convinced that I had 'great natural talent,' then going into enthusiastic rhapsodies about my potential ability. He had my head completely turned. I was, of course, developing my dramatic art, and you can put that in quotes, Mr. Mason, under his tutelage. I was also becoming a young woman. I was learning about emotion. I was getting a mature outlook. I was becoming conditioned for Hollywood. And all the line that goes with it.

"Then he got a brilliant idea. He had an opportunity to get in on one of the big studio deals. It was going to take a little money. But I would become a stockholder.

That would be a short cut. That would catapult me into fame. I gave him my money to make the investment, and you can also put that in quotes, Mr. Mason."

"And then?" Mason asked.

"Then he vanished. That was the last I ever saw of him," she said. "Of course the police investigated. They found out that Hollywood had never heard of Staunton Vester Gladden. The people whom he was calling by their first names didn't even know he existed. The police told me it wasn't a particularly novel approach."

"And so you lost your Hollywood ambitions?"

"I thought I had. I waited on tables. I learned about life the hard way, and I suppose it did things to me. I would look at myself in the mirror and compare what I saw with the fresh, young girl I'd been when I was thinking of a career on the screen and building all those air castles. Well, that's the way it goes, Mr. Mason.

"However, I was always restless. I never want to stay in one place. I keep roaming around the country. So finally I asked myself, 'Why not see Hollywood after all?' So I made it in two hops."

"Two?" Mason asked.

"First," she said, "I went to Needles. I worked there, acquired a little dough for a stake, and then I got sick. By the time I finished with doctor and hospital bills. I had a jalopy that will get you over the road if you're patient and persevering, a few clothes and nothing else.

"I should have known the answer then. I should have known that Hollywood was a hoodoo. But I decided I would never be any younger and that I'd start for Hollywood. I got as far as Corona. The jalopy's rear end went out and I had to wait while they sent to Los Angeles for parts. So I stopped at this motel. Well, you know the rest of it."

Mason regarded her thoughtfully. "They did find an article of the stolen jewelry in your suitcase?"

"Sure," she said. "I was broke. I was desperate. I had

just about enough money to pay for the car repairs, to pay for the motel, and get to Hollywood. Then I was hoping to get a job. I knew that wouldn't be easy. They say that the town is filled with broken-hearted girls who come on here to be prima donnas and wind up being waitresses—provided they can get jobs.

"Well, the second day I was there I went into the bathroom to take a shower. I noticed a drawer in the chest of drawers in the bathroom was open a little way and there was a gleam of light reflected back from the interior of the drawer. It came from this diamond bracelet."

She hesitated, thinking back over the occurrence.

"Go on," Mason said.

"Well, there I was, broke, desperate, and suddenly filled once more with that ambition that I'd had years before."

"And you intended to appropriate the bracelet?" Mason asked sharply.

"Don't be silly! I thought I could get a reward. I thought that some rich woman had been in that motel the day before I took the place and had taken off her bracelet when she started to take a shower. Then she'd gone away and forgotten it. I also felt pretty certain that she didn't know where she'd left it because if she had she'd have telephoned back to the motel and the motel would have recovered it."

Mason nodded.

"At first, of course, my idea was to dress and go to the office of the motel and explain to them what I'd found, ask them to notify the person who had last occupied the motel. Then I thought, Why be foolish? That bracelet probably belongs to some rich woman. She'd be grateful. She'd give a fifty- or a hundred-dollar reward. The manager of the motel would pocket the reward and I wouldn't even get a thin dime, or so much as a thank you. No one would know I even existed."

"So you decided to find out who had been in there before and collect the reward?"

"That's right. I didn't think they'd tell me if I asked, and if I asked I knew the manager would get suspicious. So I intended to take the bracelet to Los Angeles with me, then get someone who had some official position, an attorney or a detective or something, to get the information for me. Then I'd approach the woman directly, return the bracelet and everything would be swell. Well, you know what happened. I—"

The phone rang and Della Street nodded to Mason. "Here's your party."

Mason took the telephone. "Good morning, Counselor," he said, "and congratulations. This is Perry Mason talking."

Frank Neely was all but inarticulate with his thanks. "You know," he said, "you were right, Mr. Mason. That fellow Boles was a phony. At least he was testifying to something he couldn't substantiate. I am completely satisfied that he couldn't identify the person he saw, and the jury was, too. Thanks to the line of attack you worked out for me."

"I'm afraid you're taking too little credit for yourself," Mason said. "What about the defendant?"

"She left town right after her release."

"She's in my office," Mason said.

There was a moment of embarrassed silence, and then Neely said, "Well, of course, I couldn't resist telling her about you, and what you had done for her."

"You didn't tell anyone else, did you?"

"No, not a soul."

"Don't," Mason said, "because I didn't do much and you're the one who secured the verdict."

Neely said, "I wish I could tell you how much it meant to me, Mr. Mason. You'll never know. It wasn't only this case but my entire career. I felt so helpless standing up there trying to ask questions and getting nowhere, and then all of a sudden after you talked to me it seemed as though the scales had dropped from my eyes, and then—well, I guess I got fighting mad. The first thing I knew I had ceased to think about myself any more. I was simply standing up there throwing questions at him and he was squirming and twisting all over the witness stand. I could see the jurors beginning to believe he was a terrific liar. It gave me my self-confidence back."

"What," Mason asked, "are we going to do with Evelyn Bagby? She tells me she would like to have things cleared up."

"You do anything for her that you can," Neely said. "'I've done everything I can."

"Have you talked with any of the parties interested about—?"

"No, I haven't talked with anyone."

"I'll see what I can do at this end," Mason said. "You'll be associated with me."

"Please remember me to her," Neely said. "I don't suppose there's anything more than can be done."

"I'll keep you posted," Mason promised and hung up. He smiled at Evelyn Bagby. "Neely wants to be remembered to you."

"He's a nice young fellow," she said. "I'm everlastingly grateful to him, but—well, I know who inspired him."

Mason frowned thoughtfully. "Who signed the complaint which resulted in your arrest?"

"Irene Keith. She was the bridesmaid. That is, she was to have been the bridesmaid. It was one of those movie affairs. Helene Chaney, the actress, and Mervyn Aldrich, the boat manufacturer. I'd been reading about it just the day before in one of the Hollywood columns. I certainly didn't think I'd ever get mixed up in it. I—"

The telephone rang, a series of quick, short rings.

Della Street picked up the instrument, said, "Yes, what is it, Gertie . . . ? Oh, tell him to hold on."

She turned to Perry Mason and said, "Frank Neely

from Riverside is calling you back, says he has to speak with you right away."

Mason nodded, picked up the extension telephone, said, "Yes, hello, Neely. What is it?"

Neely's voice was excited. "Irene Keith is calling on the other line," he said. "She said that since Evelyn Bagby had been acquitted she was thinking about giving her a little money to use in getting out of town. She mentioned a figure of seventy-five or a hundred dollars. What shall I tell her?"

Mason grinned. "Tell her that Perry Mason is your associate in the matter and that she is to call me. But don't get your mind set on any big fee because I doubt if it's in the cards. Don't discuss any figures with Irene Keith. Just tell her to call me; that you're associated with me in the matter."

"Okay. Will do," Neely said. "I guess that's another place where I overlooked a bet, Mr. Mason. With all of those Hollywood personalities mixed up in the case, and having signed a complaint accusing Miss Bagby of a felony—well, anyway, I'll make up for it now."

"Don't tell her anything," Mason said, "except that she is to call me. Don't discuss figures, don't discuss facts. Just state that I am associated with you and that she can communicate with me."

"That's fine," Neely said. "I'll tell her."

Mason hung up the phone, turned to Evelyn Bagby. "Well," he said, "someone has evidently put a bee in Irene Keith's bonnet. She's been in touch with Neely, talking about a settlement. She mentioned a figure of seventy-five or a hundred dollars to enable you to get out of town."

Evelyn Bagby's eyes were wistful. "Every one of those hundred dollars would look as big to me as a dinner plate right now, Mr. Mason, but—well, I can get by. I always have. I know I'll get work somewhere."

"How much actual cash money do you have?" Mason asked.

She smiled. "It's hardly worth mentioning, Mr. Mason."

"How much?"

"Under five dollars."

"You have a car?"

"A jalopy."

"How did it happen that wasn't taken for the expenses of your trial and—?"

"I have an equity in it," she said. "That is, if you can dignify my interest in it by calling it an equity. No one wanted to assume the payments."

Mason was thoughtful for a moment. "You want to get a job?"

She nodded.

"Doing what?"

"Anything."

"You've worked in a restaurant?"

"And how!"

"You consider yourself an expert waitress?"

"I've worked in all sorts of restaurants at all kinds of jobs. I know my way around, Mr. Mason. I can get something."

Mason said to Della Street, "See if you can get Joe Padena for me, Della."

"Will he be up now?" she asked.

"Probably just about getting up," Mason said. "Get him on the line and we'll see just what the situation is up there."

A few moments later Della nodded to Perry Mason, and Mason took the line. "Hello."

"Hello, this is Joe Padena. What you want with Joe Padena?"

"Perry Mason," the lawyer told him. "I want a favor."

"You want a favor from Joe Padena? You get a favor from Joe Padena. Joe Padena doesn't forget his friends. What you want?"

"You have an opening for a waitress?" Mason asked.

"You bet your life. If she's a friend of yours, yes. For a good waitress who is your friend I have an opening, right now."

"I'm sending a girl out to see you," Mason said "an Evelyn Bagby."

"She's a girl or she's a waitress?"

"She's both."

"That's fine. Maybe Joe Padena is not doing you a favor. Maybe you're doing Joe Padena a favor if you get a *good* girl. You understand this place is up in the sticks. The girl lives here. My wife she is cashier. Joe Padena he doesn't make passes, but she lives here. She is like one of the family. Other people make passes. Joe Padena, no."

Mason grinned. "I'll explain it to her. I'll send her up there."

"How soon?"

Mason glanced over at Evelyn Bagby. "How soon could you report for work?"

"Right now," she said.

"She'll be there within an hour," Mason told him.

"That's fine. Now, Mr. Mason, you do me a favor."

"What?" Mason asked.

"This girl, what does she look like?"

"Good."

"I thought so. You tell her not to ask for Joe Padena. You tell her ask for Mrs. Joe Padena. You understand?"

"I understand," Mason said. "She'll be right out."

"Okay. Good-by."

Padena hung up.

Mason said to Evelyn Bagby. "This is rather an interesting place. Joe Padena is a client of mine. He and his wife run a place called the Crowncrest Tavern. It's up on top of the mountains back of Hollywood. It's right up on the crest. It overlooks the San Fernando Valley on one side and Hollywood on the other. Quite a lot of the movie people go out there. It's rather a small place but it has a lot of atmosphere. It's very high-class and all the really famous movie stars get up there every so often. You'll have to live out there on the job because when you get off it's after midnight and—"

"That's okay by me," she said. "It sounds like a wonderful opportunity."

"When you go out there," Mason said, "ask for Mrs. Padena. Don't pay any attention to Joe. Mrs. Padena is the cashier. She likes to hold the purse strings and—"

"And wears the pants?" Evelyn Bagby asked, laughing.

"Exactly," Mason said. "You'll be perfectly safe out there. Joe won't make passes at you. I suppose some of the patrons will. You—"

"They all do," she said casually. "You get accustomed to that. It goes with the job. How much does it pay?"

"I don't know," Mason told her. "It's a top spot. They know you're a friend of mine. It'll pay enough. Now I want to keep in touch with you. You'd better telephone me as soon as you've had your interview, and let me know whether you're going to work there or whether you aren't. Until we get a settlement in this case I want you to be where I can reach you at any time. Day and night I want to know where you are. I may have to reach a quick decision and—"

"If you can get any cash, take it," she said, "but at least make a stab at getting me a screeen test. I know that's going to be tough and I know that even if they promise it, they'll probably dog it. They'll fix it up with some second-rate outfit to put me in front of a camera, have me read a few lines, show my legs, register anger, surprise and love, kick me out and I'll never hear from it again. It'll just be an act they'll put on as part of a settlement. But—"

"If I get them to agree to a screen test," Mason interrupted, "it'll be a *real* screen test. You won't need to worry about that."

She smiled gratefully. "I should have known," she said. "You *wouldn't* do things by halves. How do I get to this Crowncrest Tavern?"

Mason said, "Della Street will draw you a map. You can drive the long way up Mulholland Drive, which is the way most of the traffic goes, but there's a short cut up a steep, narrow road that saves quite a bit of distance. If you're going to be working there you should know the short cut because it saves quite a bit of time."

"Mr. Mason, there's something I think I should tell you."

"What?"

"I may have made a botch of things and I keep wondering if that could have had anything to do with—still, I don't see how it could, but I—"

"Go on," Mason said.

"Well, the day I got to Corona and my car broke down, I had some time to kill so I was reading one of the movie magazines and there was an article in it about Helene Chaney—one of those sob sister, poor-little-rich-girl type of things. It discussed her attempts to find happiness, and intimated that she was now in love and was hoping that this time it would be the genuine thing. There were pictures of her first two husbands, and there was something about the picture of her second husband, Steve Merrill, that looked terribly familiar."

"In what way?"

"He looked like Staunton Vester Gladden."

Mason's eyes narrowed. "What did you do?"

"I called up the office of the movie magazine, got the address of a casting agency where they thought I could locate Mr. Merrill, and finally got an address where I could get him on the telephone."

"Go on," Mason said, keeping his voice completely without expression.

"I called him. I told him who I was and where I was staying. I told him that my car had broken down, that I was broke, and that I expected him to make some immediate payment on account. I also told him that I expected him to get me the rest of the money within six months or I was going to take it up with the police."

"What happened?"

"He said I must be crazy, that he was not accustomed to paying blackmail, that he had never heard of Staunton Gladden or of Evelyn Bagby in his life. Then he slammed the phone in my ear. I'm wondering, Mr. Mason, if perhaps somehow that call might not have had something to do with—well, you can understand it's all mixed up—but in case he really is Staunton Gladden—"

"There's a doubt in your mind?" Mason asked.

"Yes. There is now. At the time I thought I'd made a mistake. I walked out of the phone booth with my cheeks burning. After all, you can't depend too much on a likeness in a photograph."

"And now?" Mason asked.

"I've been thinking a lot about it the last few hours. Do you suppose that some of my troubles could have come from—I mean, in case Merrill really is Staunton Gladden. After all, you can put two and two together. The man was stage-struck just the same as I was, only his approach was different. He must have been desperate when he embezzled my money. It's only logical to suppose that he would have used the money to go to Hollywood, and, of course, he'd have taken another name and—well, I can't help wondering."

Mason said, "It's worth looking into. How positive are you?"

She laughed. "Not positive at all. Not from the picture. If I could see him I could tell."

Mason said, "That's a fact we'll file away for future consideration."

"You think it's significant?"

"Very."

"Well, I thought I'd tell you—that you should know."

"We'll find out," Mason told her. "In the meantime there are more pressing matters to be considered. You're going to need some money to finance you until your first pay check comes along."

Mason turned to Della Street. "Make Miss Bagby a check for a hundred dollars, Della. Get her to endorse it and then give her the hundred dollars in cash."

Evelyn Bagby's blue eyes widened. "What's *that* for?"

"That's on account of a settlement I'm going to make," Mason said, "and you may want to start work with a little money to spare."

"I don't like to run in debt," she told him. "It's always been a policy of mine to pay as I go. I've tried to—"

"This isn't a loan," Mason told her. "This is an advance on a settlement Frank Neely and I are going to get for you. You may want to—"

As he hesitated she looked down at her clothes and laughed. "I get you," she said. "I'm to buy some new clothes. These are things I picked up in Needles, Mr. Mason. They were supposed to be cheap and stylish. They were cheap and they *looked* stylish until they went to the cleaner for the first time, I suppose people have told you that you're a very, very wonderful man, Mr. Mason, so I'm not going to take any more of your time telling you how *I* feel, but I think you know."

She stood in front of him, her eyes, blue, serene and steady, looking into his. Then she put out her hand and shook his with firm, strong fingers. "You're grand," she said.

Della Street handed her the map and the hundred dollars. "Sign here on the back of the check, Miss Bagby."

Evelyn Bagby signed, took the money and the map, said abruptly, "I'll call you, Mr. Mason," and left the office without looking back.

Della Street took a piece of blotting paper and placed it on the back of the check.

"Ink?" Mason asked, as he noticed the expression on Della Street's face.

She shook her head. "A teardrop," she told him. "It spilled out—and somehow I'll bet that girl doesn't do very much crying."

"Poor kid," Mason said, "I guess she's had her share of tough breaks. Perhaps we can get her a decent deal for once."

"And now, Santa Claus," Della Street pleaded, "if you can tie up the reindeer long enough to just *look* at that pile of important mail—"

The telephone rang. Della Street said, "Who is it, Gertie? Mr. Mason is . . . Who . . . ? Just a minute."

She turned to Perry Mason, cupped her hand over the mouthpiece. "I take it you'll want to speak with Irene Keith personally."

Mason's mouth broadened into a wide grin. "Put her on my line," he said, and picked up his personal telephone.

"Hello, Miss Keith," he said.

Irene Keith's voice was steady, calm, confident. "Good morning, Mr. Mason. I believe you're representing a Miss Evelyn Bagby?"

"I'm associated with Frank Neely of Riverside," Mason said. "Do you have some attorney who generally looks after your business?"

"I look after my own business, Mr. Mason."

Mason said, "Miss Bagby is virtually without funds. There has been a certain stigma attached to her name and reputation. She's looked for work here in the city. I gather that you want to do something to help."

"I might be charitable."

"Perhaps you'd better be just."

"Is this a threat?"

"Not as yet."

"Is she thinking of suing me?"

Mason said, "I'll be frank with you. I am not familiar with the facts of the case, but I intend to investigate them. If you have some attorney who looks after your business affairs you might suggest to him that he give this matter his consideration."

"I'd prefer to handle this myself. Are you going to be in your office today?"

"Yes."

"Could I see you if I came in?"

Mason said, "I'm very busy. I've tried to impress upon you that this is a matter where you'll need a lawyer, and—"

"I don't want a lawyer. I'd prefer to pay the girl rather than have some lawyer charge me a fee to tell me to settle. I'm not much good at talking on telephones. I'll pay a little money, but it's not going to be much. How about it? Do you want to talk?"

"Come on in," Mason said. "I'll see you, but remember I would much prefer to talk with your lawyer."

"I'll get a lawyer when I need one," she said. "I think I can make a better settlement with you personally than I can through a lawyer."

"Why?" Mason asked, puzzled.

"Because although my lawyer is good, he has no sex appeal." She laughed. "I'll be in this afternoon at two-thirty. That'll give me time to get to the beauty shop. I've warned you, Mr. Mason."

Perry Mason laughed. "Okay, I'll see you at two-thirty."

Mason hung up the telephone.

Della Street firmly pushed the pile of correspondence into his hands.

"After you have dictated answers to the first four letters, which are very, very important," she said, "I'll let you read the Hollywood gossip column in the paper."

Mason raised his eyebrows. "Something about the case?"

"Not about the case particularly, but the columnist uses the verdict in the case to comment on Helene Chaney's romance."

"Yes?" Mason asked. "Tell me about it."

"Helene Chaney," Della Street said, "was to marry Mervyn Aldrich. That was to be her third marriage. Her second marriage had been to Steve Merrill, who was a second-rate actor at a time when Helene Chaney was just on the point of being discovered. She was then a starlet.

"The marriage to Merrill lasted about a year, then she found out he was a heel and kicked him out. He wanted to remarry and she financed a quickie divorce in Mexico so he could do so. Then she began to doubt the legality of that divorce and filed suit herself here in California. She published summons, got an interlocutory decree and was to have had a final decree of divorce issued.

"Mervyn Aldrich, the boat manufacturer, became interested in Helene Chaney and it was rumored they were going to get married. Then Merrill filed papers claiming there had never been a legal marriage to him because her first husband was still living and she had only obtained a Mexican divorce—they were greatly in vogue around that time.

"Therefore Merrill claimed they had been partners rather than husband and wife, that his earnings had financed Helene Chaney in her career and he was entitled to a half interest in all the property.

"Helene Chaney's final decree of divorce was to have been issued the day she reached Las Vegas. Her attorney was to get the final decree at 10:00 A.M., phone her, and she was to have married Aldrich at 11:00.

"Now the thing is in a legal muddle because Merrill is suing for an annulment on the ground of her first husband still being her legal spouse. He may have something. Merrill has tied the whole thing up with a mess of legal proceedings.

"Incidentally, Merrill's suit was filed in court two days after the tentative wedding date Helene Chaney and Mervyn Aldrich had arranged in Las Vegas. That wedding, it is pointed out, was called off because of the theft of the jewelry. It disrupted the whole wedding ceremony, and before another date could be fixed Merrill had filed his suit.

"Now wouldn't it be a real thriller if it should turn out Steve Merrill was really the villain who had betrayed the young country girl who was so stage-struck. In that event your Evelyn Bagby—"

"Wait a minute," Mason interrupted. "What do you mean by saying *my* Evelyn Bagby?"

"I mean your Evelyn Bagby," Della Street said. "You should have seen the look in her eyes! What's more, girls who have been batted around as much as she has don't spill tears over checks unless they've had an emotional shock.

"Now, please, Mr. Perry Mason, will you return to this pile of mail and give it your personal, prompt and immediate attention?"

4

TWO-THIRTY FOUND MASON TWO-THIRDS OF THE WAY through the stack of letters in the urgent file. Then the telephone rang and Della Street, after talking with Gertie the receptionist, turned to Mason.

"Irene Keith is out there," she said. "Could you keep her waiting while you got out a couple more letters? That one to Judge Carver is rather important."

Mason shook his head. "No, Judge Carver can wait. I said two-thirty and she's right on the dot. Go bring her in, Della. We'll write Judge Carver later. Have you, by the way, heard anything from Evelyn Bagby?"

"Yes. She phoned at noon and left a message with Gertie. Joe Padena gave her a job. He was shorthanded and was tickled to death to get her."

"All right," Mason said. "Let's take a look at Irene Keith. She warned me she was going to turn on the charm. I want to see how it works."

"It'll work," Della said. "It has so far. You were going to save the day for mail, and—"

"This is an emergency," Mason said.

Della Street sighed, put down the correspondence and went out to escort Irene Keith to the inner office.

When she returned she seemed visibly impressed. There was something almost approving in the way she said, "Miss Keith, Mr. Mason."

Irene Keith stepped forward. Her personality filled the office, pushed the somber dignity of the leather-backed books, the desks and filing cabinets into the background.

"Hello," she said. "I've been to the beauty shop and had my deadly weapons burnished."

She came forward with outstretched hand. "I've heard a lot about you, Mr. Mason. You look just like your pictures. Isn't that an inane thing to say? What I mean is your pictures look just like you. Well, why shouldn't they?"

Mason smiled and indicated a chair. "After all," he said, "that's the purpose of having pictures made."

"No, it isn't. You'd be surprised at the number of people who want pictures that *don't* look like them. They want to be glorified, idealized—but let's get down to business. You're busy. You want me to do something for that young woman."

Mason nodded.

She looked at her watch. "Mervyn Aldrich is going to meet me here. You don't mind, do you?"

"Aldrich?" Mason raised his eyebrows.

"He's the groom," she said laughing. "He was all set to

commit matrimony. He was saved by the gong—the gong in this case being the theft of all of the jewelry."

Mason glanced at Della Street, who flipped a switch that turned on a hidden recording device so that every word spoken was recorded on tape.

"Go ahead," Mason said.

"Merv is a good guy," she went on. "You may have heard of him. He makes yachts down at Newport Beach."

"The Aldrich cruiser?" Mason asked.

"That's it. The Aldrich cruisers. He knows what the boys want and he sure gives it to them. Lots of boat for a little money. How he does it no one knows. Of course, volume helps, but he's really cleaning up."

"And he was to have been married?"

"That's right. He was the groom, I was the bridesmaid, and the bride was Helene Chaney."

"What happened?" Mason asked.

"We were to meet in Corona. Merv Aldrich was driving up from Balboa through the Santa Ana Canyon. Helene and I were driving from Hollywood in my car. We were going to make our rendezvous in Corona and then drive over to Las Vegas. Everything was arranged in Las Vegas. It was going to be quite a wedding."

"Go on," Mason said.

"Well, after all, Mr. Mason, I don't see where these facts really make any difference. Most of the story is in the movie section of the morning paper. After all, the jewelry was stolen and this girl was tried and acquitted and—"

"But I'd like to know the facts."

"Okay," she said, "you asked for it," and laughed nervously.

"Go ahead."

"Well," she said, glancing at her watch. "I guess I was driving rather fast. That car of mine is really souped up, and when it starts purring along the road it goes places. I can't seem to hold it down. It isn't exactly a law-abiding car, Mr. Mason. And, of course, we left a little early so we'd have time—in case of a puncture."

Mason nodded.

"I suppose you know all about Helene. She had a meteoric rise from a bit player to a star. Steve Merrill is a heel. He was a second-rate ham. He's broke. He'd like to chisel in on Helene's property. In an ordinary court action he wouldn't stand a whisper of a chance. But if he can gum up the works on Helene's marriage to Mervyn Aldrich he has some hopes of being bought off.

"You probably won't believe all this, but Helene really wants a home and security and—of course, she's a tramp in the eyes of the public because of the roles she plays on the screen. However, that's the way it goes. She's always cast in the part of a doll with tight sweaters and loose morals and that's the way the public wants her. I've told her dozens of times not to let them type her that way, but the pictures kept coming along and she liked it—well, here I go, rambling off on a tangent."

"You were to rendezvous in Corona," Mason prompted.

"That's right. We got there a little too soon. We didn't dare to keep Mervyn waiting. He won't wait for anyone."

"You assumed Mervyn Aldrich would be on time?"

"Right on the dot," she said. "He's a stickler for time. He'd synchronized watches over the telephone so that we could meet there and start right out."

"And you were early?"

"Twenty minutes—actually it was twenty-one minutes, I believe. Well, anyway, we parked the car, and decided we'd have a drink. Helene thought it was indicated under the circumstances and she didn't have to twist *my* arm."

"You went into this cocktail lounge and had a drink?"

"That's right."

"You came out, and what happened?"

"I noticed that the lid of the trunk compartment was raised, and we had—well, we had Lord knows how many presents in there, all of my jewelry, and Helene's, and the suitcases.

"Like a fool I decided to notify the police. Well, that was where I made my big mistake.

"That chief of police moved right in. I guess he saw a chance for publicity, glory and fame. He herded us all down to police headquarters. He had me give him detailed descriptions. Merv showed up and he was furious. You've never seen such cold rage."

"Why?"

"Well, he's peculiar. And he didn't like the police, the publicity, or the delay. When Merv does anything he wants the plans to go through like clockwork."

"So the wedding was off?"

"I'll say it was off. Why, the police held us there until after midnight. Helene was wild, Merv was furious and all the small-town police and newspapermen were having a field day."

"Couldn't you have broken away?"

"Probably we could have if it hadn't been for the police digging up this witness and then arresting Evelyn Bagby and insisting I sign a warrant. I told the others to go on ahead and I'd stay behind and wrestle with the technicalities of the law and the police, but Helene wouldn't go on without me, and the whole atmosphere had ceased to be romantic. Mervyn Aldrich won't wait for anyone. He says the average man spends ten per cent of his productive time waiting for other people, either directly or indirectly. He won't wait as much as five minutes for anyone."

"Then what happened?" Mason asked.

"I guess you know the rest of it."

"The wedding was called off. I remember reading about it. There was a postponement and then almost immediately Helene Chaney's second husband filed his legal action. What about that action?"

Irene Keith's lips became hard. "It's blackmail action," she said. "Steve Merrill! That heel! What a ham! What a heel! The prize—"

The telephone rang. Mason nodded to Della Street, who picked up the receiver, conversed briefly with the receptionist, then said to Mason, "Mervyn Aldrich said he was to meet Miss Keith here."

Mason glanced at Irene Keith. "You want him to come in now?"

She said hastily, "I think it would be a fine thing, Mr. Mason, to—well, I'd like to get everything all sort of straightened up, and I know Merv would want to know what's going on. He might—just might resent it if I made some sort of settlement without consulting him."

Mason nodded to Della Street, who went out to escort Mervyn Aldrich to the inner office.

While she was gone Irene Keith seemed to have forgotten Mason, but sat with her eyes on the door through which Della had left.

The door opened.

Irene Keith jumped from the chair, walked swiftly forward. "Hello, Merv!" She gave him both of her hands. "Come on over and meet Mr. Mason."

Mervyn Aldrich, fully as tall as Mason, slim-waisted, broad-shouldered, standing erect, his face tanned to a healthy, outdoor color, took Irene Keith's hands in his, smiled down at her for a moment, said. "Hello, beautiful! How's the bridesmaid?" then advanced to shake hands with Perry Mason.

Following the preliminaries, Aldrich sat down, glanced at his wrist watch and took charge of proceedings with the crisp, businesslike efficiency of a chairman of a board conducting a directors' meeting.

"Let's see, Irene," he said, "your phone message said there was something about making a settlement with this young woman who stole the wedding presents?"

"She didn't steal them, Merv."

"How do you know she didn't?"

"She was acquitted," Mason said.

Aldrich's smile was more eloquent than words.

"Merv," Irene pleaded, "I *know* she didn't do it. I feel it in my bones. There was something phony about that whole business."

Aldrich turned to Mason. "May I ask just how *you* got into this act?"

"I was drafted," Mason said.

Irene Keith said by way of explanation, "Merv, of course, feels pretty much put out about this whole business. You see, it stopped the wedding."

"Irene and Helene left all that jewelry in the back of the car and—"

"I'd locked the baggage compartment. I know I did, Merv," Irene said.

He merely nodded a crisp acknowledgment of the statement, then went on speaking to Mason. "The girls felt that the theft had to be reported to the Corona police. Trying to get a description of all the stuff and details consumed more than an hour and a half. Then this man showed up—what the devil was his name, Irene?"

"Boles, Harry Boles."

"That's right. He'd seen this young woman fooling around the baggage compartment, at least he said he had. He went all to pieces on cross-examination at the trial yesterday. The jury turned the defendant loose. She certainly was lucky! Where is she now?"

"Working," Mason said.

"Where?"

"In the city here."

Irene Keith said impulsively, "Merv, I want you to trust me in this. I have a very definite feeling that—well, I think there was a frame-up."

Mervyn Aldrich shook his head.

"Merv, won't you trust a woman's instincts in the matter?"

His eyes, which had been steely hard in their appraisal

of Mason, turned to Irene Keith and softened. "You're such a big-hearted girl," he said. "You always look for the best in everyone. You're simply incapable of understanding what really goes on in this world of ours."

"Now, please, Mervyn. I feel very deeply about this."

Aldrich smiled tenderly at her for a moment, then turned once more to Mason. His manner was coldly contemptuous. "Just what's your proposition, Mr. Mason?"

Mason said, "Irene Keith signed a felony complaint accusing Evelyn Bagby of a crime. Evelyn Bagby was imprisoned, then tried and acquitted. That leaves the situation in rather an unsatisfactory state."

"Unsatisfactory from whose viewpoint?" Aldrich asked.

"From the viewpoint of all parties concerned."

"Irene didn't have any malice toward this woman. She'd never seen her. The deputy district attorney told Irene to sign and she signed. Any claim against her wouldn't have a legal leg to stand on. Any lawyer would tell her that."

Mason said, "I tried to get Miss Keith to give me the name of her lawyer and let me talk to him. Since she preferred to discuss it personally, I am keeping it on that basis."

"That's all very pretty," Aldrich said. "But you can't hold Irene for a thin dime as damages. She didn't even know the girl. She had no malice. She swore to the complaint on the advice of the authorities."

"Are you," Mason asked, "trying to tell me the law?"

"Yes."

"I thought so."

Mason got to his feet.

"Now, wait a minute," Aldrich said, "perhaps I'm misjudging you."

"I think you are, but it's too late for that to make any difference now," Mason told him.

"Look," Irene said pleadingly to Mason, "I think you're being unduly disturbed about this."

"I don't," Mason replied.

Mason walked over to hold open the exit door from the private office.

Irene Keith glanced at Aldrich, turned impulsively to Mason. Mervyn Aldrich took a firm hold of her arm. "Come on, Irene," he said. "Let's go."

Mason watched the door click shut behind them. Della Street threw the switch which shut off the recording machine.

"Well!" she said.

Mason stood frowning at the door through which his visitors had departed.

"Chief," Della Street said, "if she wanted to settle, *why* do you suppose she asked Mervyn Aldrich to meet her here?"

Mason turned to regard Della Street with thoughtful concentration. At length he said, "Thank you, Della."

Her eyes were puzzled. "For what?"

"For pointing out a key to the situation. One which I all but overlooked."

"I don't get it," she said.

"Mervyn Aldrich," Mason told her, "is extremely punctual. He never waits more than five minutes for anyone. He keeps his appointments right on the dot."

"Well?" Della Street asked. "I still don't get it."

"Irene Keith's appointment," Mason said, "was for two-thirty. She asked Mervyn Aldrich to meet her here. He showed up some fifteen minutes later. Therefore she must have told him to meet her at two-forty-five.

"You remember Irene Keith told me she was going to a beauty parlor and get her deadly weapons burnished. She warned me she was going to use sex appeal."

Della nodded.

"So," Mason said, "she planned on having fifteen minutes to dazzle me with her personality, to get acquainted, to act the part of a broad-minded, generous woman who was very anxious to make amends for any wrong that might have been done Evelyn Bagby.

"Then Mervyn Aldrich who, either by preconceived plan or by natural temperament, was nasty, cold, supercilious, sarcastic and utterly impossible, entered the picture and all offers of settlement were promptly knocked in the head."

"Then you think this was all planned?"

"Very definitely," Mason said. "It was a little too opportune to have just happened."

"Well," Della Street said, "I can tell you something more, something from a woman's standpoint."

"What's that?" Mason asked.

"Irene Keith is, very, *very* much interested in Mervyn Aldrich. I suppose that the theft of the jewels played into Steve Merrill's hands in that he had time to file his suit before Helene could get married, but I'll bet you that when the wedding was called off Irene Keith didn't become dehydrated because of shedding tears."

Mason's eyes narrowed. "Now that opens a highly interesting field for speculation, Della. I think under the circumstances we'll engage in a little investigative work and see if we can't uncover some facts which might be of value."

She smiled. "In other words, we have a job for Paul Drake."

"Exactly. Run down the hall and see if Drake's in his office. Drag him away from whatever he's doing and get him down here. The plot, it would seem, has begun to thicken."

"Which," she observed over her shoulder, as she went through the door, "is the way some people I know like it."

5

PAUL DRAKE, HEAD OF THE DRAKE DETECTIVE AGENCY which had its offices on the same floor of the building occupied by Perry Mason, slid into the clients' overstuffed chair, swiveled around on the small of his back so that he was sitting sideways in the big chair, his knees over one rounded arm, his back resting against the other.

"Okay, Perry," he said. "Shoot."

Mason started to say something, paused thoughtfully, selected a cigarette, lit it, and studied the smoke for a few moments, said, "You know Helene Chaney, Paul?"

"The actress?"

"Yes."

"Not personally."

"What do you know about her?"

"Not too much. There's a lot of stuff released from time to time by her publicity director. That doesn't mean a damn thing. On the screen she's sexy, sultry and seductive; she has come-hither eyes, and wears low-cut dresses, but always within the pale of respectability. She also fills out tight sweaters.

"That means that her publicity department works overtime taking photographs of her being a busy little homebody, wearing an apron, high-necked blouses, long skirts, and things of that sort. She just *loves* to cook. It's one of the great tragedies of life that her career keeps her from staying home and being a housewife. She's portrayed as being sexy on the screen. Actually she's a sweet little homebody. Whenever she has a few minutes she loves to knit something for friends, little knickknacks. She—"

"Don't," Mason said. "It's too much of a pattern."

"Isn't it." Drake grinned. "You'd think they'd develop a new wrinkle. I understand she's about to commit matrimony again."

Mason nodded. "It was all set for a splice in Las Vegas but somebody stole the wedding presents. That put a stop to the Las Vegas wedding safari. Then her second husband, a chap by the name of Merrill, entered the picture with legal proceedings and snarled everything up with red tape. What do you know about Merrill, Paul?"

"Nothing much. He was an actor, if you want to call it that—I guess he still is. Helene, you know, wasn't top billing until she made that picture where she played the part of the Korean newspaper correspondent."

Mason nodded.

"Why, what's the pitch?" Drake asked.

Mason said, "Evelyn Bagby was arrested for theft of jewels from Irene Keith's car. She was acquitted yesterday."

"That's right," Drake said. "tried up in one of the cow counties, wasn't she? I read about it in the paper."

"Make it an orange county," Mason said, grinning. "She was tried in Riverside."

Drake nodded.

"Now then," Mason went on, "I'd like to get some sort of a settlement for Evelyn Bagby."

"Does she have a case?"

"Not at present. She can't prove malice. There probably wasn't any. Irene Keith swore to the complaint but she did so on the advice of the deputy district attorney."

Drake nodded.

"But," Mason went on, "if I know more about the facts in the case I *might* find there was a frame-up. Then Evelyn Bagby would be in a different position. If the girl was guilty that's one thing. If she was innocent, and the evidence so indicates, then someone deliberately tried to frame her. The person who planted the bracelet in her motel room certainly tried to frame her, and Harry

Boles, the man who identified her as having opened the suitcase taken from Irene Keith's automobile, may have been the victim of an honest mistake or he may have been in on the frame-up."

Drake nodded.

"Find out," Mason said.

"How soon?"

"Fast."

Drake heaved himself out of the chair. "You're so good to me," he complained, as he turned the knob on the exit door.

"And here's another thing," Mason called as Drake opened the door, "find out about Steve Merrill. See if he ever went under the name of Staunton Vester Gladden."

Drake turned back to the office. "What name?"

"Staunton Vester Gladden."

Drake jotted the name in his notebook. "I suppose you want *that* information within thirty minutes."

Mason grinned. "Tomorrow night will do on that one, Paul."

6

AT FOUR-FORTY-FIVE THAT AFTERNOON MASON'S UNlisted telephone rang sharply. Mason nodded to Della Street to answer it.

Della said, "Hello. . . . Okay, just a minute, Paul."

She turned to Mason. "Paul Drake says one of his men has information from Corona."

Mason took the phone, said, "Hello, Paul."

Drake said, "Hi, Perry. One of my men has uncovered

pay dirt at Corona. The 3D Motel, right across from the tavern, rented a unit at 11:30 A.M. on the day the jewels were stolen to a young woman wearing dark glasses, who seems to have given a phony name and address. A maid says she saw this woman coming out of Evelyn Bagby's unit at the motel. The maid wouldn't have paid any attention to it only the woman seemed so self-conscious. She explained she'd made a mistake and walked into the wrong place. She was just taking her stuff in from her car."

"What time?" Mason asked sharply.

"It must have been when this woman rented the place, around eleven-thirty. Some time between then and eleven-forty-five. The manager can't be absolutely certain. She remembers that the unit had just been made up. The checking out time is ten o'clock. The maids come to work at ten o'clock and it takes them until about two to get things finished. So when this person showed up at eleven-thirty in the morning the manager had to find one unit that was already made up so that she could rent it to her. She remembers the time from that."

"How about a description?" Mason asked.

"I'm coming to that," Drake said. "She was tall. About five feet six. She wore dark glasses, good clothes, and was driving an expensive make of automobile. The manager can't be sure which. The tenant listed the car on the registration slip as a Cadillac, but the manager is inclined to think it was a Lincoln. She's just not sure."

"What about the license number?"

"I've checked it," Drake said. "It's a phony."

"And the address?"

"Fictitious."

"What else about the description of the girl?"

"Well-dressed, smartly tailored, well-modulated voice, and kept dark glasses on all the time. The manager thinks she was about twenty-nine or thirty. She remembers one thing about her. The woman wore a distinctive pair of alligator-skin shoes. The manager noticed those. They were expensive shoes. The girl had pretty feet and ankles and the manager noticed the shoes because she was trying to size this woman up. You know they don't like to rent motel units at that hour in the morning to an unescorted, attractive young woman who might get the place into trouble."

"But she did rent a unit to this one?"

"That's right. The woman said she'd been driving most of the night, that she was going on into Hollywood and she wanted to get two or three hours' sleep, that she was perfectly willing to pay for a full day on the unit, even though she would only be there a few hours. She said she wanted to rest her eyes and relax for an hour or so."

"And how long was she there?"

"That's the significant thing," Drake said. "She evidently had checked out by one o'clock."

"How come?"

"At twelve-thirty one of the maids noticed that this unit was vacant, that the key was on the outside of the door. Someone had taken a shower and left towels on the floor. But the bed hadn't been disturbed at all and there wasn't any baggage in the place."

"And this woman did go in Evelyn Bagby's cabin?"

"Apparently so. The maid saw her coming out. She thinks it was this same woman who rented the cabin at such an unusually early hour."

Mason said, "Of course, Paul, at that time the jewelry hadn't been stolen."

"I know. I thought you'd be interested."

"I am. Where was Evelyn?"

"Apparently out to breakfast. She slept late while she was there, told the maid she'd had to get up by an alarm clock for years and was going to enjoy life while she had the chance."

Mason said, "Get pictures of Irene Keith, Paul. See if

the maid can identify this mysterious tenant as Irene. If she can we're off to the races."

"Remember this woman was wearing dark glasses, Perry."

"Well, keep after it."

"I will," Drake promised. "You going to be there for a while?"

"I'll let you know when I leave," Mason told him. "In fact, I'll drop by your office on my way out. You keep working on this angle."

"What's new?" Della Street asked as Mason hung up.

Mason relayed Drake's information on to her, said, "Try getting Evelyn Bagby on the phone, Della."

"Do you want to talk with her personally?"

"No. Tell her there are some new and very interesting developments in her case. Tell her that Irene Keith may approach her personally and try to dazzle her with an offer of settlement. Tell her that no matter what happens or how extravagant the offer may seem, she isn't to make any settlement."

Della Street nodded, started for the outer office. "I'll put through the call out there, Chief, so it won't disturb you."

"Then get Frank Neely at Riverside," Mason said. "Tell him that we're working on a hot lead."

Della Street went into the other room to put through the call. Mason started pacing the floor, his eyes narrowed in thought.

A few minutes later Della Street returned. "Chief, I got Joe Padena on the phone. Evelyn isn't there."

"No?" Mason asked, pausing in his pacing.

"No. Evelyn worked from twelve until three. She goes on again at eight and works until one in the morning. You can figure what happened. You gave her a hundred dollars and got her a job. She's out getting new clothes."

Mason grinned. "That, Della, we could regard as elemental."

"Here's another bit of information Padena gave me. I asked if anyone else had been asking for Evelyn—if there were any messages. He said a man called and left word that S. M. was willing to settle and would they please see that Evelyn got the message."

"S. M.?" Mason asked.

"Yes, just those two initials."

"Steve Merrill," Mason said. "How the devil did *he* know where he could reach her?"

"Perhaps she called him again."

"She could have."

"Or," Mason said, "that message about settling could have related to the matter of the arrest—and if we can identify that woman who went to Evelyn's cabin in Corona as Irene Keith I wouldn't settle for twenty-thousand dollars."

"Shall we leave a message for Evelyn Bagby?" Della Street asked.

"She might call S. M. first," Mason said.

"So what do we do?"

Mason looked at his watch, reached a quick decision.

"Della, take my car. Hop out there. Take the short cut. The minute Evelyn Bagby shows up give her my message. Be sure she gets that message before she sees anyone else or gets any message. Call me when you've talked with her and we'll meet for dinner out in Hollywood—or are you free?"

"Yes, I'm free. I'm also hungry. I'm on my way. I'll be calling you, probably within an hour."

She adjusted her hat and coat, opened the exit door, flashed him a smile, then said, "Heavens, I didn't call Neely. I got this report from Joe Padena, and—"

Mason motioned her on her way. "Gertie can get Neely. You get going, Della."

Mason stood for a moment looking at the closing door, then crossed over to his desk, picked up the phone and said to Gertie at the switchboard, "Get Frank Neely at Riverside for me. I'll hang on to the line."

Mason advised Neely that because of "certain developments" it would be unwise to even discuss a settlement at the present time.

"That's okay," Neely told him, laughing. "I'm leaving everything in your hands, Counselor. If they asked me I wouldn't even tell them what time it was. I'm just tagging along as associate counsel as a matter of courtesy."

"You're tagging along in this," Mason said, "because you're going to get some cash to compensate you for the work you did in defending Evelyn Bagby."

"You think things look promising?"

"Oh, it's difficult to tell," Mason said noncommittally, "but we *may* be on a lead that will enable us to get a fair settlement."

"Well, I hope so on account of the girl. She needs the money," Neely said. "But you must know some law that I don't. I'm darned if I see how you can bring an action for malicious prosecution when the complainant in the case acted under instructions from the deputy D.A."

"I don't know any law you don't," Mason replied, "but I've been in the practice long enough to realize that it's advisable to get *all* the facts, and *then* apply the law."

"I'll remember that," Neely said.

Mason laughed. "It takes a long time to learn that. It isn't in the law books. I'll keep you posted."

He hung up, settled back in his chair, locked his hands behind his head, and concentrated. After a while he lit a cigarette, smoked contemplatively, his mind probing the various facets of the situation that had been uncovered.

Gertie tapped on the door of Mason's private office, entered and said, "Irene Keith is in the office. She wants to see you about something she says she'll have to explain personally."

"Is she alone?" Mason asked, flicking the switch which turned on the hidden tape recorder.

Gertie nodded.

"Send her in," Mason said, grinding out the cigarette he was smoking, "and Gertie—"

"Yes, Mr. Mason."

"If, within a few minutes, a Mervyn Aldrich should come in, stating that he was to meet Irene Keith, just tell him I'm in conference and left word that I wasn't to be disturbed."

Gertie nodded.

"The same holds true for anyone else," Mason went on. "I'm about to have a conference with a young woman whose conscience is probably giving her twinges of remorse, and this time I want to be damn certain I'm not interrupted by someone who has a mental callus where his conscience should be. Do you get me?"

Gertie smiled and turned toward the door. "Very definitely."

There was a cool, long-legged efficiency about the manner in which Irene Keith came striding into Mason's private office, which indicated she had a carefully thought out plan of campaign.

"Hello, Mr. Mason," she said, coming forward to give him her hand. "I'm terribly sorry about what happened."

Mason raised his eyebrows.

"About Merv. Mervyn Aldrich, you know."

"What about him?" Mason asked.

"That manner of his, that way of looking at the thing with such a completely detached, dehydrated viewpoint. He squeezed every bit of human relationship out of the situation and regarded it as a dry problem in detached economics."

"Do sit down," Mason said.

"Mr. Mason, I want to do something for that girl."

"I think," Mason told her, looking down at the alligator-skin shoes she was wearing, "that you'd better let me talk with your attorney."

She settled herself in the clients' big chair, crossed her knees, smiled at Mason and said, "Why? Are you afraid of me, Mr. Mason?"

"No, but the situation may be a little more complicated than I had at first supposed and—well, I think you should have an attorney."

"I don't. I handle my own business affairs very nicely. I go to an attorney if I get in trouble."

"You're in trouble now."

She raised her eyebrows.

"I think it is only fair to tell you, Miss Keith, that since my last talk with you I have uncovered some evidence that would make it seem that Evelyn Bagby has a very good cause of action for defamation of character, malicious prosecution, false arrest and imprisonment."

"My, you sound formidable."

"I intend to."

"And whom would the action be against, Mr. Mason?"

"I believe you signed the complaint."

"Oh, if you want to get stuffy and technical," she said, smiling, "I signed the complaint on the advice of a public official. The deputy district attorney told me to sign. In fact he made out the complaint and then pushed it across to me and said, 'Sign here,' and I signed there."

Mason nodded.

"Doesn't that completely eliminate any question of malice, Mr. Mason?"

Mason said, "You seem to have an unusually clear concept of the law relating to prosecution for malicious arrest."

"Oh," she said, laughing, "I know the *law*."

"You do?"

"Oh yes, I've been to my attorney on that."

"I see," Mason said dryly.

"I don't think you do. You see, I retain an attorney to

tell me what the law is. As far as deciding what to do, I think my business judgment is better than that of my attorney. I have made more money for myself than he has made for himself."

"Money, of course, isn't everything," Mason said.

"It's a darn good yardstick."

"Financial success depends on a lot of things. People may have initiative, judgment and skill and still be unsuccessful so far as money is concerned. There's an element of daring and of luck in financial success."

"That's exactly right, Mr. Mason. I'm glad to hear you say so. I have more initiative, more judgment, more skill than my attorney, and I have a darn sight more daring, and so far I've done all right on luck."

"So you saw your lawyer and asked him about the law."

"Oh yes."

"And he advised you?"

"That's right."

"What did he say?"

She laughed and said, "Do you want to know exactly what he said?"

"If you wish to tell me."

"He said I was to tell you and your client, Evelyn Bagby, to go to hell."

"So then you decided to come over here?"

"Yes."

"Why?"

"To make a settlement."

"It may be a little more difficult than you think."

"Oh, stuff and nonsense, Mr. Mason. I'm going to give that girl a thousand dollars. That will compensate her for all the annoyance and trouble she's had. It will make my conscience feel a lot better and it will give you a fee. Here's the check. I've made it out to you as attorney for Evelyn Bagby, and I've endorsed on the back of it that by acceptance, endorsement and cashing of this check you, as Evelyn Bagby's attorney, warrant that I will be held forever harmless from any action by or on behalf of Evelyn Bagby because of false arrest, slander, malicious prosecution, false imprisonment, or anything else growing out of the events in connection with a loss of jewels in the County of Riverside, and that she will and does release any and all claims she may have against me from the beginning of the world to date."

Mason laughed and said, "That endorsement I take it, was dictated by your attorney."

"Oh certainly."

"Yet you preferred to handle negotiations yourself."

She nodded.

"I think," Mason said, "you'd better let your attorney tell me to go to hell personally."

"What's the matter, Mr. Mason? Aren't you going to accept this thousand dollars?"

"I don't think so."

She looked at him with every semblance of complete stupefied surprise. "Good Lord, Mr. Mason, there's a thousand dollars for your client! I'm handing it to you on a silver platter."

"I don't see the platter," Mason said.

"I was speaking figuratively of course."

"So was I."

Her eyes met his. "Are you bluffing, or do you have an ace in the hole?"

"I have an ace in the hole."

"And you're going to refuse to accept this check on behalf of your client? Are you going to turn down a settlement without even consulting your client?"

"I'll submit the offer to her and advise her to reject it."

"May I ask why?"

"Where were you on the day of the theft, at say eleven o'clock in the morning?"

"Helene Chaney and I were in a beauty shop getting our weapons sharpened. You can check with the operators there if you wish. Then we went to lunch and then—well, you asked about the morning?"

"Yes."

"That's the answer. Was I supposed to be alarmed or to try to evade the question?"

"Not necessarily. I asked for information."

"And you got it. Are you going to accept this thousand-dollar settlement?"

"Probably not. I'll have to—"

"Now wait a minute," she interrupted. "You're not going to play that kind of poker with me, Mr. Mason. I'm giving you exactly five hours to accept or reject. I'll be at my home until ten-thirty. If you don't telephone me by ten-thirty that you are accepting that compromise, I'll instruct the bank to stop payment on the check. My telephone number is Halverstead 6-8701."

The private, unlisted telephone on Mason's desk rang sharply. Since only Della Street and Paul Drake had the number of that telephone its ring always commanded precedence over anything Mason was doing. He said, "Pardon me," picked up the receiver, said, "Hello," and heard Della Street's voice.

"Hello, Chief. Is it all right to talk?"

"For you."

"Not for you?"

"No."

"Someone's in the office with you?"

"Yes."

"Someone connected with the Evelyn Bagby business?"

"Yes."

"Well look, Chief, I'm out here at the Crowncrest Tavern. Evelyn Bagby is back from her shopping," Della Street said. "She just came in. I've had a chance to exchange only a few words with her, but I've found out that the message from S. M. is from Steve Merrill all right.

Evelyn picked up some back number movie magazines after she left our office, found some more pictures and became more certain than ever that Steve Merrill is really the Staunton Gladden who embezzled her money. So she called his number. He was out but a woman who answered the phone said she'd take any message.

"Well, Evelyn left her name and the place where she was working and told the woman to ask Mr. Merrill to tell Mr. Gladden to call her there no later than five o'clock today."

"Just that message?" Mason asked.

"That's all, just that message. But it did the work. Merrill called and left that message for Evelyn—that he'd settle."

"Well," Mason said, "I think you'd better get in here and we'll discuss that phase of the matter."

"You want me to come back right away?"

"That's right."

"I'm coming," she said, "and shall I tell Evelyn Bagby to do nothing until she hears from you?"

"That's right, nothing."

Mason hung up the telephone, paused, waiting for Irene Keith to say something.

Abruptly she arose, gave him her hand. "I think you're bluffing," she said. "I liked you a lot this afternoon. Now I'm not so certain."

"That," Mason told her, "is one of the disadvantages of conducting your own negotiations. If you had permitted your attorney to call on me we could have retained our pleasant personal relationship."

She opened the door, turned to look at Mason over her shoulder, then archly blew him a kiss. "Good night, Counselor," she said mockingly.

"Good night," Perry Mason said.

The door slowly closed, shutting out the sound of Irene Keith's heels as they clicked rapidly down the corridor.

7

At this time of the year it got dark at an early hour and Mason, waiting for Della Street to return, walked over to the office window and stood moodily looking down at the tangled mass of blaring, congested traffic in the street below.

Strangled by traffic, the tortured streets seemed to deplore their futility as the whole business district of the city became snarled in a bottleneck of slowly moving cars and pedestrians.

After a few moments Mason went to the outer office to see if Gertie, the receptionist, was still at the switchboard. She had gone home. The board was fixed for the night. The office was dark.

Mason walked back through the law library, paused to glance at the thousand-dollar check on his desk, then started slowly pacing the floor, turning various angles of the case over in his mind.

From time to time he looked at his wrist watch, impatiently awaiting Della Street's return, knowing that the time was running out when he had to either accept Irene Keith's compromise offer or reject it.

It was after six o'clock when Della Street reached the office.

"Gosh, Chief, I sure had to fight through traffic."

"I was afraid you'd have trouble. How's our client?"

"Well, of course, she's all worked up about this Steve Merrill business. I guess she needs money pretty bad. She intimated even a partial payment from Merrill would be a lifesaver."

Mason said, "Irene Keith was in. She left a thousand dollars by way of settlement. And she was wearing alligator-skin shoes."

"Oh-oh!" Della Street said.

"The check's on my desk there. Take a look at what's written on the back of it."

Della Street read the endorsement on the back.

"Now *isn't* that something."

"We have until ten-thirty tonight to accept or reject it," Mason said. "She left her telephone number and said she'd be waiting."

"Nice of her, wasn't it?"

Mason said, "The deuce of it is, Della, we're in a spot. I presume that thousand dollars will look big as a barn to Evelyn Bagby. If I tell her about it she'll instruct me to go ahead and accept the settlement, acting on the theory that a bird in the hand is worth two in the bush. If I don't tell her about it and we can't get enough additional evidence to make a good case and get a better settlement, I'd have to make up the thousand dollars out of my own pocket."

"Why?"

"Because I took it on myself to turn down an offer of compromise without communicating with a client."

"That means you'll have to tell her?"

"I suppose so."

"Want me to get her on the phone?"

"No," Mason said. "I've been thinking—what's that noise, Della?"

Della Street said, "Someone is ringing the board in the outer office. When it's connected up for the night and a call comes in it makes that buzzing noise, but that's all. Shall I see who it is?"

"It might be a good idea," Mason said. "We have so many irons in the fire that anyone who is that persistent deserves to be encouraged."

Della Street went out to the outer office, plugged in

the switchboard and Mason could hear her say, "Good evening. Perry Mason's office."

A moment later Della Street hurried back into the office. "It's Evelyn Bagby," she said. "She's terribly excited. She says she simply has to talk with you right away, something that's vitally important."

Mason said, "Put her on this phone, Della," and picked up his desk phone.

Della Street hurried back to the office to make the connection.

"Better listen in, Della," Mason called. "See what she has to say. Take notes—if there's anything you need to take notes on."

"Okay," she called, and plugged in the connection.

"Hello," Mason said.

"Oh, Mr. Mason," Evelyn Bagby exclaimed her voice quavering wtih excitement. "Something has happened. I don't know what to do. I—"

"All right," Mason said. "Tell me, what about it?"

She said, "I went shopping today and—"

"Yes, I know."

"I came back and Miss Street was here and—"

"Yes, yes, I know. Get to the point."

"Well, I want you to understand just how it happened. I had some new clothes I'd purchased, so I went into my room and took a shower and got ready to put on these new clothes and looked in my bureau drawer and—I found something."

It was impossible for the lawyer to keep skepticism out of his voice. "You mean *more* of the stolen jewelry?"

"No, no, Mr. Mason. Please understand me. I'm leveling with you."

"What did you find?"

"A gun."

"A gun!"

"Yes."

"Where was it?"

"Tucked right in the middle of a lot of folded garments I'd put in the drawer and—"

"No chance that it was in the drawer when you put your things in?"

"None whatever. It very definitely was placed there while I was uptown shopping."

"Where is it now?" Mason asked.

"I have it here with me. It's in my purse. I'm talking from the telephone booth upstairs."

"Take a look at it," Mason said. "Tell me what kind of a gun it is and whether it's loaded and whether it has been shot."

"I've already done that, Mr. Mason. It's a Colt. It's very, very light, almost no weight to it at all. It's fully loaded. It's a .38 caliber. It has a very short barrel, I guess about a two-inch barrel—the kind that officers carry with them. There are six cartridges in the cylinder."

"Has it been fired lately?" Mason asked. "Can you smell and—"

"No, I've smelled the barrel. It just has a smell of oil."

Mason said, "You have a car out there. Can you bring it in at—"

"I doubt if I can make it all the way into your office and then get back here in time to go to work at eight o'clock. I'll have to leave it for you somewhere."

Mason said, "This is important. Get out of there immediately. Jump in your automobile and drive to Hollywood. There's a restaurant known as the Joshua Tree Café at 6538 Pemberton Drive. Joe Padena can tell you how to get there. Ask for Mike, the headwaiter. He knows me. He'll show you to a table. Della Street and I are on our way out there. We'll get there very shortly after you do. Get started immediately."

"Very well," she said. "Is there anything else?"

"Yes," Mason said. "Before you start, look through your room carefully. Make sure that nothing else has been planted there."

Mason hung up the phone.

Della Street called from the outer office, "Do you want me to call Mike at the Joshua Tree?"

"Please," Mason told her.

"Okay. I'm putting through the call right now."

Mason carefully folded the thousand-dollar check, placed it in his billfold, got his hat and coat, then took Della Street's coat from the closet and was holding it ready for her when she returned from the telephone.

"Okay," Mason said, "slip into this. How's the weather, Della?"

"It looks like rain. It's dark as a pocket and there are heavy clouds with a south wind. It may start raining any minute. Feels like it, too. The air's damp and heavy."

"All right," Mason told her, "let's go. We'll meet Evelyn at the Joshua Tree Café."

Della Street adjusted her hat. Mason switched out the lights as soon as she had finished and they walked down the corridor, stopping in at Drake's office to have a quick word with Paul Drake.

Mason deftly piloted the car through traffic, avoiding the freeway, taking the through boulevards which were not quite so crowded at this time of night.

"She'll be there before us?" Della Street asked.

"She should be."

"What do you think of that gun, Chief?"

"She called Merrill once and got framed for a jewel theft. She called him a second time and—well, she says she found a gun—and she was out most of the afternoon."

"My but you're cynical!"

"A lawyer is trained to look at facts with a good, healthy cynicism."

"But she said the gun hadn't been fired."

"That's what she *said.*"

Della Street looked at him sharply, then lapsed into silence.

Mason concentrated on driving the car, speeding for

traffic signals whenever he had a chance, avoiding cars that were going to make left turns, threading his way in and out of traffic, yet carefully observing the traffic laws.

The doorman of the Joshua Tree Café was glad to see them. He took Mason's car and said obsequiously, "Good evening, Mr. Mason. Good evening, Miss Street. Looks as though it might rain tonight."

"It does for a fact," Mason said.

"Staying for dinner?"

"That's right."

"Yes, sir. I'll have the car all ready when you come out."

Mason entered the restaurant and Mike, the headwaiter, came hurrying over toward them.

"You have a young woman waiting for me, Mike? A redhead?"

The headwaiter glanced quickly at Della Street, then back to Mason, shook his head.

"The deuce! She should have been here. I—here she comes now," Mason said as Evelyn Bagby walked in the door. "How about a nice table for three over in a corner, Mike? We want to be where we can talk."

Della Street hurried over to Evelyn Bagby. "You didn't find anything else, did you?"

Evelyn Bagby shook her head.

"We thought you'd be here before us."

"I . . . I had an experience."

Della Street piloted the redhead over to Mason, and Mike ensconced them in a corner booth.

"Della and I are Bacardi cocktail fans," Mason said to Evelyn Bagby. "Do you—?"

"I love them," she said. "Could I have a double one?"

"Three double ones," Mason said. "It looks like rain. We'll keep warm within."

Della Street made a gesture of surrender. "Good-by now," she said.

Mason looked sharply at Evelyn Bagby. "What's wrong?"

She laughed nervously.

"Where's the gun?"

"Here in my purse."

"You're sure it hadn't been fired?"

She said, "It has now," and leaned forward, putting her chin on her hand. "I'm shaking like a leaf. I—I'm supposed to be pretty hard-boiled but I'm not too certain I'm not going to faint."

"Whoa. Back up!" Mason said. "What's the trouble?"

"Everything. Is it all right if I wait a minute before I try to tell you? I can do a lot better after I've had that Bacardi cocktail."

Mason said sharply, "The details can wait, but I want to know generally what happened and I want to know right now. We may not have too much time."

"I was held up."

"And you fired the gun?"

She nodded.

There was a moment of silence. She was apparently trying to get herself nerved up to a point where she could tell about it.

"I never had such a shock in all my life," she said. "Someone tried to kill me. I said it was a stick-up but I think it was an attempt to kill me."

"Wait a minute," Mason told her. "Take it easy. Who was this? Did you get a look at him?"

She nodded.

"Was it anyone you know?"

"I couldn't tell. His face was covered. He tried to kill me. He tried to run me off the road."

"Is that what took you so long?"

"I guess so. I searched my room."

"Find anything else?"

She shook her head.

"And then what?"

"I got in my jalopy and started down the grade and—I'll tell you in a minute. Let me sort of get my breath."

Mason and Della Street exchanged glances.

The waiter brought three double Bacardi cocktails.

"Like steaks?" Mason asked her.

"I won't eat here," she said. "I'll go on back. I'll have something light and then eat when I go off duty. You see I get meals with the job up there."

Mason said, "You're not going back on an empty stomach. Can you eat a steak?"

"I can *always* eat a steak."

"Medium rare?"

She nodded.

Mason said to the waiter, "Three steaks, medium rare, with French fried onions, baked potatoes, lots of butter and paprika, some Tipo Chianti—a big bottle of the red wine. Coffee later."

The waiter nodded and moved away.

"Here's how," Mason said.

They raised glasses. Mason noticed that Evelyn Bagby's hand was trembling so that she had to steady the cocktail glass with the tips of the fingers of her left hand.

"Let's see the gun," Mason said.

Evelyn Bagby fumbled in her purse, took out the gun, passed it across to Mason under the table.

"Oh-oh," Mason said as he balanced the gun in his hand.

"What's the matter?" Della Street asked.

"It's one of those new aluminum alloy jobs," Mason said. "This is the Colt 'Cobra.' A gun that, believe it or not, weighs only fifteen ounces. It has sufficient tensile strength to fire high-speed ammunition. This is a dream of a gun. Has the number been filed off or anything?"

"I didn't look."

Mason turned the gun so that he could get the light reflected on the number. "Take this down, Della," he said.

She wrote down the number as he called it off. "Number 17474-LW."

Mason said, "This gun hasn't been out very long. Whoever bought this did so recently. . . . Della."

"Yes, Chief."

"Skip to the telephone. Try and get Paul Drake before he goes out for dinner. Give him the number on this gun. Tell him to get an operative started on it right away. I think we can find out who purchased it. It's probably a stolen gun, but at least we can find out when it was sold and where."

"Will the records be open this time of night?" Evelyn Bagby asked as Della Street slid out from behind the table and hurried to the telephone.

"Some of them will," Mason said. "When they sell a gun they make out slips in triplicate, giving the number of the gun, the name and address of the purchaser and all of that. One of them is filed with the chief of police, the other with the sheriff. I think Paul can get action on a recent sale of this sort. That is, if it was sold in any nearby county, which takes in quite a lot of territory."

Mason swung the cylinder out, looked at the shells.

"Fired twice," he said.

"That's right."

"Do you want to tell me now?"

She tossed off the last of her drink. "Would it be terribly piggish if I asked for another?"

"It wouldn't be terribly piggish but it would be damned imprudent."

"Why?"

"I want to know what your story is before I determine how much liquor you're going to consume."

"I'm not particularly hungry but I certainly could use a bracer."

"Tell me about it," Mason said. "Then we'll see about the drink."

"Well, I was there for about five minutes I guess

after I called you, getting my room checked. I couldn't find a trace of anything else that had been planted. Not so much as a pocket handkerchief. . . . Could we talk about something else for a few minutes until that drink takes hold?"

They watched Della Street returning from the telephone booth.

"Get Paul?" Mason asked.

"Yes. I gave him the number of the gun and he has a man working on it."

"Does he have any more information from Riverside?"

"Apparently not."

Mason said, "I have an offer of settlement in your case, Evelyn."

"How much?"

"It's from Irene Keith. She offered a thousand dollars cash for a complete settlement of all claims."

"One . . . thousand . . . dollars?"

"Yes."

"How much would your fees be?"

"Mine would be fifty dollars," Mason said. "I would suggest two-hundred dollars as a fair fee for Neely. That would leave you seven-hundred-and-fifty dollars."

"It isn't fair for you to take the small end of the fee. You did all the work, all the—"

"And Neely had to sit in court and try your case there."

"I'd have been convicted if it hadn't been for you. I think you and Neely should divide the compensation."

Mason reached in his coat pocket, handed Evelyn Bagby the check.

"You have no idea what that money is going to mean to me at this time, Mr. Mason."

"You haven't got it yet," Mason said. "Turn it over and look at the back."

She turned it over and read the typewritten endorsement.

"Would that affect my claim against Steve Merrill in any way?"

Mason shook his head.

"Well," she said, "that's fine. I don't want to let Gladden, or Merrill, whatever his name is, off the hook. Since he called back and left that message I know that he's worried. He must be in a very vulnerable position. He couldn't afford to be arrested right at the present time and he couldn't afford to have the facts of his embezzlement become public."

Mason said, "I don't think you should accept this check, Evelyn."

"Why not?"

"I think we can get more."

She shook her head. "That money means too much to me right now to pass up."

Mason returned the check to his wallet.

"You want me to sign it?" she asked.

"It isn't necessary," Mason told her. "My endorsement will be sufficient. It puts me in the position of guaranteeing the settlement as your lawyer. Ordinarily I'd prefer to have you sign with me but I don't want anyone to sign until a few minutes before ten-thirty tonight. I want to wait for the deadline."

"Why?"

"Something may turn up," Mason said, watching her sharply.

"What *could* turn up?"

Mason laughed. "We've got a lot of irons in the fire. Almost anything can turn up. Now tell me about your holdup."

"Well, as I told you, I got in my jalopy and started out in a hurry, driving down the hill, taking that short cut you told me about. I hadn't gone very far from the turnoff from Mulholland Drive when I noticed there was a car behind me, a car that was coming very, very fast, with the headlights on the high adjustment so that they were bothering me a lot, reflecting from my rear-view mirror and windshield. I pulled off to the side of the road, slowed down, lowered the left-hand window, thrust out my arm and motioned with my hand and wrist for him to go on ahead.

"Instead of that he came almost alongside of me and then veered sharply so that he was crowding me off the road."

"What did you do?" Mason asked.

"I put my foot on the gas—thank heavens I had presence of mind enough to do that—and shot ahead. I turned my head long enough for just one brief glimpse, and what I saw completely paralyzed me."

"What did you see?"

"I saw a man with his head covered with a sack or pillow slip or something. There were two holes cut for the eyes and the thing was held in place around his forehead with a band of some sort, a ribbon or a rubber band. I just had that brief glimpse and that was all. Every time I think of it I get the jitters."

"So then what?"

"So then I started streaking down that mountain road and this man took after me. Fortunately I remembered this gun. I got it out and about that time this man came up alongside me again, driving like crazy, and this time I knew he was going to try to push me into the bank or off the road or something, so I just stuck the gun out of the window and fired two shots just as fast as I could pull the trigger."

"You were driving then with one hand?"

"That's right. I put my right hand on the wheel. I took the gun in my left hand, and I pushed it just as far as I could out of the window so that he'd be sure to see that I had a gun. I pointed it back in the general direction of his car and pulled the trigger twice."

"And what happened?"

"That did it," she said. "As soon as he knew that I was armed, he lost all interest in the chase."

"He put on his brakes?"

"Put on his brakes so hard that he skidded. I saw the headlights weaving back and forth and falling rapidly behind."

"You kept on going?"

"I'll tell the world I kept on going. I tossed the gun onto the cushions, put both hands on the wheel, and took the curves just as fast as I dared."

"You don't think he continued to follow you?"

"I know he didn't because I was watching in the rear-view mirror. His headlights never showed up around the curve."

"Well, that's fine," Mason said. "You frightened him off. However—perhaps it isn't so fine."

"What do you mean?"

Mason said, "You have a gun which was planted in your drawer and which has now been discharged. If later on you should be called on to explain the circumstances under which that gun had been discharged, there would, of course, only be your word for it. That wouldn't be so good. I think we'll notify the sheriff's office that someone tried to hold you up and that you had a gun and fired a couple of shots that frightened him off. Della, would you mind letting me out? I think I'd better be the one who telephones."

Della Street slid over on the cushioned seats so that Mason could get out.

He went to the telephone, called the sheriff's office and said, "This is Perry Mason, the lawyer. I am at the moment out at the Joshua Tree Café. I have a client with me who had an annoying experience up on the mountain roads back of Hollywood. Someone tried to hold her up. A masked man. He tried to either run her off the road or to crowd her into the guardrail at the side of the road so she'd be forced to stop. Fortunately she had a gun with her and she fired a couple of wild shots which served to frighten this man off. Do you want to do anything about it?"

"You bet we want to do something about it," the man at the other end of the line said. "I'll have a couple of deputies out there to talk with you within the next ten or fifteen minutes. We've been having a lot of trouble on mountain roads. There have been a good many sex cases that we've had to keep out of the papers because of consideration for the victims. This may be the break we've been looking for. You say she fired a couple of shots?"

"Just a couple of warning shots," Mason said, "wild shots, but—"

"I'd give two weeks out of my own salary if she'd taken time to aim and really hit him," the man said. "The fellow who is operating up in that country is a bad actor. Now where can we find you, Mr. Mason?"

"At the Joshua Tree Café. Just ask the headwaiter."

"That's fine. I'll have someone out right away, within fifteen minutes, twenty minutes at the latest."

"We'll be here," Mason said.

Mason hung up and walked back to the table. The waiter was bringing their food.

"Let's have this understood," Mason said. "Evelyn Bagby was carrying this gun at my request. She was coming down a dark road. I suggested that she have this gun with her. If anyone wants to think that I gave her the gun it's quite all right with me. Right at the moment we don't discuss the gun or how she happened to find it. Is that straight?"

"You mean the officers are going to question *me?*" Evelyn Bagby asked.

Mason nodded. "They'll be out here within ten or fifteen minutes. It won't be any kind of an ordeal. It seems they've had some trouble on the isolated roads, other cases of this sort, and they're very, very anxious to get information that will enable them to run down the culprit. They'll want a description of the car and anything else you may have noticed, and they'll probably want to have you show them exactly where the attack took place."

"Gosh, I can't tell them anything about the car," Evelyn Bagby said.

"Well, you know whether it was an open car or a closed car, whether it was a small model sports car or a standard or—"

"Oh yes, I know it was a medium-sized car, one in the medium-priced field, and it was a closed car. I don't think it was a coupé. I think it was a sedan. But that's about all I can tell them."

"What about the driver? Could you give a description of him?"

"No, I can't. That sack or pillow slip, or whatever it was, was over his head and down on his shoulders, and you just couldn't tell a thing about him. He had on an overcoat. The top of the sack was held in place around his forehead with some kind of a dark band, which may have been an elastic or may have been a piece of ribbon."

"Well, that's fine," Mason told her. "Don't worry about it."

"Oh, I'll get over it all right. I've got over worse things than this, but I'm a little shaky, and—well, I hope they do go back to look at the place and ask me to point it out to them. That will give me an opportunity to have an escort back up to the tavern. I think, Mr. Mason, that from now on I'm going to use the well-traveled roads and lay off of that short cut."

"I don't blame you," Mason said. "Apparently it's rather dangerous, judging from what they said over the telephone. There's been a lot of trouble. Well, let's forget all about stick-ups and officers and all of that and concentrate on eating."

"Mr. Mason, if I don't have a chance to tell you again you'll accept that compromise offer, won't you?"

"Well," Mason said, "let's leave it this way. We'll wait until the last minute."

"It's all right to wait until the last minute, but don't wait too long. That money will mean a lot to me."

"You're hard up?"

"I'm desperate for ready money."

"Well, what about Steve Merrill, or Staunton Vester Gladden?"

"I think I've thrown a scare into him. I doubt if he has any great amount of cash. He's probably on a shoestring himself."

"That's right," Mason said. "He never did get in the big-time stuff—just second-rate—but, of course, he's trying to shake down Helene Chaney. He may be able to get something there."

"In which event I want my share."

Mason said, "I notice that he refers to himself as Stephen V. Merrill. I wonder if he's kept the middle name of Vester? You don't know whether that's a family name, do you?"

"I don't know anything about him, Mr. Mason. That is, I know a lot about him, but everything I know is false. All of the stuff he told me about knowing his way around Hollywood and all of the stuff he told me about his vast experience as a dramatic coach, was just that much hooey.

"Of course, as a young girl I believed that he could direct me through scene after scene, that he could tell me what was wrong and how to hold my hands, where to look with my eyes, and just what expression to put in my voice, and— I thought he was wonderful."

She laughed bitterly.

"Well, let's go on with our dinner," Mason said, "and forget the disagreeable subjects."

For some minutes they ate in silence, Evelyn Bagby

obviously nervous, Della Street watching her thoughtfully, Mason apparently thinking only of the fine food.

Mike, the headwaiter, came to the table escorting a rather studious-looking individual who seemed much more like a statistician than a deputy sheriff.

"Good evening," the man said. "My name's Ferron, from the sheriff's office."

He produced a leather folder which contained a badge and identification as a deputy sheriff.

"Sit down and join us," Mason invited. "Can I order you something?"

"No thanks. I'm on duty. What's this about a holdup?"

"I'm Perry Mason," the lawyer said, getting to his feet and shaking hands. "This is Miss Street, my secretary, and Miss Evelyn Bagby, my client."

"I've seen you in court several times, Mr. Mason. I'm glad to meet you, Miss Street. What about the holdup?"

"Miss Bagby was held up," Mason said. "That is, someone either tried to hold her up or crowd her off to the side of the road."

"Where?" Ferron asked, taking out a notebook.

"Miss Bagby," Mason said, "has just started to work up at the Crowncrest Tavern. You know where that is?"

The deputy nodded.

"She was coming down the back road, that steep grade that—"

"I know."

"Not many people use that and she was driving down there—"

"What time?"

"What time was it, Evelyn?"

"I didn't look at my watch, but I would say it was about forty-five minutes ago."

"What happened?" Ferron asked, looking directly at her.

Mason said, "She's a little upset. I think I have the picture fairly clearly. Someone tried to crowd her off the road and almost did it."

"What stopped him?"

Mason said firmly, "Miss Bagby fired two shots."

"Two shots from what?"

"From a gun she was carrying."

"You carry a gun?" the deputy asked Evelyn Bagby sharply.

"Not ordinarily," Mason said, "but I think she will now. As a matter of fact, this was a gun that Miss Bagby was carrying at my request."

"You have no permit to carry a gun, Miss Bagby?"

"Oh for heaven's sake," Mason protested, "what is this? We call to report an attempted holdup and possible attempt at murder, and you start trying to put the victim on the defensive. Skip it. Cancel the report. Say the victim refuses to make a complaint."

"I have to report the facts. I was just trying to get them."

"Well, she had a gun. It was at my request she was carrying it. I had a special reason for asking her to carry it—and on my advice she isn't going to answer any more questions about the gun.

"Now then, do you want to know about the holdup?"

"Of course we do. That's why I burned up the roads getting out here. We're very much interested in these holdups on the dark roads above Hollywood. We've had some bad crimes. Speaking unofficially and off the record, Miss Bagby, if you took two shots at this individual I'm hoping that both shots were bull's-eyes."

"Oh, but they weren't," Evelyn said. "I just shot wild in order to frighten him and keep from being crowded off the road."

"Now then, Miss Bagby, here's the important thing. Can you give us any kind of description of the car or the man who was driving it?"

Evelyn Bagby said, "The car was a closed car. I think

it was in pretty good shape. It looked shiny. The bright lights were on and they had been flashing from my windshield and rearview mirror right into my eyes. I wanted the car to go on past, so I opened my window, put out my arm and motioned with my wrist and hand for him to go on by."

Ferron nodded.

"And," Evelyn Bagby said, "he came up rapidly behind me. I put on my brakes and slowed. He still had the bright lights on. Then, all of a sudden, he swerved over directly against my car."

"What did you do?"

"If I'd continued to put on the brakes I think he'd have pushed me right over the grade. As it was, I stepped on the gas and shot ahead and I think that disconcerted him. I had turned to shout at him, caught a glimpse of a hooded man, and got cold in the pit of my stomach. I saw that he was deliberately trying to crowd me off the road."

"What's this about a hooded man?" Ferron asked.

"He had a flour sack or pillow slip over his head. There were two round holes cut for the eyes and the thing was held in position around the forehead with a rubber band or a ribbon of some sort. It was the weirdest, most awful thing you could imagine."

"So what did you do?"

"I pushed the throttle all the way down to the floorboard and almost without thinking I grabbed this gun and—"

"Where did you have the gun?"

"In my purse, on the seat, right beside me."

"And what did you do?"

"I put it in my left hand and I shot once out of the window, just as I got the gun pushed out of the window. I think that must have been about at right angles to the road, and then just as fast as I could pull the trigger I turned the gun a little back and shot again."

"Shooting at the person?"

"Heavens no! I wasn't aiming. The first shot I fired completely wild, and the second shot I pulled the gun down, trying to shoot at—well, at nothing in particular, but I guess just above the headlights. It hit something that gave a plinking sound, a rock or something."

Ferron shook his head. "We've had quite a few instances of a vicious criminal annoying women on these lonely roads and—"

"With their faces covered by sacks?" Mason asked.

"No," Ferron said. "That's a new angle. Most of the time this fellow's not even masked. This one man in particular that we'd love to get is a desperate, cruel thug. You've probably read something about it in the paper, but a lot of it doesn't get in the paper. Girls who have been attacked don't like publicity and notoriety, and we keep a lot of that stuff confidential."

Mason took the gun from Evelyn Bagby's purse. "Want to look at the gun?" he asked.

"No," Ferron said, "that doesn't make any—why, hello, that's one of those new short-barreled aluminum alloy guns."

"That's right," Mason said.

"A swell little gun." Ferron reached over and balanced it in his hand.

"The gun," Mason said, "had been picked up by Evelyn Bagby in accordance with my instructions."

"Well, it's a darned good thing she had it with her," Ferron said, returning the gun to Evelyn Bagby. "I suggest you keep it with you. Where did all this happen?"

Evelyn Bagby said, "Just about—well, there's a private driveway with a white arch over the—"

"Yes, yes, I know that place. An artist lives up there. She's rather elderly. Lives there all alone. That's rather isolated but it's out of the county. It's in the city limits. Was it near there?"

"Just about a hundred yards or so below that."

"Well, we'd better take a run up that road," Ferron said. "There isn't one chance in a hundred that your man will be still prowling around there. In fact you've probably thrown such a scare into him that he'll lay low for a week. What happened after you shot, Miss Bagby?"

"He slammed on his brakes. He must have put them on awfully hard because I could see the headlights weaving as though the car might be skidding."

"And then what?"

"Then I swept around a curve in the road, and—well, believe me, I went just as fast as I dared, but the headlights never came around that curve behind me."

"That's fine. You really threw a scare into him. He's accustomed to picking on defenseless women who get paralyzed with fright the minute they realize what they're up against. Then they're like putty in his hands. If this is the guy that I think it is I'd sure like to get an opportunity to get him lined up in *my* sights."

"I hope," Mason said, "that we can handle this so there won't be any publicity?"

"Oh sure," Ferron told him. "In fact, things of this sort the papers don't pay much attention to. Except, of course, in this case Miss Bagby being a client of yours might make good copy. But you don't need to worry, we'll put this on a confidential report."

"I wish you would."

"You are going to take a run up there?" Mason said.

"Oh sure, we'll run on up. We'd like to have Miss Bagby come along and show us exactly where it happened and, of course, since it's in the city limits we'll have to report to the city and let the city police handle it. However, we have an understanding on this lonely road bandit and we work hand-in-glove with the city.

"You see, this prowler is my special detail. My partner and I have been working nights, patrolling these roads a lot, and hoping we'd run on to one of these fellows while he's at work."

Mason beckoned for the waiter, added a twenty per cent tip to the check and signed it. "Come on," he said, "let's go. You have a partner, Ferron?"

"Yes. Outside."

"Well," Mason said, "Miss Bagby has her car. I have my car. You and I can ride with Miss Bagby. Your partner can drive your car and Della Street can drive mine. In that way you can have Miss Bagby available for any further questions while we're on our way up the mountain."

Mason took the gun, swung open the cylinder displaying the two empty shells and the four loaded cartridges.

Ferron seemed to have but little interest in the gun. "You've certainly kept your head nicely, Miss Bagby. I only wish there were a few more women like you who had enough presence of mind to pull the trigger under proper circumstances, and who had a gun with them."

Mason took the gun, casually slipped it in his coat pocket.

Ferron got to his feet. "Well, if you folks are ready, let's go."

8

THE CAVALCADE OF THREE CARS SWUNG OFF THE MAIN road and dropped into low gear as they ground their way up the winding stretch of narrow mountain road. For the most part the occupants were silent.

Mason said, "Just tell us when we come to the place, Evelyn."

"I will. I'm not too certain about—I think it was—wait—a minute, it was right around this turn where I was making time and— Slow down a bit as we get around the turn because that's where—"

"Hey, wait a minute," Ferron said. "Did you see that?"

"What?" Mason asked.

"That guardrail."

"I didn't notice it."

"Well, it's broken. Stop a minute. Just hold your car here. Keep your foot on the brake. This is a steep grade."

Mason signaled the cars behind as Evelyn Bagby braked to a stop.

Ferron got out and disappeared into the darkness.

"Did you see it, Mr. Mason?" Evelyn Bagby asked.

Mason said, "I can look back and see it. It looks like a car has gone through that guardrail."

Evelyn Bagby's hand on Mason's arms was suddenly trembling with apprehension.

"Oh Mr. Mason, do you suppose there's any chance, any chance that someone else took my place? He could have waited until some other woman came along, tried to crowd her into the rail and hit her car too hard. That would mean that—if I hadn't had that gun, I'd be—down there!"

Mason said in a low voice, "Sit tight and don't do *any* talking. If there's anything down there you're going to be completely prostrated. You leave things to me."

Ferron came running back up the hill to the car. "You're going to have to wait here, Mr. Mason," he said. "A car sure as hell went down that grade. Seems to have gone through the guardrail almost head-on. I'm getting my partner and a searchlight out of the car. We'll see what we can find down there. You'd better back your car so the rear wheels are up against the bank there. This is too steep a grade to hold your car simply with the brakes."

"Can I help you?" Mason asked.

"Probably not now. We'll see. It looks very much as if your bandit really was intent on running someone off the grade. He may have mistaken Miss Bagby for someone else, or he may have tried to force some other girl into stopping, and—anyhow, we'll know the answer pretty soon."

Ferron ducked away into the darkness. Mason said, "Now remember, Evelyn, keep a cool head, but if you have to, use all the feminine wiles of tears, hysterics, or anything else."

Ferron and his partner moved their car over to the side of the road, took out a powerful searchlight, and, standing by the break in the fence, swung the beam of the searchlight down the steep mountainside.

Della Street came walking up to join Mason and Evelyn Bagby. "What is it?"

"Another victim, perhaps," Mason said.

Della studied Evelyn Bagby. "You weren't aiming?"

"Heavens no! I just pushed the gun out of the window and let it go."

Mason caught Della's eye. "I'll go over to take a look, Della. You stay here and talk with Evelyn."

Mason crossed over to the broken guardrail.

"See anything?" Mason asked.

"Yes, there's a car down there at the foot of the ravine," Ferron said. "We're going to get out a coil of rope and tie it to the support for the guardrail so we can get down there without falling all over ourselves. Okay, here we go."

Ferron's partner appeared with a coil of rope. He made a bowline knot around one of the supports for the guardrail, then snaked the coil down the mountainside, where it rolled and twisted down toward the wreck.

"Let's go," Ferron said.

The two deputies eased themselves down the grade, holding to the rope to keep from slipping.

Mason could see the beam of the searchlight playing

around in the darkness down the deep canyon. From time to time he heard excited voices, but no one reported on what they had found. Apparently the two deputies had completely forgotten the people waiting above.

Mason glanced toward Evelyn's car where Della Street was sitting next to Evelyn Bagby. He could hear Della's voice as she kept up a stream of conversation, keeping Evelyn Bagby's mind occupied.

Mason gripped the rope, eased his weight over the edge and started working his way down the steep slope. The night was dark as a pocket. The only illumination was furnished by the intermittent wandering beam of the searchlight and a faint reflection from the lights of Hollywood which stretched out below, blazing colored signs, twinkling lights.

By shielding his eyes so he could look down into the darkness, Mason could see where the wheels of an automobile had left tracks, then swung sideways. For another fifty or sixty feet the car had evidently been in the air. Then it had struck and left a gouged out place in the hillside.

Mason continued to work his way on down, holding to the rope, feeling his way cautiously. The sound of voices at the bottom of the ravine was plainer now and Mason could hear comments.

". . . darned good job if you ask me."

"Must have gone through . . . right window . . . open . . ."

"Better get Homicide. . . . It's in the city limits."

Mason moved through sagebrush and greasewood, came at length to the bottom of a ravine where a heavy growth of chaparral had broken the impact of the rolling car.

"Well, what are you finding?" he asked.

Ferron's voice was suddenly harsh. He asked, "Are you alone?"

"That's right. The girls are up there in the car."

"It looks like she made a bull's-eye all right," Ferron said.

"The devil!" Mason exclaimed.

He followed a crude path that the man had chopped around the side of the car, which was resting on its top, the wheels up in the air.

The beam of the searchlight, shining through the splintered glass of the broken windshield, showed a crumpled figure with a pillow slip tied over its head. There were two holes for the eyes and one side of the pillow slip was soaked with red.

"That right-hand window is open," Ferron explained, "but it's on the underside. The car's upside down, but tilted so the left side is quite a bit higher than the right side. We've been chopping a trail so we could get around. We've got to get a window open. He's dead as a mackerel all right, but we've got to make sure before we go back and notify the coroner. And, I suppose, technically we've got to notify Homicide. How's that girl going to take it when she knows what happened?"

Mason said, "You mean that just shooting wildly with her left hand, she made a bull's-eye like that?"

"That's the most dangerous way to shoot," Ferron said. "Tests show that when a person gets excited and shoots instinctively, it's something like pointing your finger."

Ferron's partner said, "We can pry this door open, Bill, or we can smash in the glass."

"I hate to smash in the glass. Let's try prying this door."

"The front one's jammed. The rear one we can get open, I think."

Using the ax with which they had chopped the trail, the men managed to pry the left rear door open. Ferron squeezed inside, then stretched out a hand to feel the wrist of the body.

"No pulse," he reported. "He's dead all right."

"Can you get at that steering post and get the registration certificate while you're in here?"

"I'll try. Keep that door open. I think I can make it."

Ferron stretched himself until his fingers were able to encounter the certificate of registration snapped to the steering post of the automobile. He unsnapped the fasteners which held the Celluloid envelope in place, then, inching his way backward like some caterpillar, squeezed out through the door in the car.

"Gosh," he said, straightening and brushing himself off, "I'm all out of breath. Getting a little out of condition, I guess. That was quite a stretch."

"What have we got?" his partner asked.

"Car registered in the name of Oscar B. Loomis," Ferron said, reading the license. "We've got a local address here. Suppose there's any chance this guy is Loomis?"

As he spoke, the first drops of rain came rattling down, striking the overturned car, pattering on the leaves of the dry chaparral.

"Those are big drops," Ferron said. "When it starts that way, it means there's a heavy shower right behind. Let's see if we can get up the hill before this dust storm turns to mud and gets the rope slippery.

"If it rains this is going to be one hell of a mess, trying to get the body out of the car and getting the car back up to the road."

"We'll get the body out of the car," Ferron said, "and let the wrecking company wrestle with the car."

"Have you decided what happened?" Mason asked.

"There's nothing to it," Ferron told him. "The window on the right-hand side of this car was down. This guy probably had a rod of his own and was intending to force her off to the side of the road and then make her get out of her car and get into his car. That's the way he worked. Her bullet hit him right in the side of the head and he probably never knew what struck him. He slumped over against the steering wheel and when she described the car as weaving back and forth and thought it was because he had applied the brakes too suddenly, it was probably because the car slammed into the bank, then caromed off, hit the guardrail, smashed through and plunged on down."

The tempo of the falling raindrops increased.

Mason said, "Well, I'll lead the way going up unless you fellows want to go first."

"No, you set the pace," Ferron said.

Mason started up the steep slope, pulling his weight up by the rope, scrambling with his feet, trying to keep some semblance of a foothold in the loose, dry soil.

The rain suddenly freshened, then abruptly began to pour down in torrents.

Mason said, "Perhaps you fellows had better go ahead of me and—"

"No, you're doing fine," Ferron said. "Just be careful you don't slip on the wet rope and lose your footing. This is a steep slope and you could take a nasty fall."

Mason worked his way upward carefully. The dust that was on the rope had turned to a thin coating of mud as the rain came down in sheeted torrents.

"Gosh," Ferron said, "we should have put on our raincoats. We're all going to be wet."

Mason said, "I don't think it's much farther."

"Carrying this searchlight is a chore," Ferron's partner complained. "I've got it on my back and around my shoulder, but it keeps thumping and—"

"We're right near the top," Mason said. "I can see the guardrail up above. Here we are, I'm at the top. Can I take that searchlight?"

"No thanks, it is only a step or two."

The men heaved their way up to the top.

The rain was pelting down, striking the pavement and spattering into mushrooms.

Mason turned up his coat collar, said, "Well, you know

where you can reach me. Evelyn Bagby is at the Crown-crest Tavern. We're going to make a run for it."

"Go ahead," the officers told him. "We're going to get on our two-way radio and get our office to notify the coroner and the city police."

They diverged, making a run through the rain.

Mason panted his way up to the car where Della Street and Evelyn Bagby were seated.

"Chief," Della Street exclaimed, "you're all wet!"

"And out of breath," Mason said. "That's a steep slope."

He paused for a moment, panting, then said, "Della, you ride up to the Crowncrest Tavern with Evelyn. In that way, you won't get wet. I'll sprint back to my car and join you up there."

"No, you're all wet now. You mustn't—"

"Go ahead," Mason told her, and ran back down the grade.

As Mason passed the officers' car, he saw them sitting inside with the dome light on, putting through a call on the two-way radio to the sheriff's office.

Mason ran down to where Della Street had left his car, opened the door, and slid in behind the steering wheel. Evelyn Bagby's car was already moving slowly up the grade.

Mason turned on the motor, switched on the head-lights and the brilliant illumination showed the narrow strip of road. The falling rain made a gray curtain above the water-lashed, hard-surfaced road.

The lawyer pulled on past the county car. The wind-shield wipers of his car, beating in metronomic monotony, were unable to keep the water from the windshield sufficiently to give good driving visibility even when working at high speed. The rain assumed the proportions of a cloudburst.

With Evelyn Bagby leading the way, the two cars slowly wound their way up the curves of the mountain grade until it reached the summit and joined Mulholland

Drive. Then, after a few yards, the lighted front of the Crowncrest Tavern colored the raindrops with a red and blue aura.

Mason parked his car near the entrance. Evelyn drove her car around to the side, parked in a space reserved for employees' cars.

Mason, making a run for the front door, encountered Joe Padena.

"Hello, Joe," Mason said. "Nice weather for ducks."

"This rain," Padena said angrily. "You think it starts raining at one or two o'clock in the morning and clears up by ten or eleven o'clock? Hell no! She starts six, rains like hell until Joe Padena closes. Then she lets up. Next morning the sun is bright. The sky is blue. The food is ruined. Tonight I plan a big special—roast ribs of beef. You know what is for lunch tomorrow? I'll tell you. Cold roast beef. Next day roast-beef hash.

"A night like this, lots of food goes to waste. Profits go out the window. People don't drive up this road when it rains."

"That's too bad," Mason sympathized.

Evelyn Bagby and Della Street came in from the side door

Joe Padena looked at his watch.

"She's late but it's my fault," Mason said. "How's she doing?"

"Doing all right. This noon she does good. Nice-looking girl. Knows how to use a smile, gets good tips. That's a job. Use too big a smile, they make passes. Use too small a smile, they get sore. Kid them along just right. That's what I tell the girls. When they get too fresh, get in a hurry. Be busy. You can't make passes at a busy woman. When they're nice, take more time. Keep everybody happy. That makes business for the house, tips for the waitress. She's a good girl."

Mason started toward them.

"You want dinner?" Padena asked hopefully.

Mason said, "I'm sorry, Joe, we've already had dinner."

Padena made a face indicating a remonstrance, accompanied by a shrug of the shoulders.

"However," Mason told him, "I'm going to have a couple of hot buttered rums at the bar."

"That's fine."

"And I want to talk with Evelyn Bagby and—"

"You don't have any drinks when you're talking with the girl," Padena said. "That makes her a B-girl. You want to talk with her, you go down to her room. Then you come back up, have the hot buttered rum."

"Okay," Mason said.

He crossed over to where Della Street and Evelyn Bagby were standing.

"I want to talk with you for a minute, Evelyn," he said. "Joe says I'll have to talk with you in your room. It's all right. I told him it was my fault you were late."

She nodded, led the way across the all but deserted dining room out to the porch where water striking the roof and pouring down in rivulets bore witness to the intensity of the rain.

Leading the way, Evelyn opened a door, walked down a flight of stairs, turned to the left in a passageway, then opened a door at the end of the passageway.

"Will you walk into my humble abode?" she asked.

Mason stood aside for Della Street to precede him into the room, then entered and abruptly caught Della Street's wrist, drawing her back against the wall.

"What's the matter, Chief?" she asked.

Mason indicated the big picture window at the south corner on the east side of the room.

"What is it?" Evelyn Bagby asked.

"That window," Mason said. "Draw the drapes."

She crossed over, took hold of a cord, and pulled drapes across the big window.

"That's the first time it's been draped?"

"You mean since I came here?"

Mason nodded.

"Yes. After all, Mr. Mason, no one can see in unless h stood directly outside the window on a box or some thing. The ground falls away so fast that—"

"But why put drapes on the window if no one can se in?"

"Oh," she said, "if you want to be technical about it there's a spot of ground about a hundred yards ove there where they're building some new houses. Anyon with binoculars could look in here, but after a girl's live in the places I have, you don't have a great deal of per sonal modesty left. I'd hate to be annoyed by having Peeping Tom flatten his nose right against the window but if someone wants to look at me with binocular from a hundred yards off while I'm dressing, I guess he' entitled to some return on his investment."

She laughed.

Mason didn't laugh. He said, "Show me where yo found the gun."

She opened a bureau drawer. "There are more thing here now than when I found the gun. I've put som things in the drawer since then. You see, I went shop ping with the hundred dollars that you gave me, Mr Mason."

Mason said, "You're going to have to go back to wor upstairs. You may be called on to answer some questions."

"What sort of questions?"

"For one thing," Mason said, "you may be interrogate over and over about exactly what happened from th time this car drove up behind you."

She said, "All right, let's have it."

Mason said, "There was a body in the car down in the ravine. The body was that of a man who had been kille by one shot in the right side of his head. He was wearin a pillow slip mask and—"

"Good Lord," she exclaimed. "You mean that I— that I—"

Mason said, "The police believe that one shot, probably your second shot, went through the open window on the right-hand side of this man's car and killed him. Right at the moment, they feel you're something of a heroine and you're *persona* very much *grata*."

She stood looking at him, her eyes wide with consternation. "Mr. Mason, to think that I—that I've killed someone, even if I—if I didn't intend to—"

"Just how *does* it make you feel?" Mason asked.

"I don't know. I haven't become accustomed to the idea yet. I can't believe—why are you looking at me like that, Mr. Mason?"

Mason said, "Right at the present time, as I told you, you're *persona* very much *grata* with the police. They think you've disposed of a particularly obnoxious, ruthless bandit who was preying on parked cars, robbing the men and raping the women. A little later on they may not be so certain."

"What do you mean, Mr. Mason?"

"One thing hasn't occurred to the officers yet."

"What's that?"

Mason said, "The lights weren't on on that car that was lying down at the bottom of the barranca."

"Well, then it couldn't have been the same one. . . ."

"But this man answers the description of your bandit perfectly. He had the pillow slip over his head, the slip had two holes cut for eyes, and it was held in place with a rubber band."

"Then it must have been the same one. I just don't see how I could have possibly hit him, Mr. Mason. I was shooting blind. The first shot, I know, was ahead of the car. I just poked the gun out of the window and shot. The next time I moved the gun back a little bit. That second shot hit something with a *clink*."

"Were you looking in the direction in which the gun was pointing?"

"No. I told you I was pointing the gun with my left hand. I had my right hand on the steering wheel."

"And the bandit's car was just about abreast of yours at that time?"

"Not quite abreast I would say, but pretty close, yes."

"And you could have sent a bullet crashing into that man's head?"

"Well, if . . . if the police say I did, I suppose I did, but—why are you adopting that attitude, Mr. Mason? Couldn't the lights have gone off because of the plunge down that mountainside? Couldn't the battery have been torn out of the battery box or cables ripped loose or—"

"Something like that might have happened," Mason said, "but I don't think it did."

"Why?"

"Because I took occasion to look at something that hadn't at the moment occurred to the officers. I looked at the light control on the dashboard of the car and the lights hadn't been turned on."

"They . . . they didn't notice that?"

"They didn't at the moment," Mason said, "but they've probably thought of it by this time."

"But they *had* to be on, Mr. Mason. I know they were on. Unless this man turned them off after I shot because he—"

"That man didn't do anything after the bullet struck him," Mason said.

"Then—there's something wrong. There has to be."

Mason walked over to the head of the bed, jerked back the bedcover which had been rolled over the pillows. One pillow had the pillow slip on it. The other one showed only the blue and white striped heavy cloth which covered the feathers.

"Good heavens!" Evelyn Bagby exclaimed.

"Where's the other pillow slip?" Mason asked.

She simply shook her head.

"Was it on when you came in here?"

"Heavens, Mr. Mason, I don't know. I didn't even look at the bed. I came in here and unpacked my things and read the paper and then I went out and started telephoning and—Mr. Mason, do you suppose they're going to adopt a position that I . . . that I've been lying?"

"Do you know of any reason why they shouldn't?" Mason said.

Abruptly she reached a decision. "There's only one thing to do," she said.

"What's that?"

"Get another pillow slip from the linen closet and put it on that pillow. I think I know where she keeps the linen and—"

She started for the door. Mason grabbed her arm, pushed her back.

"Why not?" she asked.

Mason said, "You're trying to buy yourself a one-way ticket to the gas chamber."

"But, Mr. Mason, we can't let them know. We don't dare let them know. We—why, don't you see the position I'm in? It looks as though I had killed someone and then put a pillow slip over his head, sent the car crashing down into the canyon, then told you that I'd found the gun planted in the drawer and then fabricated this whole story about having been pursued in order to account for the two times the gun had been fired."

"Exactly," Mason said.

"And if—good heavens, if that should turn out to be anyone—"

She broke off abruptly.

"Go on," Mason said.

"Suppose," she said, "it should be someone I know!"

"That's exactly what I'm thinking," Mason said.

"Oh my Lord!"

"So," Mason told her, "the minute you start fabricating evidence, the minute you start trying to put yourself in a better position, you may be walking right into the gas chamber."

"But the way things are right now, I haven't any way to substantiate my story. I haven't—"

"That," Mason told her, "is the thing that bothers me."

"*You* don't think I'm guilty of fabricating all of that evidence, of building up that impossible story, of having committed a cold-blooded murder?"

Mason said, "I'm keeping an open mind for the moment. Now then, do you suppose you could take the part of a highly nervous, hysterical young woman who is completely swept off-base by the knowledge that she may have killed someone? Do you suppose you could work up to such a nervous fit of hysterics that a doctor would give you a big hypodermic and tell you to keep quiet until noon tomorrow?"

"I can try. I think I'm a pretty good actress."

"All right," Mason told her. "I've told you that you've probably killed a man. You begin to get hysterical. Go all to pieces. Call Mrs. Padena. Bring her down here. Ask her if both pillows had slips on them."

"You think the pillow slip on that man's . . . body . . . is from this bed?"

"Why not?" Mason asked. "They framed everything else on you so far. They've got the murder gun in your possession and have you admitting that you fired it twice. If they've gone to all that trouble to put you in an impossible position, then why wouldn't they have taken the pillow slip from this bed? Somebody sure did."

She said, "I'm not going to have to do any acting to become hysterical. This thing has really thrown me."

Mason said, "All right, get busy and do your stuff. Get Mrs. Padena down here. Show her the pillows. Then Della Street is going to bundle you in your car and drive you to see a doctor who is a friend of mine. He'll know what to do. He'll give you a shot to quiet you. You'll be out of circulation for a good twelve hours. But the point is, *before* you leave, you'd better call the sheriff's office and tell them about the theft of the pillow slip. You're going to have to be half-hysterical over the phone. You're going to have to tell the sheriff's office that I've just given you the information that you may have killed a man. Can you do that?"

"I can try."

Mason said, "Your acting ability is going to be given an audition beginning as of now. If you're going to put this across you'll have to be *good.*"

"I . . . I'll try."

"Now here's one more thing to bear in mind," Mason said. "Shortly after you wake up, the police will catch up with you. Under ordinary circumstances I tell my clients not to talk to the police or to the newspaper reporters.

"In your case, it's different. When you are questioned be loquacious. Talk. Tell them all you know."

Mason turned to Della Street. "You know what to do, Della."

She nodded.

"Tell the doctor I need a twelve-hour head start," Mason told her. "Then after you have put Evelyn Bagby to bed, take a taxi to Paul Drake's office. I'll be waiting for you there. Don't let anyone know where I am."

Again she nodded.

"Then afterward where will you be?" Evelyn Bagby asked.

"I'll be out digging up the answers to some of the questions you're going to be asked," Mason told her. "But don't worry about where I'll be. You'll be dead to the world."

9

MASON SWUNG HIS CAR INTO THE OFFICE PARKING SPACE, slammed on his brakes, shut off headlights and ignition, jumped out of the car, and hurried into the office building.

The janitor who operated the elevator said, "Good evening, Mr. Mason."

Mason handed the man five dollars.

"What's that for?"

"You made a mistake."

"Made a mistake in what?"

"In identity. I'm not Mr. Mason," Perry Mason told him. "I may look like him but I'm not Mr. Mason. My name is Harry Marlow, and I'm going to see Mr. Drake of the Drake Detective Agency."

The janitor winked. "I understand, Mr. Marlow. I'm sorry. I thought you looked like Perry Mason, the lawyer, when I first looked at you, but now I can see that it's just a superficial resemblance."

Mason said, "Quite a few people tell me I look like Mr. Mason. I'd like to see him some day. What sort of a chap is he?"

"Oh, wonderful," the janitor said, pocketing the five-dollar bill. "Very generous. Would you mind signing the register, Mr. Marlow?"

Mason signed the register. The elevator came to a stop. Mason left the elevator and made a beeline for Drake's office.

"Paul in?" he asked the night operator.

She nodded, busy for the moment with the switchboard.

"Tell him I'm on my way," Mason said. "If anybody else asks if you've seen me, you haven't—except Della. When she comes in send her down to Drake's office, or, if she should call, connect me. If anyone else asks for me, you haven't seen me."

The operator nodded.

"And that means *anyone* else," Mason told her.

She hesitated. "The police?"

"The police."

"Would you mind going out again, Mr. Mason?"

"Why?"

She said, "Then I could tell them that you came in, were only here for a minute and then went right out again, and that's the last time I saw you. When you come back in I'll make it a point to be in the rest room. I don't like to lie to the police. Mr. Drake doesn't like me to."

"Okay," Mason said. "I'm going out."

He left the office, waited in the corridor for some thirty seconds, then turned and entered the Drake Detective Agency's office for the second time. This time there was no one at the switchboard.

Mason walked over to the gate which opened into a corridor containing a series of cubbyhole offices, walked down the corridor to the last corner office, and opened the door.

Drake, seated at his desk, was munching a hamburger sandwich and drinking coffee.

"Hello, Perry. What's the excitement?"

"Plenty."

"Let's have it."

"You first," Mason said. "What did you find out about the gun? Anything?"

Drake said, "If it's any of my business, Perry, you'd better quit monkeying around with Mervyn Aldrich. He's bad medicine."

"Who's monkeying with Mervyn Aldrich?" Mason asked.

"You are."

Mason slid into the one chair in Drake's cubbyhole office, elevated his long legs to the corner of the desk, grinned at the detective, and lit a cigarette.

"You have me mixed up with two other people, Paul."

Drake shook his head. "Those guns."

"What guns?"

"The guns you were asking about."

Mason's feet suddenly came down off the desk. He sat upright in the chair. His eyes were hard. "Go on, Paul."

"You telephoned in the number on a gun," Drake said. "I was able to trace it because it was a recent sale, a sale made at a sporting goods store in Newport Beach, the Golf, Gun and Gaff Sporting Goods."

"Go on."

"Mervyn Aldrich bought two guns just alike on the twenty-fifth of last month."

"Two guns?"

"That's right."

"And one of them was the gun I telephoned about?"

"That's right."

"And what about the other one?"

"You telephoned in about gun number 17474-LW. He bought that, and also gun number 17475-LW."

Mason remained thoughtfully silent, his eyes studying the smoke which eddied upward from the cigarette in his fingers.

"Well?" Drake asked.

"What the devil did he want with *two* guns?" Mason asked.

"You can search me," Drake said, "but he bought two guns and paid for them in cash."

"You don't know whether he said anything to the clerk who waited on him about—?"

"Have a heart, Perry. The store is closed. It might take

a long while to locate the clerk who made the sale. However, my operative did get to see the files in the sheriff's office. He checked back on the numbers and located the sale of this gun. Then just as he was preparing to take the information and start back, he noticed there was another sheet also bearing the signature of Mervyn Aldrich, so he checked the number on that and it was the sale of another gun of the same make and model."

Mason said, "That means he wanted one for himself and one for somebody else. Now who?"

"Someone whom he felt was in danger along with him?" Drake asked.

"Probably," Mason said. "My best guess is he wanted the other gun for Helene Chaney. Paul, I want to get in touch with Helene Chaney tonight. I want to make sure that Mervyn Aldrich calls on Helene Chaney while I'm there."

"That's quite an order," Drake said.

"No it isn't," Mason told him. "I'll call on Helene Chaney. You telephone Mervyn Aldrich and give him an anonymous tip. Tell him that Perry Mason is out calling on Helene Chaney, trying to set some information out of her. That will send Aldrich out there on the run."

"Provided we can locate him," Drake said.

"How do you go about finding out whether or not we can locate them?" Mason asked.

Drake picked up the telephone, said to the girl at the switchboard, "Ring Helene Chaney, the motion picture actress. She has an unlisted number. You'll find it in our confidential file. Tell her you're connected with the studio, that there's a script they're very anxious to have her look over. Ask if she's going to be home tonight.

"Then ring up Mervyn Aldrich. His phone is listed. Tell him you're the Post Office Department, that you have a registered, special delivery letter that can be delivered only to him personally. Ask if he'll be home so that it can be delivered. If he's out, try the gag on whoever answers the phone and ask where he can be reached."

Drake dropped the telephone back into position and took another bite from his sandwich.

"That simple?" Mason asked.

"It may be," Drake said, sipping the coffee, then pouring more coffee from the Thermos bottle. "Had dinner, Perry?"

"Uh-huh."

"I'll bet," Drake said. "While I'm gulping down cold, greasy hamburger sandwiches and stale coffee, you're out eating thick steaks with French fried potatoes and—"

"French fried onions tonight," Mason said. "I like them."

"Were they good?"

"Wonderful."

"You should be a detective and eat the kind of stuff I do at odd hours," Drake told him. "Then you'd really appreciate good food."

"What good does it do to appreciate it if you never get it?" Mason asked.

"That's what I want to know. Are you going down to your office?"

"No. I'm hiding. Della Street is going to join me here shortly, then we'll be on our way."

"Doing what?"

"Ringing doorbells."

"I don't like to have you hide out here if you're dodging the police," Drake said.

"I know," Mason told him. "Your switchboard operator told me to go back out. I came in, went out, then sneaked in again. There was no one at the switchboard. She doesn't know I'm here."

"It's a nice gag," Drake said. "The only trouble is the police won't ride along on that kind of stuff."

"They won't know I'm here, Paul."

"I hope not. Where's Della?"

"Putting a young lady to bed."

"What's cooking, Perry?"

"Evelyn Bagby was held up tonight. A man whose head was concealed with a pillow slip tried to run her off the road back in the mountains above Hollywood."

"What happened?"

"She had a gun. She shot twice to scare him."

"Did she scare him?"

"The police think she killed him."

Drake put down the coffee cup. "What the hell?"

Mason shrugged his shoulders.

"Serious?" Drake asked.

"Could be."

"Of course, if he was trying to push her off the road it would be justifiable homicide," Drake said. "Any witnesses?"

Mason shook his head.

"What happened to the guy in the pillow slip?"

"Dead. One shot in the side of the head—very effective."

"That took some shooting," Drake said.

"That's what bothers me."

"How come?"

"She said she poked the gun out of the side of the automobile and shot at random, just trying to scare him by letting him know she had a gun."

"And hit him dead center?"

"That's apparently what happened."

"From a moving automobile?"

"Yes."

"And he was in a car?"

"That's right. And the gun was in her left hand."

"That doesn't sound very reasonable."

"I know it doesn't. But we're going to need additional facts in order to have a peg on which to hang an explanation. How about finding out, Paul, and not letting anyone know you're searching? Can you do that?"

"Probably," Drake said. He picked up the telephone asked for an outside line, dialed a number, then, after a while, said, "Hello, Jim. This is Paul Drake. Are you covering police tonight . . . ? Uh-huh. . . . Anything new . . . ? I see. . . . Uh-huh. . . . I see. . . . That sounds interesting. Can you get me the dope on it . . . ? Don't let anyone know I've made an inquiry but find out every fact in the case and phone me, will you . . . ? All rights, thanks. . . . 'By now."

Drake hung up.

The phone rang.

Drake picked up the phone, said, "Hello. . . . Uh-huh. . . . Okay. . . . Thanks."

Drake scribbled with his pencil on a pad of paper, said, "Helene Chaney will be home until ten-thirty. She'll be glad to receive the script any time up to ten-thirty, or the script can be left with her butler.

"Mr. Mervyn Aldrich is not home. He is not expected to return home until a very late hour. It was suggested that we *might* be able to contact him through Helene Chaney."

Mason grinned.

"Forming a pattern?" Drake asked.

"A pattern," Mason told him. "Ten-thirty seems to be the witching hour. Irene Keith gave me until ten-thirty tonight either to accept or reject a thousand-dollar compromise on behalf of Evelyn Bagby."

"You going to take it?"

Mason looked at his watch. "Probably not."

"Does she know about it?"

"Who?"

"Evelyn Bagby."

"Uh-huh."

"What does she want to do?"

"Wants to take it."

"You're sticking your neck out if you turn it down Perry. My man out of Riverside has some information which makes that Evelyn Bagby case look a little phony but that's all. We can't seem to get any more."

Mason nodded.

"A thousand dollars doesn't grow on bushes," Drake went on.

"It does with Irene Keith," Mason told him. "What's she worth, Paul?"

"Plenty."

"Any idea how much?"

"She inherited a bunch of dough and she's a darned good businesswoman herself. They say she's more than doubled her money in the past five years. She's a daring, shrewd operator."

Mason nodded.

"She has advisors but she makes up her own mind as to what she's going to do. She consults her lawyers about the law and then reaches her own decisions. Same thing with her stockbrokers."

Mason said, "A thousand dollars wouldn't even be noticed by her."

"I bet it would by Evelyn Bagby. How come that pillow slip business, Perry? That sounds phony. A man wanting to conceal features would wear a mask. A pillow slip over the entire head is clumsy, bizarre and— There must be some reason for it."

"Could be," Mason said.

"Any ideas?"

Mason said, "A mask would conceal part of a man's face, but his neck and shoulders would be visible."

"Well?"

"On the other hand, a pillow slip," Mason said, "would conceal the neck, the hair, all of the features."

"For why?"

"It might have been a woman."

"Oh-oh," Drake said. "Do you think it was?"

"I don't know. I'm just speculating. I think one reason they used a pillow slip was because they wanted to put Evelyn Bagby in bad. The pillow slip was from her bed."

"The devil it was."

"Uh-huh."

"Well now," Drake said, "that puts an entirely different face on the situation."

"Doesn't it?"

"You don't suppose she had someone she wanted to get rid of, so she took a gun and popped him in the head, then put a pillow slip over the head, ran the car down the grade and came in with a trumped-up story of a stick-up, do you?"

"The police are getting sold on that theory right now," Mason said.

"I'll have some dope in a little while. My friend who covers the police beat likes to pick up a little dough on the side."

"Uh-huh."

"Where is Evelyn Bagby?" Drake asked.

"Where the police can't find her—I hope!"

"How come?"

"She became very nervous and hysterical."

"That won't buy her anything."

"Della Street took her to a doctor."

"Oh-oh!"

Mason looked at his watch, got up from the chair, ground out the cigarette, started pacing within the narrow confines of Drake's office and said, "It's a wonder you wouldn't have an office big enough to turn around in. A man can't do any thinking here."

"I think all right."

"You can't walk the floor," Mason complained.

"You don't have to walk to think. Practice thinking in one place. It saves wear and tear on carpets and shoe leather."

"I have to move when *I'm* thinking," Mason said.

Drake brushed crumbs off his desk, put the napkins in

the wastebasket, walked over to a washstand, rinsed out the coffee cup, dried it with a dish towel, and returned to his desk.

The telephone rang.

Drake answered it, said, "Uh-huh. . . . Thanks. . . ." and hung up.

"Anything?" Mason asked, raising his eyebrows.

"Switchboard operator," Drake said, "reporting that newspapermen are frantically trying to contact you. She said she saw you earlier in the evening but didn't know where you are now."

Mason looked at his watch, said, "I told Della to move fast. She'll do a good job."

"Suppose she couldn't reach the doctor?"

"She can," Mason said. "We have three doctors. They're all clients. They're very sympathetic to cases of hysteria."

"Suppose they don't give her the treatment you want?"

"They will. Della Street will reach one of them and he'll know what to do."

"What will Della do with her?"

"Put her to bed in her apartment."

"Won't the police look there?"

"Probably. But they won't smash in the door without a search warrant. The doctor will leave orders that she can't be moved or disturbed until she comes out from under the influence of the hypodermic."

"How long will that be?"

"Twelve hours."

"You can't do much in twelve hours," Drake said.

"I'll have to," Mason told him.

The telephone rang two short, quick rings.

Drake picked up the receiver, said, "Uh-huh. . . . Okay."

He dropped the receiver in place and said, "Della Street's on her way."

Mason sighed with relief. "Okay," he said. "I'm going places."

"Be careful you don't get into trouble," Drake told him.

"I'm already in trouble."

The door opened. Della Street smiled at Perry Mason.

"Everything fixed, Della?"

"Everything's fixed."

"Where is she?"

"Fortunately one of my neighbors is out of town for the week. She asked me to feed the parrot and left me the key to her apartment. I put Evelyn in there."

"The doctor was all right?"

"Very understanding."

"What did he do?"

"Took one look and jabbed, said that she wasn't to be disturbed under any circumstances."

"How did Evelyn do?"

"One swell job," Della said. "She's a beautiful actress. She even had me fooled—or else . . . or else she really was completely hysterical and upset. She had me frightened for a while when I was driving. She was crying and laughing, and once she fainted."

"That's good," Mason said. "You can testify to it if you have to."

"Chief?"

"What?"

"She's a dandy actress. Perhaps a little too good."

Mason smiled. "She may need to be. How's the weather, Della?"

"Still raining."

"Okay," Mason said. "Skip down to the office. Don't turn on lights. Get your raincoat and mine. If any newspapermen are covering the office don't stop in here. Go right downstairs and telephone. Otherwise come back."

"On my way," Della Street said.

"Well," Mason told Drake, "you keep plugging away. I'll be in touch with you later on."

"Keep your nose clean," Drake warned.

Mason laughed. "When you're working at high speed you have to take a chance once in a while."

"You sure as hell give a client full coverage, don't you, Perry?"

"I try to," Mason admitted.

10

MASON SWUNG HIS CAR INTO THE DRIVEWAY OF HELENE Chaney's house.

"One nice thing," he said, looking at his watch, "Mervyn Aldrich is a stickler for a time schedule, wants everything right on the dot. That means we can time our little act to the best advantage."

"Chief," Della Street asked, "do you have a definite plan?"

"I have the plan all right."

"What?"

"I want Mervyn Aldrich to give Evelyn Bagby an alibi in case the police try to get rough with her."

"He'd die first—if he knew what he was doing," she said.

Mason grinned, braked the car to a stop.

"Sure puts on the dog, doesn't she?" Della Street said, sizing up the house.

"She had to," Mason told her. "She has to keep up appearances, maintain a front, have a place where she can give interviews to the press."

"She certainly has come a long ways in the last two or three years!"

Mason nodded, switched off the motor, crossed over to hold the door open for Della Street. They climbed the steps of the big porch and pressed the mother-of-pearl button on the right-hand side of the front door.

Melodious chimes sounded on the inside of the house.

The door was flung open by a radiant brunette, whose expression underwent a sudden change as she saw Mason and Della Street standing on the threshold.

"Oh, pardon me, I thought that—I was expecting—Just a moment."

She turned and called, "William."

A dignified butler appeared from the hallway. "Yes, ma'am."

"You wished to see someone?" Helene Chaney asked.

"You," Mason said.

She shook her head. "I'm sorry, I have an appointment tonight and I'm expecting to go out. William, will you please show these people— Wait a minute, aren't you Perry Mason, the lawyer?"

Mason nodded.

She hesitated. "That makes it a little different. You wish to see me?"

"Yes."

"I can give you a few minutes," she said, "a *very* few minutes."

"That may be all that's necessary," Mason said.

"William, will you show them in, please?" She gave them a dazzling smile. "I'll be with you almost immediately."

The butler escorted Mason and Della Street into a big living room and within a matter of seconds Helene Chaney came to join them.

"This is my secretary, Miss Street," Mason introduced.

Helene Chaney extended a cordial hand. "I'm very pleased to meet you both. Won't you be seated?"

They sat down. Helene Chaney waited somewhat stiffly.

Mason said, "I wanted to ask you a question, Miss Chaney."

"Yes?"

"It has to do in a way with Mervyn Aldrich."

She smiled, said, "Let's be frank, Mr. Mason. I understand your position perfectly. You're representing that waitress, aren't you?"

Mason nodded.

"And I believe she owes it to you that a jury acquitted her of stealing certain jewelry. It may impress you as being significant, Mr. Mason, that that jewelry has never been found."

"It impresses me as being very significant."

"Well, Irene told me all about you. You fascinate her. She said that she had made you an offer of settlement which was to expire at ten-thirty tonight. Irene likes to find out what the law is, then handle her entire business matters. I am entirely different, Mr. Mason. If you want to talk over any matter of business with me in any way, I can only refer you to my attorney. I have a business manager for my financial problems, an attorney for my legal problems and an agent for my acting contracts. Under the circumstances, that leaves us very little to talk about except the weather and the weather is abominable for my purposes, though I understand the farmers are welcoming the rain with open arms."

"It leaves us one other matter to talk about."

"What's that?"

"The gun Mervyn Aldrich bought for you."

For a long moment she eyed him with thoughtful appraisal, then she said cautiously, "And what about it?"

"I'd like to see it if you don't mind."

"Why?"

"Because," Mason said, "it may be that I can spare you some publicity that you *may* not like."

Her laugh was melodious, seemingly quite carefree. "How quaint, Mr. Mason! Only an hour ago, a man telephoned and said that he had to see me upon a matter of the greatest importance—to me. The butler inquired what it was the caller had in mind and he explained it was to get publicity for me. Now you're talking about enabling me to *avoid* publicity."

"Exactly," Mason said.

"And may I ask exactly what you have in mind?"

Mason said, "You may not realize, Miss Chaney, that the sale of firearms is strictly regulated by law in California. Before a man can buy a gun, he has to sign for it. Each gun has an individual number. That number is registered in the name of the purchaser. Duplicates of those registry forms are sent to the peace officers in the community, the sheriff, the chief of police."

"But I don't see what all that has to do with me."

"Your gun may have been used in connection with an activity that might not be conducive to your best welfare."

"I'm afraid you're talking in riddles, Mr. Mason."

"Well," Mason said, "I'll be frank with you, Miss Chaney. I *think* it's your gun."

"*My* gun couldn't have been used in connection with anything such as you mention, Mr. Mason."

"Why not?"

"Because I have it safely in my possession."

"Would you mind verifying that?"

She hesitated a moment.

Mason said, "I think you'll find that you don't still have the gun in your possession."

She said, "Very well, if you'll wait, please. It will only take a minute."

She walked from the room, conscious of their eyes, moving with the walk of a trained actress, a walk that had been entirely foreign to her a few years ago, yet which now had been so ingrained by hours of long practice that it was second nature.

Mason looked at his watch, exchanged glances with Della Street.

Abruptly Della Street raised her eyes, beckoned silently to Mason.

Mason raised his eyebrows.

Della Street beckoned more vehemently.

Mason crossed over to her chair. She silently pointed.

There was a mirror across the room from her which, in turn, reflected the image from another mirror showing a section of the lighted hallway and framing a reflection of Helene Chaney as she frantically dialed a number on a telephone.

Mason nodded, smiled, placed his finger to his lips as a signal for silence, walked back to his chair and sat down.

Della Street continued to look in the mirror.

At the end of perhaps three minutes Helene Chaney came sweeping back into the room.

"It's quite all right. I have it, Mr. Mason." Her manner radiated confident assurance. She said, "It's just as I told you, Mr. Mason. My gun is in its proper place in my bedroom, so I'm certain that no matter what anyone may have told you, your concern about me is groundless."

She remained standing as though inviting them to leave.

Mason took the gun from his pocket, said, "In that case, there's nothing to worry about. This gun with two discharged shells can't possibly be yours."

Her eyes were mocking as they looked directly into the eyes of the lawyer. "That's right, Mr. Mason. It couldn't *possibly* be mine. Now I'm sorry, but I have an appointment. I was just waiting for—"

Mason got to his feet. "Oh, certainly," he said. "I'm sorry I bothered you. I thought perhaps I could do you a good turn."

"I certainly appreciate your consideration, Mr. Mason."

The chimes sounded on the front door as they were halfway across the living room.

Helene Chaney did not change the even tempo of her walk.

The butler stood in the hallway, and, after a half second's hesitation, Helene Chaney signaled to him. He opened the door.

Mervyn Aldrich, attired in a raincoat, black fedora hat, with a silk muffler around his neck, stood in the doorway.

"Hello, William," he said. "Is—?"

He broke off abruptly as he saw Helene Chaney, Perry Mason and Della Street moving toward the doorway.

Aldrich stepped in, removed his hat.

"Hello, Helene," he said, and then, with his eyes cold and hard, "Good evening, Mr. Mason and—I believe it's Miss Street."

"That's right," Mason said easily.

Aldrich said, "I trust that you haven't been trying to approach Miss Chaney in connection with this settlement business, Mason. After all, an attorney is supposed to deal through an attorney and not approach another client directly. I believe that Miss Chaney has advised you she retains counsel—"

"Oh, yes," Mason said breezily. "I wouldn't have thought of that, Mr. Aldrich. This was on quite another matter, a matter in which I thought perhaps I might save Miss Chaney from some publicity."

"Yes?" Aldrich asked, his voice cold, his manner belligerent.

Helene Chaney laughed nervously. "Mr. Mason thinks that my gun has been used for some dark deeds of crime."

"*Your* gun?" Aldrich said, and then turning to Mason, demanded, "What do you mean, her gun?"

"The gun that you gave her," Mason said evenly.

"I didn't give her any—"

"The little revolver that you gave me, Merv," Helene Chaney interposed quickly. "The one that you wanted me to keep in my bedroom for protection."

Aldrich said to Mason, "Who told you about that?"

"I was simply running down the number on this gun," Mason said, taking the gun from his pocket, "and found out that it was one of two that you had purchased at a sporting goods store in Newport Beach. One of them you kept and the other you gave to Miss Chaney."

Mervyn Aldrich said abruptly, "Let's talk this over for a minute."

He turned and firmly, methodically closed the door, looked at his watch, carefully checking the time.

Helene Chaney said contritely, "I'm sorry, Merv. I was ready. I was waiting. These people rang the bell. I thought it was you and so I answered the door myself, and—"

"That's all right, Helene," Mervyn said. He turned to Mason. "Now then, what made you think that I had purchased a gun for Miss Chaney?"

"Don't be silly," Mason said. "You signed the register. You purchased both guns at the Golf, Sun and Gaff Sporting Goods Store in Newport Beach. I can give you the date, the data and the numbers."

"But that doesn't mean I gave Miss Chaney one. I never—"

"Merv," Helene Chaney interposed desperately. "Please let's remember that Mr. Mason is an attorney. He wouldn't be here unless it was on a matter of the greatest importance. He asked me about the gun that you gave me, and I told him that gun was in my bedroom. I even went to verify it."

"And it was there?" Aldrich asked.

She met his eyes. "Of course it was there, Merv."

Aldrich said, "Mason is representing a woman who I think is a shrewd, dangerous—well, I won't give you an opportunity to feather her nest still further by filing suit for defamation of character, Mr. Mason. I'll finish the sentence by stating that she is a shrewd, dangerous antagonist."

"Quite all right," Mason said, smiling.

Aldrich took a step forward. "And I don't think I like the idea of you coming here and trying to get an admission from Miss Chaney."

Mason also moved forward. "I don't give a damn whether you like it or not, Aldrich. I've had just about enough of your arrogance. You run your business and I'll run mine. Now you try starting anything and I'll finish it. I came here because I thought there was an opportunity to save Miss Chaney some definite embarrassment. Here, take a look at this gun! Look at it!"

Mason swung the cylinder open. "Two empty shells in there. Two empty cartridge cases. For your information those were fired about three hours and a half ago. And that's a gun you bought and paid for. Now would *you* like to know where the bullets are?"

Aldrich recoiled from the vehemence of Mason's attack. His eyes regarded the gun as though fascinated by the two empty cartridge cases.

"You traced this gun?" he asked, plainly stalling for time.

"Of course I traced it. That's why I'm here. Look at the number on the gun. I had a detective agency check that number and run down the registration. This is one of the two guns that you bought in Newport Beach."

"There must be some mistake," Aldrich said, lamely.

"Perhaps," Mason said. "Since this gun *isn't* Miss Chaney's gun, then it must be *your* gun."

"Oh no, that's impossible. I— Let me look at that gun," Aldrich said, abruptly changing his tactics.

"Certainly," Mason said, and handed the weapon to Aldrich.

"Your gun is upstairs, Helene?"

"But definitely, Merv."

Aldrich looked at the gun for a moment, then raised his head. His eyes were half-closed in thought. Abruptly he said, "I think perhaps I owe you an apology for having been so abrupt, Mr. Mason. I'm very much afraid that this gun really is mine. In which case, it must have been stolen from the glove compartment of my automobile."

Aldrich looked at the number on the gun, took out a notebook, moved over to Helene Chaney's side, said, "I'll just jot down the number of this gun, Helene, so there won't be any mistake."

He made an entry in his notebook. "You'd better check that number, dear, so you can verify it."

She looked at the notebook, at the number on the gun. Her face reflected no faintest flicker of expression. "Yes, Merv, I've checked the number."

"That gun," Aldrich said to Mason, "very definitely has been stolen from the glove compartment of my automobile."

"When was it stolen?"

"I don't know. I left it in the glove compartment—in fact, I didn't know until just now that it was gone. But if it's one of the two guns I purchased it must have been stolen from me. Your gun is upstairs, Helene?"

"Yes, Merv."

Aldrich said, "Let me verify this." Without asking permission and before anyone could divine his intention or interfere, he whirled, whipped the door open, jerked it shut behind him, and stepped out into the rain.

"I'm sorry if Merv seemed rude when he first came in," Helene Chaney apologized. "He's rather intense and he's very nervous. He works under quite a strain."

"Yes, I can imagine," Mason said.

"He's a stickler for punctuality. So many girls keep their escorts waiting while they finish dressing. That's why I answered the door personally. I wanted him to see I was all ready to go. When you rang I thought it was he and—"

"I understand."

"And, of course, I appreciate the fact that you came out here, Mr. Mason. I can see *now* that you were really trying to spare me trouble and notoriety. May I ask what happened? Why you made reference to the fact that two shells were fired from that gun about three and a half hours ago?"

"I think one of those bullets may have killed someone."

"Indeed? Who?"

"I don't know—yet."

She frowned. "You're rather mysterious, aren't you, Mr. Mason?"

"Perhaps. I deal in mysteries."

"Yes, I daresay you do."

The front door abruptly opened.

Aldrich said indignantly, "Just as I thought. Some crook stole this gun from the glove compartment of my automobile. I've been warned not to leave it there. May I ask how this weapon came to be in your possession, Mr. Mason?"

Aldrich extended the gun, butt first to Mason.

Mason took it and slipped it in his pocket.

"Someone planted the gun in the possession of one of my clients."

"Indeed?"

"And," Mason said, "since the gun had been discharged and may have been used in a crime, I thought that it might be advisable to let Miss Chaney know exactly what had happened so that she could have her lawyers and her publicity men get together and—"

"Most commendable of you," Aldrich said, beaming. "I really owe you an apology, Mr. Mason. I'm afraid perhaps I've been a little abrupt with you, and—well, I'm *now* beginning to think I may have misjudged that client of yours, that Bagby woman. Of course, the rest of the jewelry hasn't been discovered, but there are circumstances in that case which make me feel very differently about it. I am going to get in touch with Irene Keith tomorrow. I feel quite certain that something can be worked out in that matter, Mr. Mason, a very good settlement."

"Thank you," Mason said.

"I'm afraid that I've been the stumbling block there." Aldrich turned to Helene. "Darling, let me make a call. I want to report the theft of that gun right now. Do you have the number of the gun written down, Mr. Mason?"

Mason said, "I'll give you the numbers directly from the gun if you wish to telephone. However, I believe you wrote them—"

"Of course," Aldrich said. "Stupid of me. I have them right here."

He dialed the Police Department, said into the telephone, "I wish to report the theft of a gun. I've just discovered it was taken from my glove compartment. It's a Colt Cobra. One of the new fifteen-ounce models that they've put out. And the number is—" He fumbled for his notebook, dropped it, said, "Damn! Would you mind letting me see that gun, Mason?"

Mason handed him the gun.

Aldrich read the number into the telephone. "Yes, that's right, I have a permit to carry it. This is Mervyn Aldrich of the Aldrich Cruisers Corporation. . . . Yes, I carry it for personal protection. I have to be on the road a lot at night. I left it in the glove compartment of my automobile. . . . I know that I shouldn't have done it. It was probably carelessness, but I dropped it in there and then forgot to take it out. . . . Well now, I can't tell you exactly but probably sometime within the last day or two. . . . Oh, I know where it is *now*. Mr. Perry Mason, the lawyer, has it. It was given him by a client. . . . Well, I thought I'd better report it."

Aldrich abruptly dropped the phone back into the cradle, got up, extended the gun once more to Mason, then shook hands cordially.

"I really owe you an apology. I really do, indeed, Mr. Mason."

"Not at all," Mason said. "I trust you and Miss Chaney have a pleasant evening. Good night."

Mason took Della's arm. Helene Chaney came to the porch to see them down the stairs.

"My, it's certainly raining," she said.

"It is indeed," Mason told her.

They sprinted for Mason's automobile. Mason handed Della in through the door, then ran around to the other side and jumped in.

"Well," Della Street said as they drove away, "he certainly put on a great act."

"He certainly did," Mason told her.

"Chief, did he switch guns?"

"Sure."

"But you had the number—and he copied down the number. Good Lord, she watched him write down the number. It's your word against two of theirs!"

Mason nodded. After a few minutes, he pulled the car to the side of the road, swung open the cylinder of the gun, inspected it in the light of the dash lamp. It was loaded in four chambers. There were two exploded cartridge cases in the other two chambers of the cylinder. Mason raised the gun to his nose and sniffed the barrel, then passed it over to Della.

"Like to smell?" he asked.

"It only smells of oil. It doesn't smell as though it had been fired."

"Exactly," Mason said.

"Chief, you can check the numbers on it. You can tell if he—"

"I don't have the numbers," Mason said. "You telephoned them in to Paul Drake."

"Well," she said, "I have one number written in my notebook and I could compare it with the number on this gun and we—"

"Why should you do that?" Mason asked.

"Well, we could get Paul Drake on the line and see if—"

"Why should we?"

"So we can prove that he changed the guns."

"Would that be good?" Mason asked.

"What?" she asked.

"Knowing if he had changed the guns."

"Why, of course! It would show that—" Della Street abruptly broke off, looked at Mason with wide, puzzled eyes.

"Exactly," said Mason, slipping the gun into his pocket. "We are babes in the woods, Della. *We* certainly don't know that any gun was substituted, and, of course, we wouldn't think for a minute of charging Mervyn Aldrich with having made a quick switch. Not a man of his reputation. No one would believe me, anyway. They'd think I was lying, trying to protect a client."

11

PERRY MASON SEEMED IN RARE GOOD HUMOR AS HE drove the car toward Hollywood.

"Chief, *where* are we going?" Della Street demanded.

Mason said, "Oh, I thought I'd drive up and see what's happened at the scene of the crime. However, I first want to telephone Paul Drake—I'm giving him as much time as possible to assemble the facts."

"Well, if you're going to telephone him before you go up there, this is about your last chance."

"I believe you're right," Mason said, stopping the car in front of a service-station phone booth.

"You want to phone," Della Street asked, "or do you want me to phone?"

"You telephone," Mason said. "Just get the news and tell Paul I'll be in touch with him later."

Della Street glanced at Mason sharply. "You certainly do seem elaborately casual about it."

"Well, after all, Della, as far as we know, our client took a shot at a man who was trying to assault her—probably by this time they've found he's a criminal with a long record and—"

Della Street angrily snatched the dime from Mason's hand, flounced out of the car and into the telephone booth.

Mason settled back in the car, not even bothering to watch her facial expressions as she telephoned. He selected a cigarette from his cigarette case, tapped it on his thumb, put it between his lips, lit the cigarette, blew out a cloud of smoke, and then closed his eyes.

In the telephone booth Della Street's eyes grew wide with apprehension. She grabbed a notebook, took down a few notes in shorthand, then, leaving the phone dangling, ran out to the car.

"Chief!" she exclaimed in consternation.

"What's the matter?" Mason asked.

"The man in the car, the dead man, was Steve Merrill! They've identified him through associates as being Staunton Vester Gladden, a confidence man who's wanted for forgeries and a swindle. He's the one who swindled Evelyn Bagby out of her little inheritance. She made a complaint against him and the police have a record of that complaint."

"Uh-huh," Mason said.

"The killing wasn't the way Evelyn Bagby described it at all. It was deliberate murder."

"Indeed," Mason said.

"The lights weren't on on the car when it went over

the grade and several things about the condition of the car simply don't check with Evelyn Bagby's story.

"Evelyn Bagby had telephoned and left that message for him shortly before noon. The police have learned that from the woman who took the message, a Ruby Inwood, who lives in the same apartment house. Merrill raised some money all right. No one knows how. He had seven thousand five hundred dollars in cash which he showed to some of his associates. He also said he'd have to buy Evelyn Bagby off, so he telephoned and made an appointment with her."

"An appointment?" Mason asked.

"That's right. She told him she worked until three o'clock in the afternoon, that she was off then until eight. She suggested that he meet her at four-thirty at a place along the road near the Crowncrest Tavern. She designated the place."

"Well, well," Mason said. "The police have really been doing fast work, haven't they?"

"They've got hold of some witnesses. Drake says they're going at it hammer and tongs."

"Yes, I can well imagine," Mason told her.

"And here's something else. Steve Merrill had a gun. He was showing it around. He was as proud of it as could be. Apparently it was the murder weapon. It was one of those new Colt revolvers."

"Tut-tut!" Mason said.

"What do you mean, Chief?"

"Then he must have stolen it," Mason said. "Didn't you hear Mervyn Aldrich say—?"

"Chief, you *know* that was a lie. Mervyn Aldrich was covering up for Helene Chaney. Are you going to let him get away with anything like that?"

"It's too early to tell," Mason said, "but you shouldn't accuse a reputable citizen like Mervyn Aldrich of covering up anything. What else did Drake tell you?"

"The police are hopping mad. They're looking for you.

The city police have moved in on the case. Sergeant Holcomb of the Homicide Squad is up at the Crowncrest Tavern trying to find out where Evelyn Bagby is."

"Joe Padena said you told her the man she shot at was dead and that she had hysterics all over the place, that he thought she went to see a doctor.

"Holcomb is making like crazy. They have officers staked out at the entrance to your office building and they've been trying to pump Paul Drake. He's worried."

"Well, well, well," Mason said.

"So you can see what's happened, Chief. Paul Drake is all worked up about it, and he said they've got a dead open-and-shut case against Evelyn Bagby; that she must have got Steve Merrill out on that road, killed him, put the pillow slip over his head, taken all the money from him, run the car over the grade, and then got in her car and driven back just as cool as a cucumber.

"Then at the proper time she telephoned you about having found the gun, got you to suggest that she bring it to you. Then she put on that act about having been held up and all of that."

"So the evidence would seem to indicate," Mason said.

"Paul Drake is waiting on the line. He's having kittens!"

"Well, that's fine," Mason said. "Tell him we thank him for what he's done and for him to go to bed and get a good night's sleep."

Della Street regarded Mason angrily, then suddenly started laughing.

"Now what?" Mason asked.

She said, "You can be the damnedest, most exasperating individual in the world when you start out, and, believe me, you're reaching an all-time high tonight."

With that she flounced back into the telephone booth, gave Drake Mason's message, hung up the telephone and returned.

She said, "You shouldn't do that."

"What?"

"Do things like that to Paul Drake. Drake had assumed that you'd be turning things upside down trying to get facts ahead of the police. He had been telephoning operatives right and left, getting them to dash up to his office so as to be available. He'd fortified himself with a lot of coffee because he thought he was going to be sitting up all night. He was sitting there all ready to spring into action, and you told him to go home and go to bed. That just about floored him. I think another shock like that and he'll pass out of the picture for good."

"Oh well," Mason said, "Paul should get a little sleep once in a while. After all, he works hard, Della, and that continual strain can do things to a man."

She said, "Go on, be nasty and mysterious. Don't take me into your confidence."

Mason grinned. "There's a taxi stand a few blocks down the street, Della. I'm going to drive you there. You take the taxi to your apartment. Try and get a good night's sleep."

"And where are you going?"

"Why," Mason said, "quite naturally, I'm going up to the Crowncrest Tavern to see if I can do anything to help Sergeant Holcomb. If the police are looking for me I certainly want to co-operate."

12

MASON DROVE THE CAR INTO THE GARAGE OF THE BUILDing where he had his apartment, turned the car around, said to the attendant, "Just let it stand right there, if you will, Joe. I'm going up to my apartment for just a minute."

Mason hurried up to his apartment, grabbed two .38 caliber shells from a box of ammunition and was back to his car within a matter of minutes.

Mason drove carefully through the streets of Hollywood, turned up the canyon road and started up the long, winding short-cut grade to the Crowncrest Tavern.

By this time the officers had not only removed the body but had raised the automobile from the bottom of the canyon and towed it to the police laboratory to check fingerprints and prepare photographic evidence.

There were tracks where the wrecking automobile had winched the car up the side of the hill. Empty flashbulbs scattered around near the gutter of the road indicated that newspaper photographers had been busy.

Mason brought his car to a stop, got out in the rain.

He walked up the road some twenty yards, took the gun from his pocket, took deliberate aim at a redwood post supporting a guardrail and pulled the trigger. He then raised the weapon so it was pointed toward a live oak tree and fired a second shot into the trunk of the tree.

He swung the cylinder out of the gun, ejected the two empty cartridges he had fired, replaced them with two fresh cartridges from his pocket, then casually tossed the gun in the glove compartment of his car.

He eased the car into motion and drove directly to the Crowncrest Tavern.

Heavy rain lashed the cemented parking place, pounded on the roof of the tavern, poured down in rivulets from the eaves. Mason noticed the two police cars and several newspaper cars parked around the place. There were few cars belonging to customers. Evidently Joe Padena's complaint that people didn't want to drive up to the tavern on a rainy night was justified.

Mason parked his car, switched off the lights, and shut off the motor. A newspaper photographer on the inside of the Crowncrest Tavern who had been looking out through the plate-glass window, suddenly grabbed his camera and started for the door.

A few moments later a flashlight blazed into brilliance, dazzling the lawyer. Then Sergeant Holcomb came barging out of the place like an angry bull.

"Mason," he said, "where the devil's this client of yours, Evelyn Bagby?"

Mason said, "The last I saw of her she was quite hysterical. I believe she was being taken to a doctor."

"What doctor?"

"I'm sure I couldn't tell you."

"Bill Ferron told me that she gave you the gun with which the shooting was done."

"Well?" Mason asked.

"Don't stand there like that," Holcomb said irritably. "You're a lawyer. That gun is evidence. We want it. You should have turned that in to the police."

"Didn't Mr. Ferron tell you that I asked him if he wanted to look at the gun and he said—?"

"That was before he knew a murder had been committed with it."

By this time several of the newspaper reporters had gathered around, heedless of the rain.

"A murder?" Mason asked.

"You heard me," Holcomb said. "A murder."

"Oh, I think you've completely misjudged the case," Mason told him reassuringly. "Some man tried to hold up Miss Bagby and—"

"Don't tell *me* those fairy stories," Holcomb roared. "Save them for the jury. Where the hell's the gun?"

"The gun?" Mason said, glancing toward his car, and frowning. "What you have said puts a slightly different complexion on the case, Sergeant, and—"

"I'm not going to monkey with you," Sergeant Holcomb said. "I know all about the gun. It's one of the new Colt, lightweight, two-inch barrel pocket guns of .38 caliber. It has become a vital piece of evidence in the case. I'm telling you now as an officer that a murder was committed and that this gun fired the fatal shot. That makes the gun evidence. Now then, you go ahead and withhold evidence in this case and I'll charge you with a violation of law. Are you going to produce the gun or not?"

Mason hesitated a moment, then opened the right-hand door of the car, moved his hand toward the glove compartment, then thought better of it.

"Now wait a minute, Sergeant," he said, "I have no objection to producing anything that is evidence in the case, but *if* I should produce any gun I certainly am not going to do it in response to an order from you to produce a gun with which a murder was committed. If you want to ask me for a weapon which, to the best of my knowledge and belief, is the same weapon which Evelyn Bagby referred to when she said that she fired two shots at random—"

Sergeant Holcomb lowered his shoulder, caught Mason in the chest, pushed him back off balance.

The sergeant pulled open the door of the glove compartment, reached inside, triumphantly produced the weapon, swung the cylinder open, noticed the two empty cartridges, grunted with satisfaction, and dropped the weapon into his pocket.

Newspaper photographers, crowding in, battled for position. Flashbulbs blazed.

One of the photographers said, "How about running through that action again, Sergeant. Let's have a close-up of you taking the gun out of the glove compartment."

Sergeant Holcomb was only too willing to comply.

Mason stood somewhat ruefully to one side until the photographers had secured their close-up pictures.

Holcomb turned to Mason. "Now I want you to produce Evelyn Bagby."

"I'll produce her as soon as her physician gives permission."

"That physician stuff!" Holcomb ejaculated. "That's just a bunch of hooey! You have her staked out someplace."

"I'm quite certain that I don't know where she is," Mason said, "and I don't think you had any right to reach in the glove compartment of my car and—"

"Oh, bunk!" Holcomb said. "There's no use arguing with you. I've got what I want anyhow."

He turned his back abruptly and strode into the Crowncrest Tavern.

Mason, taking advantage of the fact that the reporters and photographers were crowding around Sergeant Holcomb, wanting close-ups of the gun, walked around his automobile, slid in the driver's seat, started the car and was driving back down the road to Hollywood before anyone noticed that he had left.

13

MASON SAT BY THE HEAD OF THE BED. DELLA STREET removed the bed tray containing dishes and the remnants of a breakfast.

Evelyn Bagby, wearing one of Della Street's nightgowns, propped herself up in the bed and smiled at Perry Mason.

"How are you feeling?" Mason asked.

"Like a million dollars," she said. "A little fuzzy-headed but—boy, that was a *good* sleep."

A caged parrot, excited over the influx of visitors, craned his neck trying to see everything that went on. From time to time he would say, "Poor Polly! Poor Polly! Polly want a cracker? Pretty Polly! Watch it now, Polly! Awk-awk!"

Mason said, "You're going to have quite a day today. You'll have to prepare for it."

"Do they think that—can you tell me?"

"I'm going to tell you," Mason said, "and it's going to be a jolt."

"What?"

"The automobile at the bottom of the ravine contained a man who was quite dead. He'd been shot in the right side of the head. He was wearing a pillow slip with two holes cut for eyes, and the slip was held in place with a rubber band around the top of the head."

She nodded. "That's just the way I remember it."

The parrot burst into a shrill cacophony of parrot laughter.

"And," Mason went on, "there was a hole in the pillow slip. According to the police laboratory technician it was not a bullet hole and that pillow slip had been put on after the man had been shot."

"But wouldn't—didn't—but that bullet hole in the side of the head, wouldn't that have killed him instantly?"

Mason nodded.

"Watch it now!" the parrot screamed.

"But he was driving the car when I saw him," Evelyn Bagby protested.

Mason said, "The police have other ideas. Now here's some more. The police have identified the dead man."

"Who was he?"

"His name," Mason said, "that is, the name he was going under in Hollywood, was Steve Merrill. Evidently he was the man you knew as Staunton Vester Gladden."

She sat bolt upright in bed, her eyes searching Mason's face. "Mr. Mason, you're not joking!"

"That would be rather a grim joke," Mason said, and then added significantly, "On you."

"So *that* explained it," she exclaimed.

"What does?"

"Can't you see? I had penetrated Merrill's disguise. I had found out that he and Staunton Vester Gladden were one and the same. He had defrauded me and I had sworn out a warrant for his arrest. Heaven knows how many other people had been defrauded and had sworn out complaints against him. If they knew Gladden and Merrill were one and the same he'd be in bad. So he had to silence my lips. That's why he telephoned and left a message that he would make a settlement. Then he waited until I got in my car and had started down the hill. Then he tried to crowd me off."

"And then you shot twice," Mason said.

She nodded.

"And one bullet entered his head and the other went through the pillow slip."

"But if he was wearing a pillow slip and I had been the one who fired the shot, the same bullet would have gone through—"

"That's the point," Mason said. "That's the place where the police are going to claim that it was cold-blooded, deliberate murder; that you killed Merrill first and *then* went and got a pillow slip and put it over his head and made up this story of the attempt at a holdup."

The parrot said sympathetically, "Poor Polly, poor Polly!"

"Why, Mr. Mason, that's completely . . . that's the craziest thing. They can't get away with that for a minute."

"It would help," Mason said, "if you could explain how it happened that the pillow slip from your bed was the one which was found on Merrill's head."

The parrot said, "Watch it now, watch it now."

"Can you give me any more details, Mr. Mason?"

Mason said, "Merrill had rented a Chevvy from a drive-urself car agency. He lived in the Sternwood Apartments. Residents of that apartment house customarily parked their cars in an adjacent vacant lot.

"Oscar Loomis had a Chevvy of the same model as the one Merrill had rented. He lived in the same apartment house. He had parked his car next to the one Merrill was driving.

"At four-forty Loomis came out for his car and found it gone. He notified the police. A few minutes later, Boles, who had also rented an apartment in this house, appeared and suggested to Loomis that Merrill might have switched cars by mistake. He said he'd seen Merrill drive away a few minutes earlier and that a woman was with—"

"Boles," she interrupted. "What was he doing out there? He was supposed to be living in Riverside."

"I know," Mason said. "I had detectives look into that. I think Merrill may have staged that jewel theft to try and frame you, to get some valuable jewels, and to delay the wedding. Right at the moment I don't know how he did it, but it would seem Boles might have been an accomplice.

"Boles claims he hadn't known Merrill until after the gems were stolen and that Merrill got in touch with him when he knew Boles was a witness to what had happened.

"As a lawyer I'm very skeptical about all that. At any rate Boles and Merrill became friendly. Merrill confided in Boles, telling him about you, and about the spot he'd been put in because you'd recognized his picture.

"But Boles has an alibi. Boles was with Loomis at twenty minutes to five. Then Ruby Inwood, a girl who lives in the apartment house, joined them. The three of them went out to dinner and were together until after eight o'clock.

"This Ruby Inwood seems to be a play girl. She doesn't work, but she has a fine apartment, dresses well and has men friends. Right at present she's driving a new car which, according to rumor, was provided by some Lothario.

"Boles seems to be in the clear on Merrill's death, but I'm still working on the theory he may have been an accomplice in the jewel theft.

"Now take Aldrich. He can't furnish any witnesses as to where he was between four-thirty and seven-thirty. Irene Keith told me she'd be in, waiting for my call. I've had detectives checking her. She was out.

"However, you're the one hot lead at present. The police have issued a broadcast calling on any doctor who may have treated you to get in touch with the police immediately. They have an idea that some doctor treated you and put you out of circulation. The heat's on. I can't keep you away from the police much longer."

She nodded.

"And," Mason went on, "you're going to have to do something that's disagreeable."

"What?"

"Stay in the detention ward."

"I guess I can do that all right," she said. "I . . . I'm getting accustomed to it."

"And," Mason went on, "I want you to do something else."

"What?"

"Talk."

"Just what do you want me to say, Mr. Mason?"

"Anything, everything. I want you to tell the newspapers all about your blighted life, about how the little inheritance you had which was going to take you to Hollywood was taken from you, all about the way this man Staunton Vester Gladden betrayed you."

"But wouldn't that be playing right into their hands? Wouldn't that seem to give me a motive? Wouldn't that show I had every reason to kill him?"

"Sure it will. But they're going to find out anyway

sooner or later. It's going to look a lot better to have you tell them and tell them first.

"Now the newspapers will have a lot of sob sisters interviewing you. They'll want your life story. Give it to them. Emphasize that you've been studying how to be an actress ever since you were eighteen."

"There again I'm vulnerable," she said. "It will make it look as though I'm telling a story and have enough histrionic ability to make it look good and—"

"That's exactly what I want," Mason said. "I want the sob sisters to start speculating as to whether you're a consummate actress who is putting one over, or a sincere, straightforward girl who is telling the truth.

"The more they speculate the better publicity you'll have. The more stories they write about whether you're a naïve, truthful girl, or a skillful liar, the more they'll build up your prestige as an actress."

"Pretty Polly. Watch it now. Here's your cracker," the parrot interpolated.

"I'm not to hold anything back?"

"Tell them everything," Mason said. "Tell them the whole story. The minute you try holding back you're working under wraps. You won't be able to put your individuality into the thing. You can't really convince them. You'll be thinking all the time about mental reservations. I don't want you to have any. I want you to look them straight in the eyes and pour out your soul."

"And the police?"

"The same with the police," Mason said. "Tell them your story. Tell them that story over and over, as many times as they ask you about it. Tell them everything."

"I'm glad," she said.

"For what?"

"That you told me to do that, because, after all, Mr. Mason, I *am* innocent."

She looked him directly in the eyes, widened her own eyes slightly.

"That's a good trick," Mason said.

"What?"

"Widening your eyes just a little bit when you look at a person and want him to believe you."

"That's not a trick, Mr. Mason. I was being sincere. I—"

Mason grinned. "I am inclined to believe your story because I always make it a point to believe a client, but that gesture of widening the eyes was a trick. I've noticed you do it before."

She seemed angry for a minute, then suddenly started to laugh. "Well, I guess you may be right. I'd practiced that for so long in front of a mirror that it had become second nature to me, and for a minute I was annoyed when you intimated it was a conscious expression. Actually that was one of the things that I practiced for Staunton Gladden in front of a mirror. Isn't it funny that I should be called on to use that same trick now in connection with . . . with his death."

Mason said, "The doctor who treated you is on pins and needles. The police have broadcast a description of you and the doctor feels that he has to communicate with the police, particularly in view of the fact that you're now ready to be discharged from his care. The police will be here shortly. The doctor will tell them that Miss Street took you up to this apartment, put you to bed, and that he gave you a hypo."

"How long do I have?"

"Just long enough to take a bath and get dressed."

She started to get out of bed.

"Okay," Mason said, "Della and I will go out. You take a shower and dress. The officers will be here within twenty minutes."

Mason held the door open for Della Street, closed it gently behind her. She looked at him and raised her eyebrows.

Mason said in a low voice, "We're stuck with the case

now, Della. We can't back out. As far as I'm concerned I'm taking her at face value."

"The *face* value is good," Della Street conceded, "and the *figure* value isn't bad either."

From behind the door came the shrill scream of the parrot, followed by demoniacal laughter.

14

FRANK NEELY WAS SUFFERING FROM AN ACUTE ATTACK of stage fright.

Because the Evelyn Bagby case involved a screen personality, and seemed to be so filled with contradictions, the newspapers had given it a good coverage. Neely's eyes as he entered Judge Kippen's courtroom beside Perry Mason were blinded by a succession of flashbulbs exploding in his face.

"Lord, Mr. Mason," he said in a whisper, "I don't know what to do. It even seems presumptuous to be in the same courtroom with you. I—"

"Just act like a veteran," Mason told him, smiling. "Take it easy. The main thing is to watch the evidence like a hawk and try to manipulate things so you can protect the interests of your client."

Neely said, "If Sergeant Holcomb's reconstruction of the crime is at all correct, then things look rather bad for our client."

Mason nodded. "If the police contention in any case is correct, things always look bad for the defendant. About all we can do is to watch the facts. Well, here we go, here's the judge."

Judge Kippen entered the courtroom.

"Case of People versus Evelyn Bagby," the judge called after Court had been called to order.

"Ready for the prosecution."

"Ready for the defense," Mason said.

"Call your witnesses," Judge Kippen announced.

Geoffry Strawn, a relatively new trial deputy who represented the district attorney's office, had enjoyed a brilliant career as a trial lawyer and had been reported to have expressed a desire to "tangle" with Perry Mason in a courtroom and "show him up." Now he called as his first witness, Harry Boles.

Neely leaned over and whispered to Mason, "Oh boy, I'd like to see you tear *his* can off."

Geoffry Strawn seemed to recognize this attitude on the part of the defendant's attorney. He stood up, smiled sardonically, and, after the witness had been sworn and answered the preliminary questions, asked, "Did you know Steve Merrill in his lifetime?"

"Yes, sir."

"Where is he now?"

"He is dead."

"Have you seen the body of Steve Merrill?"

"I have. Yes, sir."

"Where?"

"At the county morgue."

"You recognize that as the body of Steve Merrill?"

"I do."

"Cross-examine," Strawn said to Mason.

Mason smiled at Boles.

"How long had you known Stephen Merrill?"

"Only a short time. It happened that he located an apartment for me in the same building where he had his apartment."

"Mr. Boles, did you ever know the decedent when he was going under the name of Staunton Vester Gladden?"

"Objected to as incompetent, irrelevant and immaterial," Strawn snapped.

Mason said, "This is cross-examination, Your Honor."

"Now just a moment," Judge Kippen announced, leaning forward and looked over the top of his glasses at Mason. "This is a preliminary examination. It's not a regular trial. The purpose of this examination is only to find out whether a crime has been committed, and if so whether there is reasonable ground to believe that the defendant participated in the commisssion of that crime.

"Therefore this Court doesn't intend to listen to a lot of technical arguments on objections, nor does the Court intend to have this case become the least bit spectacular. I'm perfectly willing to have material points argued, but I'm going to squelch any dramatic pyrotechnics, and there will be no personalities. Now then, the objection is overruled. Answer the question."

"Did you," Mason asked, "ever know the decedent when he was going under the name of Staunton Vester Gladden?"

"No sir. On the day of his death he told me he had once used that name."

"That's all," Mason said.

"Any redirect?" Judge Kippen asked.

"No, Your Honor."

"The witness is excused. Who's your next witness?"

"William Ferron."

Ferron came forward, was sworn and testified to interviewing the defendant in the Joshua Tree Café on the night the crime was alleged to have been committed.

"The defendant made certain statements to you?"

"She did."

"Were those statements made freely and voluntarily?"

Ferron smiled. "They were made in the presence of her counsel."

"Mr. Perry Mason?"

"That's right."

"And what did she tell you?"

Ferron went on to recount at some length the story the defendant had told him.

Then the witness testified to the trip up the mountain road, the discovery of the broken guardrail, the finding of the body, and the various things that happened after the discovery of the body.

"Cross-examine," Strawn said.

"No questions," Mason said.

"Call Sergeant Holcomb to the stand," Strawn announced.

Sergeant Holcomb came forward was sworn, and, with an air of glowing satisfaction, proceeded to settle himself in the witness chair as one who expected to be there for some time.

Under Strawn's direct questioning he explained his capacity with the city police, explained that the city Homicide Squad had been called by the sheriff's office when it appeared a body had been found within the city limits.

"And what was the situation at the time you arrived?"

"It was raining. The car was down the mountainside. A representative of the coroner's office was there, also police photographers."

"What did you do?"

"I went down to examine the body, then I assisted in removing the body after pictures had been taken showing the position in which the body was lying. I pointed out certain matters to the deputy sheriffs, certain things which I felt were significant, and called their attention to certain things that they should look for."

"What do you mean by that?"

"Well, I suggested that the position of the light switch on the car was a matter of the greatest importance."

"And what was the position of the light switch?"

"It was off."

"You are referring to the headlight switch of the automobile that contained the body and which was at the bottom of the ravine?"

"That's right."

"The headlights were off?"

"Yes, sir."

"And the switch was off?"

"Yes, sir."

"Now did you subsequently talk with the defendant in this action?"

"Yes, sir."

"Were any inducements made to her to make any statements to you?"

"No, sir."

"Any threats?"

"No, sir."

"Everything that was said was freely and voluntarily stated by the defendant?"

"Yes, sir."

"And did you ask her concerning the headlights on the automobile which had attempted to crowd her off the road?"

"I did. Yes, sir."

"And what did she say?"

"She said that the headlights were on, that the headlights were in the high position, that they were shining into her windshield and reflecting back from the windshield thereby causing her great driving inconvenience."

"Did you take possession of the weapon with which the crime was committed?"

"Yes, sir."

"Where did you find that weapon?"

"In the possession of Perry Mason, counsel for the defendant."

"Where in his possession?"

"In the glove compartment of his car."

"When?"

"Some time around eleven o'clock."

"Where?"

"He drove up to the Crowncrest Tavern, where the

defendant was working, and apparently tried to see the defendant before—"

"Never mind your conclusions," Strawn interrupted. "You're an officer. You understand the rules of evidence. You know you're only permitted to testify to facts. Now just go ahead and tell us what happened."

"Well, I asked for the gun which the defendant had given Mr. Mason, the gun which the defendant had handed Mr. Mason in the restaurant when she had told her story to Mr. Ferron, the deputy sheriff."

"And did Mr. Mason give you that gun?"

"Yes, sir. That is, I believe he said he had it and made a motion toward the glove compartment. So I opened the glove compartment and took it out."

"Where is it?"

"I have it here."

"What was the condition of the weapon at the time it was given to you?"

"It was in the same condition as it is now."

"Directing your attention specifically to the cylinder of the gun—there were four loaded cartridges and two empty cartridge cases in the cylinder?"

"That's right. Yes, sir."

"So the gun is in the same condition now that it was when it was handed to you?"

"Yes, sir."

"You can swear positively to that?"

"Yes, sir."

"Your Honor, I ask that this weapon be received in evidence as People's Exhibit A."

"I would like to cross-examine as to the admissibility of the weapon," Mason said.

"Very well."

Holcomb faced Mason with a certain defiance.

"You say this weapon is in the same condition now as when you received it?"

"Yes, sir."

"Nothing has been done to it?"

"It hasn't been changed in any way."

"You gave this weapon to the ballistics department, didn't you?"

"Yes, sir."

"And you know that the ballistics department fired test shells through the weapon? You were there when that was done?"

"Yes, sir."

"And in order to fire those test bullets it was necessary to remove the cartridges from—?"

"Certainly. The cartridges that were in the gun were evidence. We wanted to show that the fatal bullet had the same composition as the remaining bullets in the gun. Therefore we weren't going to shoot those bullets."

"Exactly," Mason said. "So you unloaded the cylinder of the revolver, fired test bullets, and then replaced the empty cartridge cases and bullets that had been taken from the cylinder."

"That's right."

"Who did that?"

"I did it myself."

"Now then," Mason said, "how do you know that you got the empty cartridge cases in the proper receptacles in the cylinder?"

"Why . . . why, it wouldn't make any difference."

"Then when you stated the weapon was in exactly the same condition, as when you received it, you mean exactly the same condition for all practical purposes. Is that right?"

"Yes."

"Did you try to trace this weapon by the serial number?"

"Certainly."

"And what did you find?"

Judge Kippen raised his eyebrows somewhat and said,

"Of course, this question is coming from defense counsel."

"Exactly," Mason said. "Technically the defendant might object to certain things as not being the best evidence, but I see no reason for calling in the man who sold the gun, and the gun register, and all of that. I have unlimited confidence in Sergeant Holcomb's investigative ability."

"Thank you," Sergeant Holcomb said sarcastically.

"So I'm perfectly willing to let him testify to what he found. What did you find, Sergeant?"

"I found that this weapon had been sold to one Mervyn Aldrich, by a sporting goods store in Newport Beach on the twenty-fifth of last month. I found that Mervyn Aldrich had carried the weapon for his personal protection, that he had a permit to do so, that he kept the weapon in the glove compartment of his automobile, and that the weapon was stolen from the glove compartment—"

"Now just a minute," Judge Kippen interrupted. "I see no reason for going into a lot of hearsay evidence. Is Mr. Aldrich in court, Mr. Deputy District Attorney?"

"He is, Your Honor."

"I take it that it is claimed the gun was stolen from his possession under such circumstances that in the mind of the prosecution there is reason to believe it was taken by the defendant?"

"That's right, Your Honor."

"I think that evidence should come from Mr. Aldrich himself."

"Yes, Your Honor."

Mason said, "I would suggest then that Sergeant Holcomb step down and Mr. Aldrich be put on the stand."

"Just a moment," Strawn said. 'I'm quite willing to call Mr. Aldrich. I intend to call him. He's going to be a prosecution witness, but I see no reason to call him at this time. As far as the introduction of this weapon in evidence is concerned it is only necessary to show that it was in the possession of the defendant and that it was the weapon which killed Stephen Merrill."

Judge Kippen glanced at Mason and said, "I'd like to hear the defense on that."

"As a legal proposition there's no question of the correctness of the prosecution's position," Mason said, "except that I would like to point out two things. The first is that the prosecution hasn't proved the weapon was the weapon which was used in killing Stephen Merrill. In the second place they haven't proved that the weapon was in the possession of the defendant."

Strawn said, "What are you getting at? You gave the weapon to Sergeant Holcomb yourself."

"He took the gun from *my* car," Mason said. "I'm not the defendant."

"You were representing her."

"Only as an attorney to represent her rights," Mason said, "but even so, I didn't say anything about the gun. Perhaps I can clarify that by asking Sergeant Holcomb a couple of additional questions."

Mason turned to Sergeant Holcomb, smiling affably. "Now, Sergeant," he said in a conversational tone of voice, "when I drove up to the Crowncrest Tavern you came up to me and demanded possession of the gun that had been given to me by Evelyn Bagby, didn't you?"

"Yes, I think I said the gun that had been used in the killing."

"And isn't it a fact," Mason said, "that you thereupon pushed me to one side, opened the glove compartment of the automobile and took out the gun which you now have identified?"

"You didn't hand me the gun. I had to get it," Holcomb said.

"This seems to be rather a technical point," Judge Kippen said. "Is there any serious contention on the part of the defense that this weapon is *not* the one which was used in killing the decedent, Mr. Mason? Isn't the question as far as the defense is concerned one of whether the homicide was justifiable?"

"I think," Mason said, "that as far as this weapon is concerned, Your Honor, I want to have it definitely established that it is the weapon with which the crime was committed."

"May I ask why?" Judge Kippen asked. "I think it's always advisable for counsel to get together on things about which there can be no question."

Mason said, "They have tested this gun and compared test bullets with the fatal bullet. I simply want to force them to put on that testimony at this time so the defendant will have an opportunity to study the photographic evidence in order to prepare her defense properly."

"I see your point," Judge Kippen said. "I think it's probably well taken. Mr. Strawn, you undoubtedly have ballistics evidence. Why not put on that ballistics evidence and prove that this is the gun with which the killing was committed? Then, by proving it was in the possession of the defendant, you can—"

"That's just the point, Your Honor," Strawn said. "The fatal bullet in this case mushroomed rather badly, and one side of the fatal bullet is completely flat. The other side was damaged slightly at the time it was removed from the head at the time of the post-mortem."

"You mean the fatal bullet can't be identified?" Judge Kippen asked.

"Well, I . . . I would like to ask this witness a couple more questions in order to clarify the matter if I may."

"Go right ahead."

Strawn said, "I think, if the Court please, I could bring out two or three matters here that are so incriminating there can be no question as to what happened. Perhaps I was somewhat premature in offering to introduce this weapon in evidence. Sergeant Holcomb, directing your attention to the pillow slip with which the head of the decedent was covered, do you have that pillow slip here with you?"

"I have. Yes, sir."

Sergeant Holcomb opened a small bag, took out a blood-stained pillow slip.

"Now I am going to ask you, Sergeant, if you found a laundry mark on that pillow slip?"

"I did. Yes, sir."

"And were you able to trace that laundry mark?"

"Yes, sir."

"Did you find any other pillow slips bearing the same laundry mark?"

"Yes, sir."

"Where?"

"At the Crowncrest Tavern, in the linen room."

"And did you examine the defendant's bed?"

"I did."

"When?"

"Almost as soon as I arrived at the place."

"And what did you find?"

"There were two pillows on the bed. One was covered with a pillow slip. The other was not. The slip had been removed from that pillow."

"Now in regard to the pillow slip, can you tell us whether the pillow slip on Steve Merrill's head had been put on before or after death?"

"It had been put on after death."

"Just a moment," Judge Kippen said. "Isn't this calling for a conclusion of the witness?"

"It's quite all right with the defense," Mason said. "We wish to co-operate with the prosecution in all matters concerning which there is no dispute."

"No dispute!" Judge Kippen said in surprise.

Strawn jumped up from his chair at the counsel table. "You mean you're admitting that the pillow slip was put on *after* death?" he asked incredulously.

Mason shrugged his shoulders. "I didn't object to the

question, that's all. You may draw whatever conclusions you wish. I simply stated to the Court that it is my policy not to object to questions where I feel that there is no dispute as to the facts."

Strawn slowly sat down, looking confused.

Judge Kippen said irritably, "Well, go ahead. Answer the question."

"Well now, this pillow slip has a hole in it. It is not a bullet hole. There aren't any powder marks around that hole in the pillow slip, no powder tattooing, no stain marks made by a bullet. On the other hand the scalp of the decedent showed a very evident powder tattoo. We experimented to find out just how that tattoo pattern could be duplicated, and found that it would be duplicated only when the gun was held approximately eight inches from the target, that is, strictly speaking, seven to nine inches, within that distance."

"What gun did you use in conducting those experiments?" Mason asked.

"Why, this gun right here."

"In other words," Judge Kippen said, "you were assuming that this is the gun used in the killing?"

"Oh, there's no question of it, Your Honor," Strawn said. "It's simply the fact that because of a peculiar chain of circumstances the fatal bullet is not quite as easy to identify as the others. However, I can go ahead and establish by circumstantial evidence that this was the weapon used."

"Go ahead and establish it, then," Judge Kippen said.

"Now you say that this pillow slip was put on after death, Sergeant?"

"That's right."

"And as one of your reasons you mention the absence of powder tattooing?"

"Yes, sir, and the fact the hole in it was not made by a bullet."

"Do you have other reasons?"

"Yes, sir."

"What are they?"

"When the pillow slip was put on the man's head the person who put it on had to twist the pillow slip slightly so that the two eyeholes which had already been cut would come directly in front of the eyes. In other words, this pillow slip being put on the head of a man who was dead, wasn't exactly centered, so it was turned as it was slipped over the head to bring the eyeholes in the right place. That accounts for this bloodstain on the inside of the pillow slip which follows a somewhat curved path. It's the only way to explain that bloodstain. You can see this very clearly."

Judge Kippen said, "Let me see that pillow slip."

He inspected the curved stain, then nodded his head. "Of course," he said, "the witness is testifying to a conclusion from the facts, but the facts are here and it seems evident that they admit of only one conclusion."

"I think so, Your Honor," Mason agreed cheerfully.

"But you *can't* admit that point," Strawn said. "Why, that's your whole defense."

"How do you know what my defense is?"

"Now come, come, gentlemen," Judge Kippen said. "This hearing has taken a most peculiar turn. On a matter which would seem to go to the very gist of the defense, counsel is making no point. On a matter, however, that would at first seem to be somewhat academic, counsel is making a very determined fight and insisting on availing himself of every technicality."

"I am simply insisting that my client has rights which must be recognized," Mason said.

"Yes, yes, I understand," Judge Kippen said. "However, you are not making things any easier for the prosecution in connection with identifying the fatal weapon, Mr. Mason."

"I don't intend to."

Judge Kippen looked at Strawn.

"It's all right," the deputy district attorney said grimly. "We'll prove it."

He turned once more to Sergeant Holcomb.

"Sergeant, there were two shells fired from this weapon which you are referring to?"

"Yes, sir."

"It was the contention of the police that one shot went into the head of the decedent. What happened to the other shot?"

"It stuck in a redwood post which was supporting a guardrail on the inside next to the bank at a point where there was a rather deep gutter."

"Can you illustrate to the Court the place where that bullet was found?"

"Yes, sir. I have here a photograph which was taken the next day, as soon as it became light, and which shows the hole in the guardrail. That bullet was dug out and that bullet is in an excellent state of preservation. While I personally didn't do the ballistics work I was present when that work was done, and there can be no question—"

"Well, don't testify to ballistics," Strawn interrupted hastily. "You're not an expert in that subject."

"Well, I'm an expert detective, and that includes the knowledge of a lot of—"

"Yes, yes. I understand," Strawn interrupted. "But since I intend to call a ballistics expert I only want to use your testimony for the purpose of identifying this bullet. I now show you a bullet which has certain etchings on the base of the bullet, the part which may be referred to as the back end. Do you know who made those etchings?"

"Yes, sir. I did."

"What are they?"

"Those are identifying marks to identify the bullet."

"And where did you get that bullet?"

"I removed it from the redwood post shown in this

photograph, a post which was on the side of the highway at the point indicated."

"Now I think if you'll step down I'll call the ballistics expert," Strawn said. "Let's have the gun Exhibit A for identification, the photograph Exhibit B for identification, and the bullet Exhibit C for identification."

"Just a moment," Mason interrupted as Sergeant Holcomb started to leave the witness stand. "You have now introduced a second object here, a bullet. I wish to cross-examine the witness concerning the bullet."

"Go right ahead," Strawn snapped.

"When did you *first* notice this bullet in the redwood post?" Mason asked.

Holcomb said, "You can't see a bullet in a redwood post, Mr. Mason, not until it's dug out. I didn't have the equipment for digging out bullets."

"When did you first see the hole in the redwood post?"

"Almost as soon as I arrived on the scene. The gun had been fired twice so I knew that there were two bullets around there somewhere. I looked to see if there was a possibility the second bullet had struck some object that would preserve it, and I found that it had."

"And then you quit looking?"

"What do you mean, I quit looking?"

"You didn't look around any more?"

"Well, I looked around, but there wasn't anything to look for after I'd found the second bullet."

"I see," Mason said. "That's all."

"I'm going to ask Sergeant Holcomb to leave the witness stand and I'll place Alexander Redfield on the stand," Strawn said. "Mr. Redfield is the ballistics expert."

"Very well," Judge Kippen ruled.

Alexander Redfield, a tall, thin individual, with high cheekbones, large protruding gray eyes, who moved deliberately when he walked, and spoke carefully when he talked as though afraid he might say too much, was given the oath, took his position on the witness stand, qualified himself as an expert in the science of ballistics and firearms identification, and was asked by Geoffry Strawn, "I hand you the bullet which Sergeant Holcomb has just identified and which is marked for identification People's Exhibit C. I ask you if you have seen that bullet before, and, if so, when?"

"Yes, sir. I saw it when it was recovered. I saw it when it was in place, that is, I saw the bullet hole in the redwood post, and I saw Sergeant Holcomb when he dug the bullet out of the post."

"Can you point on this map and tell us approximately the location?"

The witness took the map and marked an X at the spot.

"This map is an official map," Strawn said. "That is, it is a copy of an official map. I assume there will be no objection on the part of counsel to having it in evidence as People's Exhibit D."

"None whatever," Mason said.

Mason whispered to Neely. "Make an objection once in a while, Neely. Let them know you're in the case."

"I'm afraid to," Neely whispered. "I might be objecting to the wrong thing. You've got that prosecutor so puzzled now he doesn't know just where you're going to make your fight."

"Object to anything," Mason said, "just so it isn't important. Let them get in all the important facts whether they hurt us or not. Save your objections for the facts we already know. Throw a little variety into the case and give him something to think about. After all, your girl is watching you back there in the courtroom, and the newspapermen are taking this stuff down."

"All right," Neely said. "Tug my coattail if I start to object in the wrong place. I'll get up whenever I make an objection."

Mason settled back in his chair.

"And," Strawn went on, "you are familiar with this gun, this so-called Colt Cobra, which we are seeking to have introduced in evidence and which is marked People's Exhibit A for identification?"

"Yes, sir."

"You fired test bullets through that gun?"

"Yes, sir."

"Just how do you do that, Mr. Redfield?"

"Well, you fire the bullets into a box that is filled with cotton, a box long enough to stop the bullet without damaging it."

"And then what?"

"Then you examine the bullet for microscopic markings."

"Can you tell us something of the nature of those markings?"

"Well, there are what I refer to as class characteristics and there are individual characteristics."

"What are class characteristics?"

"Those are the marks left on a bullet by the lands and grooves of a barrel. They have a certain width and a certain pitch, a certain number and direction of twists. By the class characteristics it is possible to tell the make and caliber of the weapon from which the bullet was fired."

"And what are the individual or microscopic characteristics?"

"Those are the individual scratches on a bullet caused by little rough places on the inside of the barrel. No barrel is perfectly smooth, and, of course, these rough places are completely individual with the barrels so that these tiny, microscopic grooves which are left by these rough places give a bullet as much of an individual trademark as though the barrel had left its fingerprints on the bullet."

"Now then, did you compare this bullet from the redwood post with the test bullets fired from this gun?"

"I did. Yes, sir."

"And, as an expert, can you say whether you matched characteristics so you could tell from what gun the bullet had been fired?"

"Yes, sir, I did. I matched both class and microscopic characteristics so that I can identify absolutely that that bullet was fired from this gun."

"How about the fatal bullet? That was recovered and turned over to you?"

"Yes, sir."

"And did you conduct a series of tests with that?"

"I can state that that bullet was rather mutilated. It was in poor condition but I was able to determine class characteristics so that I knew that that bullet had been fired from a Colt .38 of this type."

"What about the individual characteristics?"

"On the strength of the individual and microscopic characteristics I am not at the present time able to make an identification. One half of the bullet is badly damaged."

"Now then, Your Honor," Strawn said, "I wish to renew my offer of this gun as an exhibit."

"That's objected to," Neely said, getting to his feet and squaring his shoulders. "It is incompetent, irrelevant and immaterial. There is no proper foundation laid. There has been no connection."

Judge Kippen looked down at the young man. His eyes were kindly but there was a certain grim determination about him.

"Let's see if I understand your point, Mr. Neely," he said. "Simply because the fatal bullet cannot be matched you object to having a weapon introduced in evidence which concededly was in the possession of the defendant?"

"We don't concede that it was in the possession of the defendant. It was in the possession of Mr. Perry Mason."

Judge Kippen shook his head. "There may be a technical distinction there, but as far as this Court is concerned I am not going to get too technical. If there is any point about that weapon not actually having been in the possession of the defendant then testimony to that effect will go to the weight of the evidence, but now you are objecting as to its admissibility."

"Because, if the Court please, no one knows that it is the weapon which killed the decedent," Neely insisted.

"There is certainly every indication that it was the weapon. This defendant told officers of firing the gun in the general direction of a car being driven by a man who wore a pillow slip over his head."

"And it is quite evident that that couldn't have been the decedent in this case," Mason said, getting to his feet.

"Why not?" Judge Kippen asked.

"Because," Mason said, "the testimony of the prosecution shows that the pillow slip was put over the head of the decedent *after* he was dead."

"It is the contention of the prosecution that this proves the guilt of the defendant," Judge Kippen said.

"Exactly," Mason said. "And it is the contention of the defendant that it proves the body could not have been that of the man at whom the defendant fired the shot."

"What? How's that?" Judge Kippen asked, suddenly sitting up. "You contend there were two people on that road wearing pillow slip masks?"

"Why not?" Mason asked. "Let's let the prosecution prove its case."

Judge Kippen shook his head. "If this is merely a technicality," he said, "I will hold that all of these objections go to the weight of the evidence rather than its admissibility, but if there is a definite point here—"

"I think there is, Your Honor," Mason said. "I would like to have the Court inspect the place where this shooting took place."

"What would be gained by that?" Judge Kippen asked.

"We intend to submit a defense," Mason said, "and I

think the Court will understand the nature of that defense after it sees the premises."

"Now just a moment," Geoffry Strawn said, getting to his feet, his voice tinged with anger. "It is a well-known fact that counsel stages theatrical legal pyrotechnics at the time of preliminary examination. That is not the function of a preliminary examination. Such examination is only to ascertain whether a crime has been committed and whether there is a reasonable ground to believe that the defendant committed that crime. I believe that with the evidence right in its present state the Court is bound to answer that question in the affirmative."

"Yes," Judge Kippen said, "the Court is inclined to agree with the prosecutor, Mr. Mason."

"Exactly," Mason said, and sat down.

"Now just a moment," Judge Kippen said. "I didn't mean to preclude you from further argument, Mr. Mason."

"There's nothing to argue about," Mason said. "In the present state of the evidence it is quite evident that a man has been murdered and there is some evidence indicating that this defendant was guilty of that crime."

"Well then, what are we arguing about?" Judge Kippen asked.

"Simply," Mason said, "that I don't propose to let the case go to the Court in the present state of the evidence."

"Oh, I see," Judge Kippen said smiling.

"Now just a moment, I object to that," Geoffry Strawn said. "I feel that—"

"Do you wish to preclude the defendant from putting on evidence?" Mason asked.

"No, certainly not, but—oh, here we go again with this spectacular request that the Court view the premises. I don't see what can be gained from viewing the premises. We have photographs here."

"Well, introduce the photographs," Judge Kippen said, "and I'll look at those. Then if I feel there's any need to view the premises I'll take a look at them."

"Do you wish me to call the photographer and identify the photographs, Your Honor?"

"That would be the proper way, unless—"

"Oh, we'll stipulate," Mason said. "We like to save time as much as counsel. If the prosecutor will give us his word that the pictures were taken under his supervision and direction by a qualified photographer, and represent a true picture of the scenes indicated therein, we'll stipulate they may be admitted in evidence."

"Very well, Your Honor," Strawn said, and then, turning to Mason with a smile, "Perhaps I was unduly critical, Mr. Mason. I appreciate your co-operation in this matter."

"Not at all," Mason said. "Perhaps you'll have reason to renew your criticism later."

Strawn said to the judge, "These photographs are numbered one to ten inclusive, and on the back of each photograph appears a description of what is shown."

"May I have copies?" Mason asked.

"Certainly," Strawn said, handing Mason ten eight-by-ten glossy prints.

Mason and Neely studied the prints.

Mason picked one photograph from the group, and, holding it in front of him, slowly arose to his feet. "Your Honor," he said, "I would like to direct the Court's attention and the attention of counsel to photograph number seven purporting to show, as is listed on the back of the photograph, the redwood post in which the bullet lodged."

"Yes, I have that photograph," Judge Kippen said. "What about it?"

"The Court will notice an oak tree in the background and a little to the left of that post," Mason said. "There is a very peculiar spot on that tree about, oh, I would say some eight or ten feet from the base of the tree on the left-hand side, a little white spot with a dark center—"

"Yes, yes, I see it," Judge Kippen said. "What about it?"

"It looks like a bullet hole to me," Mason said, and sat down.

Strawn said, "Oh, Your Honor, that is obviously some sort of a blemish either on the tree or on the photograph. This is indicative of tactics that are used for delay and to confuse the issues. It couldn't be a bullet hole because—"

Strawn ceased talking suddenly.

"Why couldn't it?" Mason asked.

"Because," Strawn blurted, "there were only two bullets fired from the gun."

"Exactly," Mason said. "One of those bullets has now been identified as having been fired from the gun and lodged in a redwood post. My client stated to the deputy sheriff that she pulled the trigger twice, shooting at random. Now then, if it should appear that the second bullet had lodged in this oak tree, then my contention would be thoroughly established—that the body found in the canyon was that of—"

"Oh, if the Court please," Strawn said. "This is absurd! I don't know whether this is one of counsel's ingenious traps or not, but counsel had that gun in his possession. What was to have prevented *him* from firing one shot into the redwood post and one into the oak tree, and then claiming there was a perfect alibi for his client?"

Mason smiled. "Simply that Sergeant Holcomb has stated that he saw this hole in the redwood post *as soon as he arrived at the scene of the crime and that he arrived there before the deputy sheriffs had left.*"

"But Sergeant Holcomb didn't say anything about the hole in the redwood post to the deputy sheriffs," Strawn blurted.

"Are you now attacking the veracity of your own witness?" Mason asked.

Judge Kippen said, "Well, under the circumstances the Court has decided to take a look at the premises. It will only take a few minutes. We'll drive out there and counsel can point out the exact spot, and while we're out there we'll take a look at that blemish on the oak tree. Mr. Redfield, the Court would like to have you along to give your opinion as to the cause of that mark on the oak tree."

"Very well, Your Honor," Redfield said.

Newspaper reporters, sensing a sudden dramatic turn in what otherwise might have been a routine trial, moved toward telephones as Judge Kippen, frowning thoughtfully at the collection of pictures, adjourned court.

15

THE CAVALCADE OF CARS WOUND ITS WAY UP THE STEEP road, came to a stop at the place where the guardrail had been recently repaired.

Sergeant Holcomb said with great importance, "The car went through right here, Your Honor."

"Where's the redwood post where the other bullet was found?" Judge Kippen said, holding the photograph. "It—oh, yes, yes, I see it."

"And here's the oak tree," Mason said.

Judge Kippen cocked a somewhat skeptical eye at the trunk of the oak tree, then began to show increased interest.

"Something has chipped off the bark there very recently," he said. "It looks as though a bullet had—well, I won't reach any hasty conclusions. Let's see what caused that mark."

Sergeant Holcomb excitedly drew Strawn off to one side.

Strawn said, "Your honor, we don't want to conceal any facts, but we certainly aren't going to be bound by any bullet hole unless we can show *when* the bullet was fired into the tree and *by whom*."

"Well," Judge Kippen said, "if you want to be technical in the matter, Mr. Strawn, I noticed that Sergeant Holcomb stated he had taken personal responsibility for searching the premises for bullets and that he found this bullet in the redwood post and then had ceased to search because two bullets had been fired and he had then accounted for two bullets. That seems to me to be poor investigative technique. I think the premises should have been searched thoroughly so the officer could have said definitely there were no other bullets or marks of bullets readily visible before he terminated his search."

"Well, of course," Holcomb retorted. "I can't keep anyone from coming out here and firing bullets all over the place—"

"That will do, Sergeant," Judge Kippen said tartly. "If there had been proper investigative technique at the time in regard to those bullets, we would have *known* whether bullets had been subsequently fired or not. Now let's get a ladder and get up that tree and see what that thing is up there."

"I think there's a ladder up at the house where there's an archway over the gate. I believe an artist lives there, a woman who— Here she comes now."

A tall, slender woman with white hair, long nose and a firm, pointed chin, came moving slowly down the walk.

"What's all this?" she asked.

Judge Kippen smiled and said, "This is an investigation into the shooting which took place up here, madam. I am Judge Kippen and—"

"Oh, yes, yes," she said, smiling. "And I am Mary Eunice. I'm an artist, living up here in retirement, Judge, and—"

Judge Kippen intervened in what threatened to be the start of a long-drawn, rapid-fire explanation. "Mrs. Eunice, we're trying to get at a place on this oak tree about ten feet up where you can see something that looks like a score in the tree. We want to see if that was made by a bullet. Do you have a ladder at your place?"

"Yes, indeed I have," she said. "I'll be only too glad to loan it to you. And if you're looking for bullets I can give you another one."

"What?" Judge Kippen exclaimed.

"Yes," she said. "It happened that night when we had all the excitement up here. I thought I heard something strike the house and I thought there was the tinkle of glass. But I really didn't think much of it. Birds sometimes fly against the house. It wasn't until this morning that I noticed one of the attic windows has a neat little hole in it, and a spent bullet is partially embedded in one of the rafters."

"That happened the night of the shooting?" Judge Kippen asked.

"Yes, Judge."

"When? What time?"

"Well—it was after dark, but very early in the evening."

"Did you hear a shot—or shots?"

"No, I didn't. There was a wind blowing, and, of course, a body always hears cars backfiring going down this grade. The exhaust seems to go *put . . . put . . . put . . . bang!* A body gets so she doesn't pay any attention to those sounds. All I want, Judge, is to live up here and be left alone. I think there's a great deal of inspiration living that way, calling upon the inner silence, the reserves of the spirit so to speak. I—"

Judge Kippen said, "Madam, if you'll be so kind as to escort us to your house I would like *very* much to see that bullet. And while we're up there, Sergeant Holcomb, I suggest that you get the ladder and put it in place against this tree. Then Mr. Redfield can go up and take a look. Now, mind you, Sergeant, I want Mr. Redfield to be the one to recover any bullet if there's a bullet in there.

"Now, Mrs. Eunice, if you'll be so kind, please."

They followed her back up the hill, a compact group of lawyers and court attendants, with gleeful newspaper photographers exploding flashbulbs from time to time.

Mrs. Eunice moved along at the head of the procession with stately dignity, her long legs carrying her up the steep grade as though it were level. She led the way through the arched gateway, up a steep driveway to the garage, then up steps, into a house which was redolent with the smell of paint, upstairs to a seldom-used attic, and pointed out the hole in the window and the partially embedded bullet in a nearby rafter.

In the attic Redfield promptly took charge. "Just a moment," he said. "Let's be very careful here. That's a round hole in the window and this bullet is lodged in the rafter. By sighting from the location of the bullet through that hole we can tell almost exactly the position from which the shot was fired."

Redfield placed a piece of string at the location of the bullet, stretched the string to the hole in the window.

Judge Kippen said, "That's the direction all right."

Redfield studied the scene. "The bullet broke that pane of glass and then embedded itself in the rafter. It had, of course, traveled over a hundred and fifty yards."

Strawn looked through the hole in the window, then sighted along the string, said, "Well, it would seem to be—of course, Your Honor, we're not accepting any responsibility for this bullet."

"I'm not asking you to accept any responsibility for any bullet," Judge Kippen snapped, "but I certainly do think that the police should accept the responsibility for a thorough investigation."

"Of course, the police didn't have the sole responsibility. At first it was assumed it was in county territory," Strawn said, "and—well, then the city police took over and—"

Judge Kippen interrupted, "The law is the science of applying justice to facts which have previously been determined and which are properly adduced in a court of law. When those facts haven't been properly collected the law is groping in the dark. That's why we have cases involving a miscarriage of justice.

"Whenever that happens public opinion blames the law. Actually the law isn't at fault. It's incorrect, sloppy investigative technique that's at fault. Now I want this case thoroughly investigated. I'm going back to my chambers and I'll reconvene court at three o'clock this afternoon. That should give you an opportunity to have this matter properly and thoroughly investigated—at least to the extent of evaluating this newly discovered evidence."

Strawn said, "I'm sorry, Your Honor. Officers talked with Mrs. Eunice before, asking her if she'd heard any shots, and at that time she didn't tell them about the bullet and—"

"Because I didn't know about it," Mrs. Eunice snapped. "I just found out about it this morning. What do you think I am? A mind reader or something? And besides, no one asked me about a bullet. They didn't ask me to look the house over to see if any bullets had struck it. They only asked me about the sound of shots. Don't you go trying to make *me* responsible for this, young man."

"No, no," Strawn said hastily. "You misunderstand me."

"Well, there's no reason for *you* to misunderstand *me,*" she retorted.

"Indeed there isn't," Judge Kippen announced with a smile. "I'll reconvene court at three o'clock this afternoon. At that time we will resume the case where we left off this morning."

16

Word had spread like wildfire and when Court reconvened at three o'clock, standing room in the courtroom was at a premium.

Hamilton Burger, the big, barrel-chested, bull-necked district attorney had entered the case personally, and was seated beside Strawn, his manner that of a man who is not going to be trifled with.

Judge Kippen emerged from his chambers promptly at three o'clock. Court was called to order and Judge Kippen, in a deceptively mild voice said, "People versus Evelyn Bagby. Preliminary hearing. Are the parties ready?"

"Ready," Strawn said.

"The defendant is ready," Mason said.

"Now the Court would like to know generally, in order to understand the evidence, what you have discovered out there at the scene of the crime, Mr. Prosecutor."

Strawn said, "In addition to the bullet which was in the house of Mrs. Eunice, and on which we want to question Mr. Redfield, there was another bullet in the oak tree. That bullet also was removed by Mr. Redfield, and we want to question him on that point."

"Very well, go ahead," Judge Kippen said. "Mr. Redfield was on the stand and the question before the Court at the present time is whether the weapon, claimed by the prosecution to be the weapon with which the shooting was done, is to be admitted in evidence. Mr. Redfield, take the stand. You've already been sworn and you have qualified as an expert."

"Now then," Strawn said, getting to his feet, "I want to ask you about the oak tree and the bullet—"

"Now let's get these straight," Judge Kippen interrupted. "Let's call the fatal bullet, Bullet Number One. Let's call the bullet from the redwood post Bullet Number Two. Let's call the bullet from the oak tree Bullet Number Three, and the bullet from the house of Mrs. Eunice, Bullet Number Four. Is that satisfactory?"

"Quite," Strawn said.

"Very satisfactory, Your Honor," Mason said.

"Very well. Let's have them so designated. You are now referring to Bullet Number Three, the one that was found in the oak tree, Mr. Redfield."

"That's right."

"What did you find there?" Judge Kippen asked, taking the questioning away from the deputy district attorney.

"Well, Your Honor, I found that there was a bullet embedded in that tree. It had entered on an angle and had chipped off a piece of bark. I found that that bullet had been fired from the revolver in question, the one that it appears the prosecution is seeking to have introduced in evidence. It is marked for identification Exhibit A."

"No question about that bullet having been fired from that gun?"

"No, Your Honor."

"Then that would make three bullets fired from that gun, with only two empty shells in it," the judge said.

Hamilton Burger arose ponderously to his feet. "Just a moment, Your Honor," he said. "I'd like to be heard on that question. I believe there has been a very deliberate attempt on the part of someone, and I am not at the present time naming that someone, although I hope to be able to do so before this case is concluded—I think there has been a very deliberate attempt on the part of someone to tamper with the evidence in this case."

"That, of course, is a most serious charge," Judge Kippen said.

"Exactly," Hamilton Burger said, "and I may state to the Court that that is why I am here in court at this time. I want to get this matter clarified so that we can fix the responsibility."

"Very well, it is your contention that the evidence has been tampered with. Now may I ask you how, Mr. District Attorney? How could that have been done?"

"Well, as to that—I'm not prepared at this time to answer the question. I think that the evidence in regard to Bullet Number Four is probably more significant than this Bullet Number Three!"

Judge Kippen turned to Redfield. "Well, what about Bullet Number Four?" he asked.

"Bullet Number Four," Redfield said, "was fired from a gun of this same type and caliber, but not from the gun that is now being introduced in evidence."

"You're certain?" Judge Kippen asked.

"Absolutely certain, Your Honor."

"All right," Judge Kippen said to the prosecutor. "Renew your motion to introduce that gun in evidence, and the Court will—"

"Just a moment, Your Honor," Mason said. "I believe I'm entitled to cross-examine this witness on this point before the weapon is received in evidence."

"Well, of course, the Court doesn't want to preclude you from cross-examination, Mr. Mason, but under the circumstances the Court certainly intends to see that this weapon is received in evidence and is impounded in the custody of the Court so that we won't have any more tampering with evidence or any more accusation of tampering with evidence."

"Exactly, Your Honor," Mason said urbanely. "I take it I may now cross-examine the witness."

"Yes," Judge Kippen snapped, and then added gratuitously, "There are things in this case that I don't like.

The Court joins with Mr. Hamilton Burger, the district attorney, in stating that it will be highly desirable to find out exactly what happened."

"Exactly, Your Honor," Mason said casually, as though he had no idea that remarks of the prosecutor and the Court were directed toward him in the least. "Mr. Redfield, when you received the weapon, Exhibit A, which is now the subject of discussion, there were two exploded shells in the cylinders, is that right?"

"Yes, sir."

"Now are you familiar with what is known in ballistics as a breechblock signature?"

"Yes, sir."

"What is it?"

"It is a means of identifying shells which have been fired from a weapon. It consists of a microscopic examination of the markings on those shells made by the breechblock.

"In other words, when a shell is fired there are expanding gases within the shell which force the bullet out through the barrel of the weapon, and, at the same time, press the brass cartridge case back against the breech of the gun."

"And each breechblock has its individual markings?" Mason asked.

"Quite frequently it happens that by examining the exploded cartridge cases it can be definitely ascertained whether they were fired from a certain particular weapon."

"And have you made an effort to examine the breechblock markings of the cartridges in the weapon marked Exhibit A in this case?"

"Why, no."

"Why not?"

"Why, it isn't necessary," Redfield said, smiling. "The empty cartridges were already in the weapon. They must have been—"

"But," Mason interrupted, "you have heard Sergeant Holcomb state that he removed the exploded cartridges from that gun, together with the unexploded cartridges."

"That was done so I could fire test shots through the gun."

"And have you any of the exploded cartridge cases in your possession?"

"They're in my laboratory, yes."

"That is near here?"

"Yes, sir."

"I would suggest," Mason said, "that if you are going to qualify as a ballistics expert for the purpose of having this gun introduced in evidence, that you compare the so-called breechblock signatures or breechblock markings—"

"Well, that can be done very easily and very quickly," Redfield said, "that is, I believe it can."

"And," Mason went on, "did you examine the markings on Bullet Number Four, that is, the individual or microscopic markings, and compare them with the fatal bullet?"

"Why, no. Of course not. Bullet Number Four very definitely was not fired from this weapon, Mr. Mason."

"But, nevertheless," Mason persisted, "it might be advisable to put Bullets One and Four in a comparison microscope just for the purpose of seeing whether you can find some identical individual or microscopic characteristics, at which point I will renew my cross-examination."

Mason said to Judge Kippen, "I take it, Your Honor, that I am entitled to have these matters at least investigated before I am called upon to decide whether I want to stipulate that this weapon may be received in evidence, or whether I want to make an objection."

"Well, the Court is entitled to it," Judge Kippen said, "and I think the defendant is, too. This simply gets back to the point that the Court raised earlier in the day, about insufficient investigation in cases which are brought before a court for adjudication. It isn't entirely a question of whether a defendant is entitled to have all of the evidence investigated and collected. The Court has some rights in the matter, too. The Court wants this matter of the bullets throughly investigated. I had assumed they would have been by this time."

Hamilton Burger said grimly, "We want them thoroughly investigated, too, Your Honor. We want to find out how it can happen that four bullets were fired from one gun with only two empty cartridge cases being in the gun."

"Oh, but they weren't fired from one gun," Mason said. "You mustn't mislead the Court, Mr. Burger. The evidence now definitely shows that at least two guns figured in the matter."

"And if one gun has been substituted," Burger said, banging his fist down on the desk, "I'm going to use every resource of my office to find out where that gun was substituted, when it was substituted and by whom it was substituted."

"I certainly hope you do," Mason said, and sat down.

"Do you have another witness you can call?" Judge Kippen asked Strawn.

"Yes, Your Honor. I would like to call Mr. Mervyn Aldrich to the stand."

"You can make those tests in your laboratory, Mr. Redfield," the judge said. "If you need more time let me know, but inasmuch as time may be a very vital factor in this case the Court would like to have the results of even a preliminary examination. Now, Mr. Aldrich, you may take the stand."

Mervyn Aldrich came forward with calm complacency as though completely unaffected by the atmosphere of tense excitement which was building to a climax in the courtroom.

He was sworn, gave his name, took the stand and sat

erect and tight-lipped. He answered the preliminary questions as to his age, residence and occupation.

Strawn said, "Mr. Aldrich, I show you a Colt revolver with a two-inch barrel, number 17475-LW and marked for identification Exhibit B. Are you familiar with that weapon?"

"I am. Yes, sir."

"According to the records you purchased that weapon."

"I did. Yes, sir."

"Where?"

"From a sporting goods store in Newport Beach called the Golf, Gun and Gaff Sporting Goods Store."

"And what did you do with that weapon after you purchased it?"

"I carried it on my person some of the time. I kept it in my house some of the time. I carried it in my automobile some of the time."

"Calling your attention to the tenth of this month, do you know where that weapon was located at that time?"

"Yes, sir."

"Where?"

"In the glove compartment of my convertible."

"And was that glove compartment locked?"

"Unfortunately it was not. I had tried to keep it locked, but apparently I was careless. When I went to my glove compartment to look for the weapon it was gone and the glove compartment was unlocked."

"When was that?"

"On the evening of the tenth."

"Of this month?"

"Yes, sir."

"And how did it happen that you went to your automobile to look in the glove compartment?"

"Mr. Perry Mason showed me this weapon and asked me if I was familiar with it. I looked at it and told him that I was, that I felt quite certain it was a weapon I had purchased."

"Was there any distinguishing mark on it other than the manufacturer's number, anything by which you could tell that this was your weapon?"

"Yes, sir."

"What?"

"You will notice if you look closely that there is a little indented line in the handle of the gun."

"What caused that indented line?"

"It was caused by a file."

"When was that line placed there and by whom?"

"It was placed there the day that I purchased the gun and was placed there by me. I went into my shop, took a three-cornered file and made this line in the handle of the gun."

"Why did you do that?"

"Objected to," Neely said, "as incompetent, irrelevant and immaterial."

"I think the objection is well taken," Judge Kippen ruled.

"Well, I'll get at the same thing this way," Strawn said angrily. "When you purchased this weapon, what else did you purchase?"

"I purchased another one just like it."

"And what did you do with the other weapon?"

"I gave it to my fiancée, Helene Chaney."

"Why?"

"For her personal protection."

"Now then, did you do anything at the time of your purchase of these guns or immediately afterward to differentiate one from the other?"

Mason leaned over to Neely and whispered, "We want to get this second gun into the evidence. In a preliminary never object to any questions calling for new evidence. Only object to the form of questions so you keep the prosecutors off balance and keep them from letting a witness have things too easy. Otherwise let them drag in everything they want. You can never tell when something will do some good. The more a witness says the first time he's on the stand the more he's apt to contradict himself the second time he gets on the stand. I think now we're getting ready to saw the limb off from under Mervyn Aldrich."

"You mean he's on a limb?" Neely asked.

Mason nodded.

Aldrich said, "I wanted to differentiate the gun which was mine from the one I was giving my fiancée, so I filed this nick in my gun."

"In *your* gun?"

"Yes, sir."

"Now when was the last time you remember having that gun in your possession?"

"On the ninth."

"Of this month?"

"Yes, sir."

"And where were you on the ninth?"

"I was in Riverside, California."

"And what were you doing there?"

"I had gone to Riverside to attend the trial of the defendant in this action."

Strawn said hastily, "I am, of course, aware of the rule that as a general proposition, the prosecution cannot introduce evidence of another crime. However, there are exceptions and I am prepared to introduce authorities—"

"There seems to have been no objections," Judge Kippen said.

"Well, there probably will be, Your Honor."

"Reserve your argument until then."

"Very well, Your Honor."

Strawn turned to the witness, "To what trial are you referring, Mr. Aldrich?"

"The trial of this defendant on a larceny charge. She was acquitted. She left the courthouse. I stayed behind to consult with the deputy district attorney and some of the witnesses. When I left the courthouse I saw her standing near my convertible. At the time I thought nothing of it and—"

"Never mind what you thought," Strawn snapped at the witness. "Just tell the facts."

"Those are the facts," Aldrich declared. "At that time she was within six feet of the place where I had left my car."

"Cross-examine," Strawn snapped at counsel.

"Go ahead. Take him in cross-examination," Mason said to Neely.

"What do I ask?" Neely asked.

"Ask him everything," Mason said, tilting back in the counsel chair and clasping his hands behind his head.

Neely said, "You purchased both of these guns on the same day?"

"Yes, sir."

"And paid for them by check?"

"Yes, sir."

"And put a file mark on one so you could tell it from the other?"

"Yes, sir."

"'And the one with the file mark on it you put in your glove compartment?"

"Yes, sir. In the glove compartment of my automobile some of the time. Other times I wore it in a holster or in my pocket."

"And why did you make a file mark on this gun?"

"So I could tell it apart from the other one. I thought that perhaps there might be occasions when Miss Chaney would be out with me and would have her gun perhaps in her handbag and there might be some confusion."

"Now as I understand it, Mr. Mason showed this gun to you on the evening of the tenth?"

"Yes, sir."

"At what time?"

"Sometime between ten and ten-thirty."

"Where were you?"

"At Miss Chaney's house."

"Where was Mr. Mason?"

"At the same place."

"And what did he do?"

"He showed me the gun."

"And what did you do?"

"I told him I thought that was the gun that was missing from my glove compartment."

"And took the gun?"

"Yes, sir."

"And did what?"

"Went to the glove compartment of my automobile, opened it and found that the gun actually was missing."

"So then what did you do?"

"I returned this weapon to Mr. Mason."

"The same weapon?"

"Yes, sir."

Neely leaned over and whispered to Mason, "I don't seem to be getting anywhere."

Mason whispered back, "You won't as long as you follow that mode of cross-examination. Whenever you ask him the same things over in the same sequence in which he testified on direct examination you'll get the same answers."

"Well, I guess I'm sunk now," Neely said.

"Ask him why he deemed it necessary to take this gun out to the glove compartment in order to find out if it was his gun," Mason said.

Neely nodded, faced the witness, said, "And why, Mr. Aldrich, did you deem it necessary to take this weapon with you when you went out to look in the glove compartment of your car to see if your weapon was there?"

"Because I wanted to make certain."

"In what way?"

"By making certain that the gun in the glove compartment in my automobile was missing."

"But you didn't need to take this gun with you in order to do that," Neely said. "All you needed to do was to look in your glove compartment and see if your personal weapon was missing."

"Well, I wanted to have this one as a . . . as a standard of comparison."

"You mean you didn't remember what your gun looked like?"

"Well, I thought I did."

"Then why did you want this gun with you at the time?"

"Because I could compare . . . I mean I wanted to—well, I wanted to make sure that this was my gun that was missing and not Miss Chaney's gun."

"But you didn't need to do that," Neely said, "since you had made this file mark on your gun for purposes of identification you could have looked at the weapon then and told instantly whether it was your gun."

Aldrich averted his eyes and was silent.

"Isn't that right?" Neely asked.

"Well, I guess so, yes."

"Then why did you take the gun with you when you went out to your automobile?"

"I guess I was confused."

"You were confused then?"

"Yes."

"You're not confused now?"

"No."

"Then can you tell us any sound reason, any single sound, sane reason why you had to take this weapon with you when you ran out to look in the glove compartment of your automobile?"

"No, sir. I guess not. I . . . I say I was confused."

Neely glanced at Mason. Mason nodded approvingly and said under his breath, "Quit."

"That's all," Neely said.

Aldrich, looking somewhat confused, left the stand.

Mason gripped Neely's arm. "Good work," he said. "When you read about that in the newspapers you'll find that the reporters have credited you with getting Mervyn Aldrich, the big executive, pretty well confused on the witness stand."

Hamilton Burger said, "Your Honor, may we have a brief, five-minute recess?"

"Very well," Judge Kippen ruled. "In view of the unusual developments here the Court will be lenient with counsel. We will take a fifteen-minute recess. At the end of that time I am hoping we will have a report which will iron out some of the confusion in this case."

Court adjourned and a couple of lawyers who had been interested spectators came up to congratulate Neely.

"A nice point you made there, Counselor," one of them said.

"Good work," the other one announced, shaking hands. "Nice cross-examination. Mr. Mason, you have a worthy associate."

"I think so," Mason said.

Neely's face was flushed with pleasure.

Estelle Nugent pushed her way through the crowd which was streaming from the courtroom and came up through the gate in the mahogany rail to grab Neely's hand.

"Frank, I'm so proud of you," she said. "You were *wonderful.*"

She turned to Perry Mason and Evelyn Bagby. "Oh, Miss Bagby," she said, "I *do* so hope this thing works out all right. And, Mr. Mason, you're so generous, so marvelous to let Frank have this chance to prove himself."

"He seems to be doing all right," Mason said.

Evelyn Bagby wordlessly squeezed Estelle Nugent's hand, then turned away, blinking back tears.

Mason patted her on the shoulder. "Take it easy, Evelyn," he said. "It won't be long now."

"You think not?"

"That's my present idea," Mason said.

A policewoman approached Evelyn Bagby. "We'll step into the defendant's room, if you don't mind, Miss Bagby."

She followed the policewoman out of the courtroom.

Neely turned to Mason and said, "When you come right down to it, Mr. Mason, why the devil *did* he take that gun with him when he went out to the car?"

Mason chuckled. "So he could substitute guns."

"So he could what?"

"So he could substitute guns," Mason said, "thinking that he could confuse the issue. He knew at once that that was the gun he'd given Helene Chaney. He knew his gun was in the glove compartment of his car.

"He thought he could save Helene Chaney some embarrassment and keep her out of trouble by switching guns. So under the guise of pretending to check and see if his gun was in the glove compartment, he broke open both guns, dumped the shells out of his gun, replaced them with the four loaded shells and the two empties from Helene Chaney's gun, then reloaded Helene Chaney's gun, put it in his pocket and brought both guns back to the house. He handed me his gun which by that time was loaded with the cartridges from Helene Chaney's gun. When he thought I wasn't looking he slipped the loaded gun to Helene Chaney so she would be able to produce it, if necessary.

"He then announced to me that he had checked and that his gun was missing from the glove compartment of his automobile."

Neely and Estelle Nugent looked at Mason in speechless surprise.

"You're certain of this?" Estelle Nugent asked.

"Of course," Mason said, smiling. "That's why I let him take the gun out to the car so he'd have an opportunity to make the switch."

"You knew he was going to?"

Mason laughed. "He was as obvious as a sheet of plate glass. You could see right through him. He and Helene Chaney exchanged purposeful glances. All the time I was talking with him she was signaling behind my back."

"But, good Lord, why did you let him do it?" Neely asked. "Why didn't you—?"

"Oh I didn't think it would hurt anything," Mason said. "And if he decided to lie about it it furnished a delightful mix-up. A defendant in a criminal case very seldom has anything to lose by letting the issues become confused."

Neely said, "But in that case the bullets . . . and the—so *that's* why you were talking about the breechblock signature on the empty cartridges!"

"Stick around," Mason said. "You're going to see some fun."

Neely and Estelle Nugent looked at each other, then at Mason.

"Well I'll be darned," Neely said, then, after a moment, "What's going to be the effect of all this?"

"It probably will give Hamilton Burger, our esteemed district attorney, a very marked increase in blood pressure," Mason said. "He is, of course, sitting over there waiting to accuse me of having fired shots from another weapon. In a moment he's going to find that the other weapon was in the custody of Mervyn Aldrich and Helene Chaney. Then he's going to be in a devil of a fix."

"And what will be the effect of all this on the case against Evelyn Bagby?"

"That," Mason said, "is going to be one of the unexpected little twists that make the practice of trial law so very, very interesting."

17

It was a good twenty minutes before Judge Kippen returned to the courtroom and announced, "Mr. Redfield has telephoned me that he is on his way over and will be here within a minute or two, gentlemen. I suggest that as it is approaching the hour for the afternoon adjournment we have court convened and ready for Mr. Redfield to take the witness stand. . . . Here is Mr. Redfield now. Come right forward, Mr. Redfield."

The ballistics expert, looking somewhat flustered, hurried forward and took the witness stand without any opportunity for a word with either Burger or the deputy district attorney.

"I have been rather hurried," he said breathlessly. "I—"

"I can understand," Judge Kippen said. "Now, have you completed your tests, Mr. Redfield?"

"No, Your Honor."

Judge Kippen frowned. "I understood you to say that—"

"I have completed my *preliminary* tests, Your Honor."

"Yes, yes, and what did they show?" Judge Kippen asked.

Mason tilted back in his swivel chair, his hands clasped behind his head, his eyes fixed on the ceiling rather than on the witness. The corners of his lips were upturned in a smile.

"I find," Redfield said, "that Bullets Numbers One and Four were probably fired from the same weapon, and that this is *not* the weapon which has been marked Exhibit A for identification in this case. I find that Bullets

Two and Three *were* probably fired from the weapon which has been marked Exhibit A for identification. I find that the empty cartridge cases which were in the cylinder of the weapon marked Exhibit A for identification definitely were not discharged by that gun but have been substituted from some other weapon."

"What!" Hamilton Burger exclaimed, jumping to his feet.

Judge Kippen blinked his eyes as he tried to adjust himself to the situation. He glanced at the bewildered Hamilton Burger, then at the smiling, completely unconcerned figure of Perry Mason.

Judge Kippen's lips tightened. "Do I understand your findings indicate that there has been a substitution of shells and that the empty cartridge cases in this gun, which has been marked Exhibit A for identification, were actually fired or discharged while they were in some other weapon and then, after having been fired, the empty cartridge cases were substituted in the cylinder of this weapon?"

"That is the only possible explanation I can think of, Your Honor."

"Then this weapon marked Exhibit A for identification is not the fatal weapon?"

"That would seem to be the case, Your Honor."

"The weapon which fired Bullet Number Four, which lodged in the attic of Mrs. Eunice's house, was the same gun which fired the fatal bullet which we have referred to as Bullet Number One?"

"That apparently is the case, Your Honor. I haven't made a sufficient examination as yet so I can't be absolutely certain. My preliminary examination certainly indicates that is the case. I may state that I have a trusted assistant working on the matter at the present time and taking photographs showing the two bullets, that is, the fatal bullet, Number One, and Bullet Number Four, in a superimposed position so that microscopic marks of identification can be followed on a photograph. However, according to a visual test, they were both fired from the same gun, and that definitely is not the gun which fired Bullets Two and Three."

Judge Kippen said, "It is quite apparent that someone has been tampering with the evidence in this case. Mr. Mason."

"Yes, Your Honor."

"This weapon which has been marked for identification was in your possession?"

"It was, Your Honor."

"Under the circumstances and since you are an interested party, the Court feels it is incumbent upon you to account for what happened during every minute of the time that weapon was in your possession."

"I shall be glad to do so, Your Honor," Mason said suavely. "I will, of course, have to call upon some witnesses in an attempt to clear this matter up. I had intended to produce some of these witnesses on the defendant's case, but in view of the situation which has developed I will respond to the Court's request by calling these witnesses at the present time. Will Helene Chaney please take the witness stand."

Mervyn Aldrich jumped up. "Helene Chaney will not take the witness stand."

Judge Kippen's gavel banged a peremptory summons. "Mr. Aldrich, come forward," he said.

Aldrich strode forward and glowered at the judge.

"What did you say?" Judge Kippen asked.

"I said that Helene Chaney would not take the witness stand."

"Mr. Aldrich, the Court observes that Miss Chaney is in the courtroom. The Court orders her to the witness stand. The Court further finds that your interpolation constitutes a flagrant contempt of this Court. The Court will not fine you under the circumstances for this one outburst because the Court understands that this case has taken a series of unexpected, dramatic, seemingly impossible turns. The Court realizes that you find yourself under something of a strain. You will, however, be seated in that chair behind the prosecutor's table, and you will refrain from making any comments, from signaling the witness, or— Miss Chaney! Miss Chaney, do not try to leave the courtroom. Miss Chaney, come back here! Bailiff, grab that woman!"

The bailiff seated by the door hurried out into the corridor. The courtroom became a scene of confusion as reporters hurried out into the corridor. Newspaper photographers stationed in the corridor blazed flashbulbs as the bailiff chased after Helene Chaney to the elevator, caught her as she was frantically jabbing at the button.

Judge Kippen tried to restore order in the courtroom as some of the spectators hurried in scrambled confusion to try to get out in the corridor to see the action.

"I'll clear this courtroom if I can't have order," Judge Kippen shouted. "Order! Spectators will be seated and will remain seated."

Hamilton Burger got to his feet. "Your Honor," he said, "this situation is one which could hardly have been anticipated unless perhaps one had engaged in other trials with *distinguished* counsel," and Hamilton Burger nodded with savage ferocity in the direction of Perry Mason. "I am going to ask the Court if we can have a recess—"

"This Court won't take any recess until that woman comes back into court and obeys the order of the Court," Judge Kippen announced. "This Court—" He broke off as the door opened and the bailiff escorted Helene Chaney into the courtroom.

"Bring that woman here," Judge Kippen ordered the bailiff.

Helene Chaney was piloted down the aisle.

"Close the courtroom doors," Judge Kippen announced. "Those spectators who were so anxious to interrupt the proceedings of this court by dashing pell-mell out into the corridor can remain in the corridor as far as the Court is concerned. Close the doors and lock them."

Judge Kippen turned to Helene Chaney. "Now then, Miss Chaney," he said, "the Court ordered you to take the witness stand and you fled from the courtroom."

She glanced uncertainly at Mervyn Aldrich, then at the judge.

"Didn't you hear me?" Judge Kippen asked.

She met his eyes. "Yes," she said in a low voice.

"Well, that's something," Judge Kippen grunted. "At least you didn't try to lie your way out of it. Now why did you try to get out of the courtroom?"

"Because I don't want to be a witness."

"Why?"

"Because I am afraid. I don't want the publicity. I—"

"It isn't a question of what you want," Judge Kippen said, "or whether you feel that you're going to be annoyed. The Court will protect you and see that no questions are asked which are going to embarrass you other than questions which are pertinent to the case. Now you take that witness stand, hold up your right hand and be sworn, and I want you to answer questions fully and frankly. You understand?"

"Yes, sir."

"Call me Your Honor," Judge Kippen snapped.

"Yes, Your Honor."

"Go over there and hold up your right hand."

Helene Chaney held up her right hand, was sworn and took the witness stand.

"Now then," Judge Kippen said, "the Court is going to question this witness. The Court will ask counsel for both sides to refrain from interrupting the Court except with pertinent legal objections to any question which may be asked. And the Court will further state that it is not going to take kindly to technical objections. The Court wants to get to the bottom of this case.

"Now then, Miss Chaney, you have heard Mr. Aldrich's testimony?"

"Yes, Your Honor."

"Mr. Aldrich gave you a Colt revolver, as I understand it, a Colt revolver very similar to the weapon which has been marked in this case for identification as People's Exhibit A."

"And where is that weapon now?"

"I . . . I—"

"Where is it?" Judge Kippen thundered.

"It is here," she said. "I have it here."

"What do you mean by here?"

She indicated her handbag.

"That weapon is loaded?"

"Yes, Your Honor."

"Why are you carrying a loaded weapon?"

"For personal protection."

"Do you have a permit to carry a loaded weapon?"

"I—Mr. Aldrich told me—"

"I'm not talking about what Mr. Aldrich told you. I'm asking if you have a permit to carry a loaded weapon."

"No, sir."

Judge Kippen said to the bailiff, "Mr. Bailiff, you will wait on the witness. You will take the loaded revolver from her purse. You will unload it. You will read the number of that revolver into the record so there will be no question of any mix-up while these weapons are in court. You will then properly label that gun for identification as People's Exhibit E. While you're doing that the Court will receive the other gun which has been marked People's Exhibit A in evidence. Now let's get this thing handled in an orderly manner."

"Will the Court note my objection to the receipt of these weapons in evidence?" Perry Mason asked.

"The Court notes your objection and overrules it," Judge Kippen snapped. "We're going to have both of these guns in evidence. We're going to have them impounded in custody where there won't be any *further* tampering with the evidence."

Judge Kippen glowered at Perry Mason.

Mason smiled back urbanely.

"Now then, Mr. Clerk," Judge Kippen said, "what's the number of the weapon that has been marked for identification People's Exhibit A and is now received in evidence?"

"Number 17475-LW."

"And what is the number of the weapon which is now marked People's Exhibit E and which the bailiff has just taken from the purse of the witness?"

"Number 17474-LW."

"All right," Judge Kippen said. "Now these two weapons are received in evidence. They're in the custody of the Court. Anyone who touches those weapons without the authorization of the Court is going to be sentenced for contempt of this Court. We'll have no further confusion of evidence. Mr. Redfield, the Court is going to turn those weapons over to you. I want a complete report from you when court convenes tomorrow morning at ten o'clock, and I wish to charge you, Mr. Redfield, that under no circumstances are you to communicate your findings prior to the time you get on the witness stand to any person whatever except to your assistants who necessarily cooperate with you in making tests, and you will warn them not to give any information to the press. I don't care to have this case tried in the newspapers.

"I know that the events of the afternoon are sufficiently dramatic so that the newspapers will give this case an enormous amount of spectacular publicity. I can't help that. I can't control that. But I certainly intend to control the publicity in regard to the further developments in this case. I don't want you to communicate with anyone. And that means counsel for the defendant or anyone connected with him, or—yes, I also mean counsel for the prosecution."

"Oh, Your Honor," Hamilton Burger protested. "After all, the prosecution is charged with putting on this case and the prosecution feels that Mr. Redfield, being the People's witness—"

"I don't care how you feel," Judge Kippen said. "This is a matter which has assumed very important proportions. The Court will take judicial cognizance of the fact that it is exceedingly difficult for any public officer to withhold information from the press. The Court doesn't care to have any information leak out of Mr. Redfield's office until court can reconvene tomorrow morning at ten o'clock. Do you understand, Mr. Redfield?"

"I understand," Redfield said.

"I take it," Mason said, "that the Court is preparing to adjourn."

"It is," Judge Kippen snapped.

"I feel that under the circumstances I should be permitted to ask this witness one or two questions on cross-examination before adjournment."

"I don't think so," Judge Kippen said. "I think the damage has been done at the present time, and I don't want to have the issues any further confused until we know what we're doing here."

"Then," Mason said, "I would suggest that the Court ask the witness *why* she deemed it necessary to carry a weapon, what the danger was that was threatening her."

"Why?" Judge Kippen asked.

"Because," Mason said, "I am satisfied that the person of whom she was afraid, and whose threats caused her to carry this gun in the first place, was none other than Stephen Merrill."

Hamilton Burger jumped to his feet. "Now there, Your Honor, is a typical example of what I have referred to from time to time. Counsel knows that this statement of his will be featured in the press. It is undoubtedly without foundation, but by tossing it as a choice tidbit of speculative scandal into the hopper of the newspapers—"

"That will do, Mr. Prosecutor," Judge Kippen said. "Mr. Mason was pointing out to the Court what he expected to prove."

"I respectfully suggest that he was doing no such thing," Hamilton Burger said. "I suggest that he was taking deliberate advantage of an opportunity to make a statement which is absurd on its face, but which, under the circumstances, the Court wouldn't permit the witness to deny. I would now like to join with Mr. Mason in suggesting that that question be asked this witness here and now so that we can at least control *this* phase of the publicity."

"Very well," Judge Kippen said, growing increasingly angry. "The Court does not like this continued reference to matters of publicity. The Court doesn't want this case tried in the newspapers. On the other hand, the Court recognizes the fact that we have a free press in this country and that this is a public hearing."

Judge Kippen whirled in his chair, confronted Helene Chaney. "Why were you carrying that gun?" he asked.

"For personal protection."

"Against whom?"

"Against anyone who might harm me or threaten to harm me."

"Had you ever carried a gun before?"

"No."

"Why did you start carrying the gun about—what was it, about twenty days ago?"

"Yes, Your Honor."

"Why did you start carrying a gun at that time?"

"Because Mr. Aldrich bought one for me."

Judge Kippen's color heightened. "Miss Chaney," he said, "you're avoiding questions. Now the Court can pin you down if it becomes necessary, but I want you to quit beating around the bush and answer questions. Why were you carrying that gun?"

"Because I'd been threatened."

"By whom?"

"Is that pertinent?" Hamilton Burger asked, suddenly scrambling to his feet. "Suppose it is entirely without the issues of this case. Suppose it was by some person who is a complete stranger to the issues here involved. Aren't we prying into Miss Chaney's private affairs and at the same time calling for evidence that is incompetent, irrelevant and immaterial?"

"You opened the door on this," Judge Kippen said. "I'm asking these questions because you wanted them asked. The objection is overruled. Answer the question, Miss Chaney."

"I was threatened by Stephen Merrill."

There was a long period of silence. Judge Kippen frowningly regarded the witness, apparently thinking over the various possibilities of an explosive situation.

"Can you tell us how you were threatened, Miss Chaney?"

She said, "Steve Merrill wanted money. At first his demands were preposterous. However, on the day of his death he telephoned me in the early afternoon. He said he had to meet a pressing obligation. He offered to dismiss the proceedings seeking to reopen our divorce suit if I would give him money."

"That isn't a threat," Judge Kippen said.

"He had made the threat at an earlier date—when he made his first demands."

"What sort of a threat?"

"It was a veiled threat. He said that I would never live long enough to marry Mervyn Aldrich if I didn't settle with him."

"Well," Judge Kippen said, "this serves to confuse the issues rather than to clarify them. I think that perhaps it would have been better if we had not opened up this channel of investigation. However, it was done at the sugestion of the prosecution."

Hamilton Burger seemed to want to say something but abruptly thought better of it.

Mason said, "I would like to have the Court ask the witness the exact sum that Stephen Merrill demanded on the day of his death."

"Why?" Judge Kippen snapped.

"Because it might make some difference," Mason said.

"I fail to see where it would."

"Suppose," Mason said, "the amount that he asked was seven thousand five hundred dollars."

Judge Kippen said, "Now there again, Mr. Mason, you are intimating certain facts adroitly introduced by insinuation."

"I'll ask her that question if I'm permitted to examine her," Mason said. "If I'm not permitted to question a witness directly I certainly have the right to make suggestions to the Court."

Judge Kippen said, "The Court will ask one more question and then Court is going to take a recess. At this time the Court does not want any more suggestions from counsel. I will ask you this one question, Miss Chaney. How much money did Stephen Merrill ask?"

"He didn't ask. He demanded. He wanted seven thousand five hundred dollars."

For several seconds it would have been possible to have heard a pin drop in the courtroom.

Then Judge Kippen banged the gavel so viciously he all but broke the handle.

"Very well," he said, "Court's adjourned until tomorrow morning at ten o'clock. Mr. Clerk, I shall hold you personally responsible for the safeguarding of those exhibits. You will deliver them to Mr. Redfield. You will accept Mr. Redfield's receipt, and you will not let anyone else have access to the exhibits. Mr. Redfield, I shall hold you responsible for the custody of those exhibits while they are in your possession. That's all."

The judge rose and strode angrily to his chambers.

The bailiff unlocked the doors of the courtroom. People who were on the outside trying to hear what was going on were swept back as the doors burst open under the pressure of spectators and reporters dashing for telephones.

Within a matter of seconds all the telephone booths on that floor, the floor above it and the floor below, were occupied with men frantically dialing numbers and telephoning to rewrite men in the newspaper offices.

Neely looked at Perry Mason with apprehensive eyes.

Mason grinned. "Well, Neely, I trust I'm not going to get you involved in a contempt of court on the first case in which you're associated with me."

"But, good heavens," Neely said, "Judge Kippen is *really* angry. He's going to make an example of somebody."

"I think he should," Mason said.

"Mr. Mason, will you think it presumptuous if I were to ask you to do something for me?"

"What?" Mason asked.

"Please give me your personal assurance that you had nothing to do with those bullets that were found at the scene of the crime."

"What bullets?"

"Well, any of them, but particularly Bullets Two and Three."

"I can't do that, Neely."

"Why not?"

"Figure it out."

"Good Lord, Mr. Mason? If you . . . if you fired those bullets, why—oh, my heavens!"

"Want to withdraw from the case?" Mason asked.

"Certainly not. I'm not a quitter. I wouldn't pull out. I—"

"Well then quit worrying about it," Mason said.

"But Mr. Mason, that means that we'll be in jail for contempt of course. It may mean that they'll start disbarment proceedings."

"On what ground?" Mason asked.

"Tampering with evidence."

"What evidence?"

"Why, the gun."

Mason said, "If that gun didn't kill Stephen Merrill we can shoot it anywhere we damn please. It isn't tampering with evidence. It's just like any other gun."

"But Mervyn Aldrich has sworn that that's the same gun you gave him. And if that's the same gun Evelyn Bagby gave you, then that *must* be the gun with which Steve Merrill was killed."

"It couldn't have been the gun that she fired," Mason said, "because the two exploded cases which are in the cylinder weren't fired in that gun."

"Then the evidence must have been tampered with."

"By whom?"

"Well, of course, once you admit firing those two bullets—"

Mason grinned. "I'm not going to admit anything for a while."

"But the prosecutor knows you did and the judge seems to feel certain that you must have done so."

Mason said, "Neely, I think I know the law. I think I know something about human nature. I know damn well that I'm not going to sit back and let a penniless defendant be convicted of murder simply because someone wants to frame a murder on her.

"I was morally certain that if Sergeant Holcomb found a bullet at the scene of the crime at any time, he would try to be a big shot and swear that he had seen the mark of that bullet when he was *first* called to the scene. He would claim he'd noticed something that all the other officers had overlooked.

"Now then, I could have cross-examined Sergeant Holcomb until I was black in the face and he'd simply become more and more positive. He'd be lying, but I couldn't prove he was lying. But by shooting a bullet into a redwood post, which bullet obviously couldn't have been there at the time Sergeant Holcomb arrived on the scene, and then letting Sergeant Holcomb swear that he had seen it as soon as he did arrive, I have laid the foundation for a cross-examination that will be effective."

"Well, it's a subtle, technical distinction," Neely said. "Perhaps technically you can claim that you weren't tampering with evidence, but—I admire your daring, but you're moving too fast for me."

Mason said, "When you're skating on thin ice the only way you can keep from breaking through is to start going like hell."

"I'm frightened," Neely said simply. "And for the life of me I can't understand what you're trying to do."

"I'm scrambling facts," Mason said.

"Why?"

"Did you ever cook eggs over a camp fire?" Mason asked.

"Yes, but what does that have to do with it?"

"And did you ever start out trying to fry eggs, break the yolks and then save your face by scrambling them and pretending you had intended to scramble them all along?"

Neely grinned. "Yes," he admitted.

"That's a damn good way to try a lawsuit when you're up against a frame-up," Mason said. "When you scramble eggs no one can tell which yolk was accidentally broken, and when you scramble facts you have at least upset the plans of the man who thought he had a perfect frame-up."

18

JUDGE KIPPEN SURVEYED THE JAMMED COURTROOM WITH disapproving eyes.

"I wish to make a few remarks to counsel and to the spectators," he said. "This Court deplores the sensationalism which has surrounded this case."

He glanced briefly at Perry Mason, then at the spectators.

"Under our Constitution, trials must be open to the public. That is to prevent Star Chamber sessions. It does not mean that the trial of every case which offers room for speculation should be turned into a species of side show for sensation-hungry spectators.

"The persons in this courtroom will understand that this is an orderly investigative procedure. It is not a show. The spectators will refrain from comment or the courtroom will be cleared.

"The Court deplores the manner in which this case was exploited in the press. The morning papers are filled with sensational reporting, speculative comment by feature writers, and interviews with various parties. The Court cannot, of course, control the press, but the Court points out to counsel on both sides that this hearing should be rather simple, purely for the purpose of determining in a preliminary way whether there is any reason to bind the defendant over for trial. The Court will frown upon any attempt on the part of counsel on either side to be spectacular or to indulge in the dramatic. The Court wants to get at the facts.

"Now then, Mr. Alexander Redfield has made certain

tests. I would like to have you return to the stand, Mr. Redfield."

Redfield returned to the witness stand.

"Do you wish me to question the witness?" Hamilton Burger asked.

"I will question the witness," Judge Kippen said. "Mr. Redfield, have you completed your ballistics examinations and your microscopic tests?"

"Yes, sir."

"What do they show in regard to the weapons from which these bullets were fired?"

"The fatal bullet, which is Bullet Number One, and the bullet in the garret of the house, which is Bullet Number Four, were both fired from the revolver identified as People's Exhibit E. Bullets Number Two and Three were fired from the revolver marked for identification People's Exhibit A."

Judge Kippen frowned as he digested the import of the testimony.

"The empty cartridges, that is, the discharged cartridge cases which were in the weapon marked People's Exhibit A, what about those?"

"Those cartridge cases were fired from the weapon marked People's Exhibit E, and were not fired from the weapon in which they were found—that is, the weapon in which they were presented to the court, Exhibit A."

"It is then your considered opinion, Mr. Redfield, that those two empty cartridge cases were taken from the weapon in which they had been fired, the one which is marked Exhibit E, and placed in the other weapon, People's Exhibit A?"

"That is the only possible solution."

"Do you know when this was done, that is, with reference to when the shells were discharged?"

"Only that it was done after the shells were discharged."

"And as to the undischarged or loaded shells you have

no way of telling whether they were or were not substituted?"

"That's right, Your Honor. I can't tell."

Judge Kippen digested that testimony for a moment, then, with his mouth straightened into a thin line of angry determination, said, "I am going to ask counsel to withhold any questions they may have for the moment until the Court can get at the bottom of this. I am now going to ask Helene Chaney to take the witness stand."

A rather corpulent individual arose from one of the chairs within the rail. "Your Honor," he said, "I wish the record to show that I, Harmon B. Passing, am appearing as attorney for Helene Chaney."

"Very well," Judge Kippen said. "She is entitled to be represented by counsel. Now will Miss Chaney please take the witness stand."

Passing said, "Miss Chaney is not here."

"What?" Judge Kippen snapped.

"I'm sorry, Your Honor, she's not here."

"Why isn't she here?"

Passing made a little gesture with his arms and shoulders. "For one thing," he said, "she wasn't subpoenaed."

"She was here yesterday."

"Yes, Your Honor. She was here and testified."

"She certainly knew that she was wanted today."

"With all due respect to the Court," Passing said, "I don't think the Court made any formal order advising her that her presence was required."

"I think I did," Judge Kippen said.

"I'm sorry, Your Honor. I had the proceedings transcribed and studied the official report very carefully."

Judge Kippen lost his temper. He leaned forward from the bench, his face colored. "You did that so that you could advise her that she could skip out and wouldn't be liable for contempt of court."

Passing said suavely, "As an attorney I was called

upon to render service to a client. I studied all of the facts in the case and advised her as to her legal rights to the best of my ability."

Judge Kippen debated the matter for a moment, then glowered at the prosecutor's table. "Miss Chaney should have been subpoenaed," he said, then turning to Passing said angrily, "I suppose it is a safe assumption that she has left the jurisdiction of the court."

"I understand she is in Las Vegas, Nevada," Passing said. "She was called there on a matter of business."

"Very well," Judge Kippen said. "Let's see what Mr. Mervyn Aldrich has to say. Mr. Aldrich, take the stand."

Passing said, "I wish the record to show that I am also attorney for Mr. Aldrich. The same situation exists in regard to Mr. Aldrich as in the case of Miss Chaney. Mr. Aldrich is not present. And I understand he, too, is in Las Vegas. I may state to the Court that I studied the transcript carefully, and as an attorney advised Mr. Aldrich that he was not under subpoena, nor had he been specifically directed to attend court. I explained to him that I felt quite certain from studying the transcript that Your Honor rather expected that he would be present today and apparently had assumed he was under subpoena. However, the Court made no direct, specific order and no subpoena had actually been served."

"How did it happen these people weren't under subpoena?" Judge Kippen exploded, shifting his eyes to the prosecution's table.

Hamilton Burger said, "Your Honor, this news is as much of a surprise to me as it is to the Court. I certainly assumed these people would be here."

"I'm not asking what you assumed. I'm asking how it happened they weren't under subpoena."

"As to that, I don't know," Hamilton Burger said. "I have a large staff and we have numerous responsibilities. It is, perhaps, one of those cases where everyone assumed that something had been done which was not done. If I may have the indulgence of the Court for the moment."

Burger bent over and whispered to Strawn. Strawn shrugged his shoulders, spread out his hands in a gesture of complete dismissal. Burger whispered angrily. Strawn shook his head, whispered something in return.

Hamilton Burger straightened. "Your Honor, I had assumed these witnesses were under subpoena. It turns out that one of my deputies, not the trial deputy who is associated with me in the case at the moment, but one of the deputies whose duty it is to prepare cases for trial, asked Miss Chaney and Mr. Aldrich if they intended to be present and had been assured that they expected to be in court. He did not wish to annoy persons so prominent by making a formal service of subpoena. We had thought that Mr. Aldrich's testimony might be needed, and that he would only testify briefly to the purchase of the weapon and its subsequent disappearance. Frankly, we didn't consider this testimony at all important because we felt there would be no question but that the possession of the gun which fired the fatal bullet would be inescapably brought home to the defendant. Yesterday's developments came as a distinct surprise to us."

"Well, after those developments took place those people should have been subpoenaed," Judge Kippen snapped.

Burger's face flushed. "Of course, Your Honor," he said, "I *could* have subpoenaed them. I assumed they were under subpoena. On the other hand, the Court could simply and very readily have directed all witnesses to return today and that would have been a Court order. I do not think my office should take the sole responsibility in the matter. Since neither of those things was done I assume that Mr. Passing is correct in his assumption that these people were free to leave the state."

Judge Kippen replied tartly, "The Court didn't make such an order because it assumed the office of the prosecutor had done what would ordinarily have been expected under the circumstances."

"I'm sorry, Your Honor," Burger snapped in a tone which showed far more anger than sorrow.

"Well, where does that leave the case?" Judge Kippen asked.

Burger said, "As far as the prosecution is concerned, it appears that a prima-facie case has been made out. This defendant told a story which was manifestly false."

"How do you know it was manifestly false?"

"Why, your Honor, her story was that this man was wearing the pillow slip. The fact is that the pillow slip was put over his head after death. She was, moreover, carrying a gun which had been discharged twice—"

"A gun which had nothing to do with the death of the decedent in this case," Judge Kippen snapped.

"Oh, Your Honor," Hamilton Burger said, suddenly realizing his position, "I think it is quite apparent that someone substituted weapons. I am not in a position to name names at the present time, but my office is certainly going to make an investigation and I am hoping we can fix the responsibility."

Burger turned to glower at Mason.

"Don't be too sure," Judge Kippen retorted. "The only person who could have substituted weapons was someone *who had access to both weapons.*"

"But, Your Honor," Hamilton Burger said, "it is obvious that the substitution must have been made *after* the two shells were fired. The defendant admitted to the officers that she had fired those shells. Since it now appears that those shells must have been discharged from the murder gun, the fact that another gun had been substituted by the time the authorities got possession of the weapon certainly isn't absolving the defendant. In fact, it indicates a consciousness of guilt and a very expert and adroit attempt to confuse the issues."

"Well, this Court isn't going to bind anyone over for

a crime until it has more evidence than it has now," Judge Kippen retorted. "That substitution was made for a purpose and was made by someone who had an opportunity to make the substitution."

"Exactly," Hamilton Burger said, and again glanced at Perry Mason.

Perry Mason met Burger's accusing eyes and merely smiled.

Burger's face reddened. "I am going to find out who made that substitution," he shouted, "if I have to devote the entire facilities of my investigative staff to it for a year, and when I find out I am going to take steps to have that person disbarred."

"Disbarred?" Judge Kippen asked, raising his eyebrows. "Are you making a definite accusation, Mr. Prosecutor?"

"I mean," Burger amended hastily, "if the person is an attorney, I intend to have him disbarred, and if he is not, I intend to have him prosecuted."

Judge Kippen looked at Perry Mason. "Do you have any statements you wish to make at this time, Mr. Mason?"

"Yes, Your Honor."

"Mr. Burger will be seated. Mr. Mason, what statement do *you* wish to make?"

Mason said, "I merely wanted to state that I had a witness I wished to call."

"Very well, the Court will hear any witness you may care to produce, Mr. Mason."

Mason said, "Call Irene Keith to the stand."

Irene Keith came forward, was sworn, took the witness stand and sat looking at Mason, her eyes sharp with antagonism.

"You are a close friend of Helene Chaney?" Mason asked.

"I was."

"And of Mervyn Aldrich?"

"Yes."

"I show you a Colt revolver, marked People's Exhibit A, and ask if you've seen that weapon before."

"I don't know."

"I show you a Colt revolver, marked People's Exhibit E, and ask you if you've ever seen *that* revolver before."

"I don't know."

"You have seen weapons which look like these?"

"I have seen revolvers, yes."

"You have seen weapons which look like these?"

"Yes."

"Which were exactly similar in appearance?"

"Yes."

"Did you ever have one of those weapons in your possession?"

"I don't know."

"I am not referring to these two specific weapons," Mason said. "I am referring to any weapon which was identical in appearance."

"Yes."

"Did you have such a weapon in your possession on the tenth of this month?"

"Oh, Your Honor," Hamilton Burger said, "Counsel is now seeking to cross-examine his own witness."

"I think it's quite apparent that she's a hostile witness," Mason said.

"The objection is overruled," Judge Kippen snapped.

"I'm afraid I can't answer that question," Irene Keith said.

"Helene Chaney loaned you a revolver, didn't she?"

"Yes."

"On the tenth of this month?"

"I believe so."

"The gun she loaned you could well have been this revolver marked Exhibit E?"

"I—well, yes."

"What did you do with that revolver?"

"I . . . I can't say."

Judge Kippen leaned forward, glared down at the witness, said to Perry Mason, "I'll examine this witness, Mr. Mason. Miss Keith, this is a serious matter. The patience of the Court has been worn very, very thin. The Court doesn't want any quibbling. Now tell us what you did with that revolver."

Irene Keith looked down at the floor, suddenly raised her eyes to Judge Kippen. "I refuse to answer," she said, "on the ground that the answer might incriminate me."

A gasp of startled surprise went through the courtroom.

Judge Kippen recoiled as though he had been struck. "You refuse to answer?" He asked incredulously.

"That's right."

"On the ground that to do so may incriminate you?"

"Yes."

"Now you have already admitted," Judge Kippen said, "that you had such a weapon in your possession."

"I had *a* weapon in my possession."

"Was it similar in appearance to these two weapons here?"

"I am not an expert on guns."

"Never mind whether you're an expert or not. Was it similar in appearance?"

"Yes."

Judge Kippen drummed with the tips of his fingers on the mahogany desk. His face was flushed with anger.

"Do you have an attorney present in court?" he asked.

"No."

"Have you consulted an attorney in regard to your testimony?"

"Yes."

"And are you acting under advice of counsel in refusing to answer on the ground that the answer many incriminate you?"

"I have been advised by counsel that I had that right if I wished to accept the responsibility."

"Well, I'd like to discuss that matter with your attorney," Judge Kippen said. "It is the Court's offhand opinion that, having answered the question that you had such a weapon in your possession on the day of the murder, you can't refuse to tell what you did with the weapon on the ground that the answer might incriminate you. There is nothing in the nature of any possible answer which could incriminate you. That is, if you gave the weapon to someone—unless, of course—"

Judge Kippen was silent for a moment. Abruptly he said, "Did you have anything to do with the murder of Stephen Merrill?"

"No, Your Honor."

"Were you present at the time he was killed?"

"No, Your Honor."

"Did you have any idea that he was going to be killed?"

"No, Your Honor."

"Did you conspire with anyone to bring about the death of Stephen Merrill?"

"No, Your Honor."

"Under those circumstances," Judge Kippen said, "I don't think that you are entitled to invoke the constitutional amendment in order to purge yourself of any contempt. If you gave that weapon to someone but did not have any guilty purpose in giving that weapon to this person, you aren't entitled to shield yourself behind the amendment. An attempt to do so, where there are no grounds for doing so, would be a contempt of court. Now I am going to ask you once more, to whom did you give that weapon?"

"I refuse to answer on the ground that my answer may tend to incriminate me."

Judge Kippen said, "This is a most peculiar situation. The Court is about to take a very drastic step. The Court is not going to be trifled with in this matter."

Mason arose. "Perhaps, Your Honor," he said, "I may be able to clear up a situation which seems to be puzzling the Court. I would like to ask the witness a question if I may."

"Go ahead," Judge Kippen snapped.

Mason said, "When you invoke your rights under the Fifth Amendment to keep from incriminating yourself, isn't it a fact that you fear that your answer, while it may not have anything to do with the murder, may incriminate you by establishing a connection with some other crime?"

Irene Keith flared into rage. "You're responsible for this whole—"

Judge Kippen banged his gavel. "The witness will answer that question," he said.

"I don't think I have to," she said.

"I do," Judge Kippen retorted.

"I've said that my answer might incriminate me and that's all you're going to get out of me. I have told my attorney the full facts and I am acting under his advice."

Judge Kippen hesitated, apparently debating whether to hold the witness in contempt of court. His eyes turned to Mason.

"Mr. Mason," he said, "you seem to have some definite idea in mind in regard to this witness. Perhaps you can ask additional questions which will tend to clarify the situation."

Mason turned to Irene Keith. "On or about the tenth of this month did you have some discussion with Stephen Merrill about some jewlery?"

"I refuse to answer on the ground that to do so might incriminate me."

Judge Kippen looked at Mason in surprise. "What *is* all this?" he asked. "What is this leading up to?"

Mason said, "Perhaps, Your Honor, I can bring it out."

Hamilton Burger jumped up. "Your Honor, I object to

counsel going on a fishing expedition. I object to him cross-examining—"

"Your objection is overruled," Judge Kippen snapped without even looking at Hamilton Burger. "Go ahead, Mr. Mason. Ask your questions."

Mason said, "Isn't it a fact, Miss Keith, that you gave Stephen Merrill a large sum of money in cash on the tenth of this month?"

"I refuse to answer on the ground that the answer may incriminate me."

"Isn't it a fact that you had a revolver on the tenth of this month and that you gave Stephen Merrill this gun?"

"Oh, Your Honor," Hamilton Burger said, "I object to this type of examination."

"The objection is overruled."

"Please, Your Honor, may I be heard?"

Judge Kippen didn't even look at him. His eyes were fastened on Irene Keith's defiant countenance. He said, "I won't preclude you from argument, Mr. Prosecutor, but I think your objection is not well taken and the Court intends to get at the bottom of this thing."

"Your Honor," Burger protested, "it is obvious as can be what Mr. Mason is doing. Knowing that this witness is in a position where she won't answer any question relating to this weapon, he is seeking to try the case in the newspapers by putting all sorts of absurd combinations together. It is just the same as though I would ask her, 'Isn't it a fact that on the tenth day of this month you bribed Judge Kippen to kill Stephen Merrill with a weapon which you funished him which was exactly similar in appearance to the weapons marked for identification in this case?' Since the witness obviously feels that she cannot answer any questions concerning a gun being in her possession on the tenth of this month without incriminating herself, she will again invoke the protection of the amendment and counsel will have made a telling point in that it will appear he has made an accusation which the witness has been unable, or has been afraid, to deny.

"It is a well-known fact that counsel for the defense is noted for his adroit ingenuity, his ability to capitalize on the dramatic. Here we have once more a case which should have been a routine matter in a preliminary examination. It has, however, been handled in such a manner that this courtroom has been turned into a three-ring circus for the benefit of publicity and for the purpose of obscuring the issues."

"Are you finished, Mr. District Attorney?" Judge Kippen asked, still with his eyes on the witness.

"Yes, Your Honor."

"Your objection is overruled. The witness will answer the question."

"I refuse to answer on the ground that my answer may incriminate me."

"Go on, Mr. Mason," Judge Kippen said.

"I have no further questions."

Hamilton Burger said, "*I* would like to ask a question on cross-examination."

"Go ahead," Judge Kippen said.

"Miss Keith, isn't it a fact that on or about the tenth day of this month you conspired with Stephen Merrill to assassinate the President of the United States, and that for the purpose of carrying out this assassination you gave to Stephen Merrill a gun which you had in your possession which was exactly similar in appearance to one of the weapons marked for identification in this case?"

Judge Kippen said, "I consider that question impertinent, Mr. Prosecutor. I consider that it dangerously borders on a contempt of this court."

Burger stuck by his guns. "I am simply trying to make my point in regard to these questions asked by counsel for the defense," he said. "I want to show that since this witness does not dare to answer any question concerning a gun being in her possession on the tenth, it is simply a matter of forensic ingenuity to tie up any sort of an absurd question covering anything that Counsel wants to establish, and have the witness, by her refusal, give some semblance of plausibility to a hopelessly absurd theory, a theory advanced purely for the purpose of securing publicity favorable to the defendant."

"I see your point," Judge Kippen said. "I saw it the first time, but in view of the attitude of this witness, the Court feels that the situation should be thoroughly explored. Your question is so completely frivolous, specious and absurd that it is annoying to the Court."

"I was only trying to establish a point," Burger said.

"You can establish it in a more dignified manner."

Mason said, "I beg the Court's pardon, but in connection with this colloquy between Court and counsel it may not have occurred to the Court that the witness has not as yet answered that question."

"Well, of course," Hamilton Burger said, "she'll adopt the same position. She has to. She—"

"Are you qualifying as a clairovyant," Mason asked, "or have *you* been advising this witness to refuse to answer questions?"

"I object to that," Hamilton Burger shouted. "Your Honor, this is an insinuation that—"

"That is perfectly justified under the circumstances," Judge Kippen snapped. "The Court begs your pardon, Mr. Mason. The witness was not given an opportunity to answer that question. Go ahead and answer the prosecutor's question, Miss Keith."

"No," she said.

Mason smiled.

Hamilton Burger looked crestfallen.

Judge Kippen said, "Look here, Miss Keith, you apparently feel that there was some contact between you and Mr. Merrill which you don't care to disclose at this time, some relationship which you had in connection with some other matter. Did you give Stephen Merrill approximately seven thousand five hundred dollars on the tenth of this month?"

"I refuse to answer on the ground that my answer may incriminate me."

Judge Kippen said, "Mr. Mason, apparently you have at least the inkling of a solution as to the conduct of this witness. The Court is simply unable to establish any valid reason for her conduct."

Mason said affably, "If the Court please, all I can say is that I think this witness has probably sought the advice of very competent counsel and that her position, within the technical limits of the law, is well taken."

Hamilton Burger jumped to his feet. "Your Honor, this is simply another grandstand. Now we have counsel for the defense coming in and stating that this witness is well within her rights in refusing to answer questions which certainly are pertinent—"

Judge Kippen banged his gavel. "The prosecutor will desist from any comments as to the tactics of the counsel for the defense. If you have any explanation as to the conduct of this witness, I would like to hear it."

Hamilton Burger said, "Very well, Your Honor. I'd like to ask one question. Miss Keith, have you at any time consulted Mr. Perry Mason, attorney for the defendant, as to your testimony in this case?"

"No."

"Have you consulted Mr. Perry Mason with reference to any other matter? Is he your attorney in any way?"

"No."

Burger hid his embarrassment by turning to confer in a whisper with Strawn.

Judge Kippen said, "The Court is going to take a thirty-minute recess. During that time the Court would like to confer with counsel for both sides in chambers. The Court specifically directs each and every person who is a witness in this case, or who has been a witness in this case, who is present in court, to be available when court reconvenes in approximately thirty minutes. Under no circumstances are witnesses to absent themselves from further attendance on the court. I trust that is plain."

Judge Kippen looked around the courtroom. "Are there any witnesses or persons under subpoena who do not understand that they are to return in thirty minutes?"

When there was silence the judge turned to Irene Keith. "You understand you are to return here in thirty minutes?"

"Yes, Your Honor."

"And that failure to do so will be punishable as a contempt of court?"

"Yes, Your Honor."

"Very well," Judge Kippen said. "The Court will take a thirty-minute recess. The Court would first like to see Mr. Burger and Mr. Strawn in chambers. After that the Court would like to see Mr. Mason and Mr. Neely in chambers. Counsel will please hold themselves in readiness."

Judge Kippen pushed back his chair, arose and stalked from the bench to the door of his chambers.

Perry Mason turned to Neely and grinned.

19

THE BAILIFF NODDED TO MASON. "JUDGE KIPPEN WOULD like to see you and Mr. Neely in chambers, Mr. Mason."

As Mason and Neely started for the door of chambers they saw Burger and Strawn leaving.

Hamilton Burger, his face flushed and angry, kept his

eyes straight ahead as he walked within some three feet of Mason.

The bailiff opened the door to chambers and Mason and Neely walked in.

"Sit down, please," Judge Kippen said.

He regarded Mason with eyes that made a searching appraisal.

"Mr. Mason, I want to put a few cards on the table. I think it is only fair to tell you that before I started on the trial of this case, the presiding judge called my attention to the fact that in several of your cases there had been a highly spectacular, dramatic series of developments in the courtroom which were, to express it conservatively, entirely out of keeping with the ordinary course of procedure in preliminary examinations."

Mason nodded.

"It was agreed between us that it would be highly advisable to put a stop to such practice," Judge Kippen said.

"I assured the presiding judge that I would carefully safeguard the rights of the defendant but that I would use every precaution to see that my courtroom did not become the background for scenes of dramatic sensationalism."

Again Mason nodded.

The ghost of a smile flickered at Judge Kippen's lips.

"It needs only a glance at the morning newspapers with their sensational headlines," he said, "to see how developments, each one of which seemed thoroughly logical, at the time, have conspired to turn this case into a highly dramatic spectacle in place of the orderly routine proceeding that had been contemplated."

Mason said nothing.

"I have not as yet seen the presiding judge," Judge Kippen said. "I doubtless will see him some time today. In thinking over in my own mind the series of developments which have taken place in this case I find myself completely unable to account for what has happened, and, furthermore, I cannot conceive of any explanation for the conduct of this witness, Irene Keith.

"She is a prominent woman. She is a wealthy woman. Her attitude in this matter is such that any comments that have heretofore been made by the newspapers will pale into insignificance beside the story which is undoubtely going to appear in the afternoon papers.

"Now, Helene Chaney, a prominent motion picture actress, has left the state in order to avoid questioning. Mervyn Aldrich, a wealthy businessman, has apparently left the state to avoid questioning. It's quite possible they will be married. Once they are married, under the law neither party can be called to testify for or against the other without the other's permission.

"Irene Keith doubtless would have left the state had it not been for your foresight in serving a subpoena on her. As she is acting on the advice of counsel, one can only assume that she has retained the best of counsel.

"Now then, I am going to be fair with this defendant. If a crime has been committed, and it undoubtedly has, and there is reasonable ground to believe that she committed the crime, I am going to bind her over. If, on the other hand, it appears that the crime was committed by someone else, I think it is only fair to the Court and to the prosecutor that the authorities be given an opportunity to apprehend that person and try to bring about a conviction."

Again Mason nodded.

"Now then," Judge Kippen said, "I have placed the cards on the table. The prosecutor has absolutely no inkling as to what is in back of Irene Keith's mind. Apparently you are the only one who comprehends it. I'd like to know what it is."

Judge Kippen made a motion with his hands indicating he had said all he wanted to say.

Mason said, "I want to explain my position. The law makes it a misdemeanor to practice fraud or deceit on a person who is about to be called as a witness so as to affect the testimony of that witness.

"On the other hand, I don't believe that an attorney is called upon to do all of his cross-examination in the courtroom and by question and answer. Now then, I had this gun, given to me by Evelyn Bagby. I didn't substitute guns, but when some other person did switch guns on me, thinking thereby to confuse the issues in the case, I took steps to see that what this person had done would inevitably be detected."

"Are you trying to tell me that you took the substituted gun and fired a bullet into a redwood post and into an oak tree?" Judge Kippen asked, his face grave.

Mason grinned. *"That's what I'm trying to keep from telling you."*

Judge Kippen suddenly laughed. "Very well. Go on."

"Now something happened on the tenth of this month so that Steve Merrill was able to secure seventy-five hundred dollars in cash. I have the feeling that he also secured the gun, People's Exhibit E, at that time."

"Then what about People's Exhibit A? How did that gun get into the case?"

Mason smiled. "You heard the testimony."

"You aren't being very much help, Mr. Mason."

Mason said, "If you want to give me a free hand, I'll go back into court and try to unscramble this thing. If I do that the presiding judge will think your courtroom has been desecrated by drama, but before we get done we're pretty apt to have the murder case solved."

Judge Kippen rubbed his chin thoughtfully. "What makes you think you can solve it?" he asked. "The prosecution doesn't have the vaguest idea."

"That's the trouble. The prosecutor's idea *is* vague," Mason said.

"Well, what do you have to go on?"

"Simply this. Whoever murdered Steve Merrill was someone sufficiently close to him to be with him in the automobile, to know about the gun, to know about Evelyn Bagby's claim against Merrill.

"It had to be someone who had Merrill's confidence. That person killed Merrill and parked the car containing the body on an unfrequented side road. Then the murderer cleaned and reloaded the murder weapon and planted it in Evelyn Bagby's room where she'd be sure to find it.

"The murderer stole a pillow slip, went over to some nearby houses that were under construction, watched with binoculars until he knew Evelyn Bagby had found the gun. Then when she started to drive away, taking the gun to me as he knew she would, he followed her, the pillow slip over his head, frightened her into taking two wild shots, then stopped his car and let her go, feeling certain she was on her way to meet me, and that I would notify the police.

"It only remained for him to go back to the car where he had left Merrill, fit the pillow slip over his head and drive his car well down the grade and let it go."

"That's a fine, ingenious theory," Judge Kippen said, "but unfortunately, it isn't implemented by facts."

"Give me a free hand and I'll get the facts," Mason said.

Judge Kippen thought it over. "If you can uncover what happened by keeping within the strict letter of procedural law, that is all right, but if Hamilton Burger objects and his objections are well taken, I'm going to sustain them."

"Thank you," Mason said. "I guess we understand each other perfectly, Judge."

Mason pushed back his chair and got to his feet.

"I'm not certain that we do," Judge Kippen said, somewhat petulantly. "You've left me high and dry in a devil of a position."

"Well," Mason told him, "being high and dry may not be a bad position to be in. Hamilton Burger has his feet wet and he doesn't know which way to turn for fear of falling in over his head."

Mason beckoned to Neely, and the two lawyers walked out of Judge Kippen's chambers, leaving the judge standing there annoyed, baffled and somewhat irresolute, watching them as they filed through the door.

20

JUDGE KIPPEN ENTERED THE COURTROOM, HIS FACE INdicating plainly that his mind was made up.

"Is there any further evidence in this case?"

Mason said, "I have one more witness, Your Honor."

"Very well."

"Call Mr. Oscar Loomis."

Loomis came forward.

Judge Kippen said, "Now, Mr. Mason, you're calling Mr. Loomis as your witness?"

"Yes, Your Honor."

"Very well. Proceed."

"Mr. Loomis were you acquainted with Stephen Merrill in his lifetime?"

"Yes."

"How long had you known him?"

"Quite a little while. We lived in the same apartment house."

"Are you acquainted with Mr. Harry Boles?"

"Yes."

"How long had you known him?"

"Two or three months."

"How did you meet him?"

"Through Steve Merrill. He and Steve were friends. He used to come to visit Steve and then on the ninth he moved into a vacant apartment on the same floor with us."

"Now at the time Mr. Merrill's body was found it was found in *your* car and you had previously reported to the police that your car had been stolen."

"Yes."

"Did you see Mr. Boles on that day?"

"Yes, sir."

"When?"

"About five o'clock, I guess. I was walking around cussing because my car had been stolen. Mr. Boles came along and started talking with us."

"You say he talked 'with us?' "

"Yes. My girl friend was with me."

"What is her name?"

"Ruby Inwood."

"You've known her for some time?"

"Oh yes, I've known her for quite a while. She lives in the apartment house, too."

"What happened after you met Boles around five o'clock?"

"Well, Mr. Boles was the first one who pointed out to me that perhaps Merrill had taken my car by mistake, that his car was—"

"Now just a minute, Your Honor," Hamilton Burger said. "I don't know what counsel is getting at, but I am going to insist that we have no hearsay evidence here. I object to anything that was said by Mr. Boles."

"Sustained."

"Then what did you do after talking with Mr. Boles?"

"Well, I rang up the police and told them maybe a mistake had been made, that I didn't want to accuse anybody of being a thief, that if Steve Merrill was in my car it might be because he had made a mistake."

"Thereafter were you in company with Mr. Boles?"

"Yes, sir."

"How long?"

"From a few minutes before five up until about, oh, I guess eight-thirty or nine o'clock."

"Who else was with you?"

"Ruby Inwood."

"Is she here in court?"

"Yes, sir."

"That's all," Mason said. "Call Miss Inwood."

"No questions," Hamilton Burger said, visibly relieved that Mason hadn't tossed some sort of a legal bombshell into his lap.

Ruby Inwood came forward and was sworn. She was an attractive brunette with snapping black eyes and was conscious of a good figure.

"You knew Mr. Merrill in his lifetime?" Mason asked.

"Yes, sir."

"Did you see him on the tenth?"

"Yes, sir."

"How long had you known him?"

"Several months."

"You know Mr. Boles?"

"Yes."

"And Mr. Loomis?"

"Yes."

"They are your friends?"

"Yes."

"Were you more friendly with Mr. Merrill than with Mr. Loomis?"

"Mr. Loomis is my boy friend," she said with dignity.

"But you were friendly with Mr. Merrill?"

"Oh, yes."

"Now on the tenth of this month did Mr. Merrill show you a sum of money, a large number of fifty- and hundred-dollar bills and tell you—?"

"Just a minute, just a minute," Hamilton Burger said. "I'm going to object to hearsay evidence. It doesn't make any difference whether Mr. Merrill showed her a lot of bills or not."

Mason smiled. "It shows motive, Your Honor."

"Motive!" Judge Kippen echoed. "What do you mean?"

"It shows motive for the murder of Stephen Merrill. If he had a large sum of money in his possession that would in itself be a good motive for murder."

Judge Kippen said, "Well, I'll permit evidence as to the money but not as to any conversation about the money."

"Very well," Mason said. "Did you see a large number of bills, Miss Inwood?"

"I did."

"Did you see this gun in his possession, and I am now holding up for your inspection a gun marked People's Exhibit E?"

"I saw a gun just like that."

"Did he tell you where he got that gun?"

"Same objection," Burger said.

"Same ruling."

"Did he tell you that he had received a terrific jolt and that he was going to have to make a pay-off to Evelyn Bagby, the defendant in this case?"

Hamilton Burger said, "I object, Your Honor. I—no, I don't either. I withdraw the objection."

"Yes, he told me that. I sometimes took telephone messages for the tenants when they were out. You see there's only one telephone on each floor of the apartment house.

"On the tenth I took a message for Mr. Merrill, a message from the defendant, Evelyn Bagby. She gave me her name, address, phone number and the message.

"I gave that message to Mr. Merrill shortly after noon. He was terribly upset. He told me something from his past life had cropped up to plague him, something he thought was dead and buried. He said he had to raise some money fast.

"Then about three o'clock he said he had the money. He showed it to me—and also the gun.

"He said he was to meet the defendant and that he was going to offer her two thousand dollars and not a cent more."

"Now then," Mason said, "You and Mr. Loomis, whom you have characterized as your boy friend, went out to dinner with Harry Boles on the night of the tenth?"

"Yes, sir."

"Where did you go?"

"To a roadhouse out on North Broadway."

"How did you go? In a taxicab?"

"No, we went in my car."

"And you were there how long?"

"Until about eight o'clock or eight-thirty."

"Then what?"

"Then we went back home in my car, and I loaned it to Harry Boles who wanted to see a woman about some money. Shortly after that the police advised Mr. Loomis that they had located his car."

"What kind of a car were you driving?"

"A Ford."

"What kind of a car are you driving now?"

"A Ford."

"The same car that you were driving on the tenth?"

"No, I have a new car."

"Oh, you have a new car now?"

"Yes."

"When was it delivered to you?"

"On the morning of the eleventh."

"Did you buy it yourself or was it given to you?"

"Oh, Your Honor, that's objected to as incompetent, irrelevant and immaterial," Burger said.

"Sustained."

"May I be heard on that question, Your Honor?" Mason asked.

"I think it is plainly irrelevant, Mr. Mason."

"When you bought this new Ford you turned the old one in?"

"Yes."

"And that car was turned in on the morning of the eleventh?"

"Yes."

"And you took delivery of the new car immediately?"

"Yes."

"Did you turn this automobile in or did someone turn it in for you?"

"Someone turned it in for me."

"Now," Mason said, "Your Honor, I would like to have the Court issue a subpoena *duces tecum* by which the agency which has this automobile will bring it into court. I propose to show that there is a bullet hole in that automobile."

"A bullet hole in that automobile!" Judge Kippen said, surprised.

"Exactly, Your Honor. We are one bullet short."

"One bullet short! I don't understand you. It seems to me that we have two too many bullets."

"No, Your Honor," Mason said. "The defendant fired two shots at the man who was pursuing her, whose face was covered with a pillow slip. One shot apparently lodged in the attic of the residence of Mary Eunice. The defendant said that when she fired the second shot she heard a peculiar metallic click. I think that shot must have hit the automobile of the car that was pursuing her. I think the reason that the car owned by Miss Inwood was traded in the next morning, without Miss Inwood having had an opportunity to see it, was that there was a bullet hole in that car.

"Now then, Your Honor," Mason said, turning and pointing his finger at Oscar Loomis, "as the reason for asking for this subpoena *duces tecum,* and to show what I expect to prove by that car once it has been brought in, I offer to prove that this entire testimony about what happened on the evening of the tenth, about Loomis, Inwood and Boles going to dinner, is a complete fabrication. I offer to prove that Boles and Miss Inwood did go to dinner while Oscar Loomis took Miss Inwood's car and went up the mountain grade to ambush Evelyn Bagby when she started down the hill. I offer to prove that after he had trapped the defendant into firing two shots he—"

"Oh just a moment," Hamilton Burger said. "Here we go again on a wild theory that—"

Judge Kippen said, "Sit down, Mr. Prosecutor. Be quiet. Let Mr. Mason finish his offer. Then you can object."

Burger gulped and sat down.

Mason said, "I offer to prove what happened by means of the testimony of the people who took Miss Inwood's car in on a trade and I want to interrogate the people who run the restaurant where they were supposed to have eaten."

Ruby Inwood on the stand, who had been listening to Mason with white-faced tensity, suddenly exploded into speech. "No, no, no!" she screamed. "Don't try to blame that on Oscar. It's just the other way around. It was Harry Boles who asked us to give him an alibi. He borrowed my car for the evening. He paid me twenty-five dollars for the use of it and agreed to furnish all the gas and oil. Then he showed up about eight-thirty and said he'd had a slight accident to the car, that he was going to get me a new car, that it would be delivered the next morning, and in return I was to say that he'd been with us all the time because he didn't want to be stuck for damages in the traffic accident he'd had. I never thought he could be mixed up in this murder. You can't blame it on Oscar. Oscar really *was* with me, weren't you, Oscar? Come up here and tell the truth."

Judge Kippen leaned forward. "Come up here, Oscar Loomis," he said, "and Boles—where's Boles?—Harry Boles. The Court orders you to remain as a witness, not to leave the courtroom. Where's Boles?"

Mason smiled and sat down.

Judge Kippen said, "Mr. Bailiff, get Boles. Bring him up here."

Someone in the back of the courtroom volunteered the statement, "He went out a few minutes ago."

Oscar Loomis said, "She's telling the truth. We didn't bargain for no murder alibi, just for keeping him out of trouble on that auto smash-up."

Hamilton Burger lunged to his feet. "Your Honor," he said, "this is—"

"Sit down," Judge Kippen snapped. "We'll get this unscrambled in a minute. I'm going to have Mr. Boles in here. Now as I understand it, Miss Inwood, you have testified to a false alibi for Mr. Boles?"

"Only for the automobile case."

"And you, Loomis?"

"The same," Loomis said.

"All right," Judge Kippen said. "I'm ordering you into custody. Mr. District Attorney, I would suggest that if Mr. Boles is not immediately available you send out a broadcast. Court is going to take a recess until the police can check on that automobile which was turned in to the Ford Agency on the morning of the eleventh. If there's a bullet hole in that car I want to know it.

"Now then, Miss Inwood, you and Oscar Loomis are in custody. Court's adjourned."

21

■

MASON, DELLA STREET, FRANK NEELY, EVELYN BAGBY and Paul Drake gathered in Mason's office.

"I suppose," Drake said to Perry Mason, "you'll claim that you knew it all along."

"No, I didn't," Mason said, "but I felt certain that Evelyn Bagby was telling the truth. I knew that Aldrich has substituted guns—in fact I felt pretty certain that he would substitute guns if I gave him a chance to do so." Mason smiled reminiscently and added, "I believe that an attorney should capitalize on anything that will give his client a break."

Drake shook his head.

Gertie appeared at the door, her eyes wide. "Miss Irene Keith on the telephone, Mr. Mason. She says she has to talk with you right away."

Mason picked up the telephone, said, "Hello," and motioned to Della Street to pick up the extension phone.

Della Street picked up the phone, then frantically started making notes in her notebook.

From time to time Mason asked questions, then at length he hung up the telephone.

"All right," Drake said, "we're bursting with curiosity. What is it?"

Mason said, "Well, we finally have the parts of the puzzle pretty well fitted together. Merrill had bribed Celeste, Irene Keith's maid, to keep him posted on developments, because Merrill was trying to get a settlement out of Helene Chaney without going to court. He waited, thinking Helene would settle. But Aldrich told Helene she wasn't to pay so much as a dime. He planned a quick trip to Las Vegas, and a wedding there.

"So at the last minute Merrill knew he had no alternative but to go to court, something that he didn't want to do.

"Then, to add to his troubles, Evelyn Bagby telephoned him from Corona where she was staying, telling him she had recognized his picture as that of the man who had embezzled her money.

"Merrill knew, through Celeste, that there was to be a rendezvous at Corona. His brain hatched out a beautiful scheme by which he could steal about forty-thousand dollars' worth of jewels, have Evelyn Bagby convicted of a felony so that if she ever tried to testify against him he could prove she had a criminal record, and at the same time delay the wedding of Helene Chaney and Mervyn Aldrich so he could file an action in Court, something he had been putting off as long as possible because he felt a court would eventually rule against him. His strongest play was to try for a settlement, using the threat of court action as a club.

"Boles was really a tool of Merrill's. On the day of the theft, while Helene Chaney and Irene Keith were in the beauty parlor, Celeste, the maid, put on Irene Keith's clothes, wore dark glasses—not particularly intending to involve Irene Keith, but by way of a disguise as a protection to herself—went to Corona, got into Evelyn Bagby's cabin with a passkey, planted the diamond bracelet, then went back to Hollywood to be there when Irene Keith returned from her luncheon with Helene Chaney.

"Celeste helped Irene pack up. Irene packed the jewelry in a suitcase. Celeste surreptitiously took it all out, closed the suitcase and put it in the back of Irene's car. She had also, of course, given Merrill a key to the trunk compartment of this car. Merrill turned this key over to Boles. It was only necessary for Boles to wait until the parties had made their rendezvous in Corona to open up the back of the car. Because Aldrich was a stickler for being on time, it was certain that Helene Chaney and Irene would arrive early so that no matter what happened they wouldn't keep him waiting. So they left the car and went to the cocktail lounge where the parties were to rendezvous.

"Irene Keith began to get an inkling of what might have happened at the time of Evelyn's trial. That was why she suddenly became so anxious to effect a settlement with Evelyn. You see, if the theft had been consummated by Irene's servant, Irene was afraid she might be vulnerable in a suit for false arrest, despite the fact that her attorney advised her to sit tight.

"Then after Evelyn was acquitted, Merrill called on Irene and put his cards on the table. He had forty-thousand dollars' worth of jewelry. He offered to return it all to her provided she would give him seventy-five hundred dollars in cash and guarantee that no questions would be asked. She consulted her attorney who advised her to put a microphone in the room, make a tape recording and then call the police. He told Irene that if she paid the money she would technically be guilty of compounding a felony. Nevertheless there was forty-thousand dollars' worth of jewelry that Irene could get back for seventy-five hundred, and she wanted to go ahead with the deal. She told Helene Chaney what was in the wind and Helene loaned Irene the gun Aldrich had given her.

"When it came time to make the settlement Merrill was suspicious. He looked around and found the hidden microphone, followed the wires to the tape recorder, smashed the tape recorder and confiscated the tape. Irene pulled the gun on him but he made a quick lunge at her and grabbed the gun. So then Irene made the deal, giving him the seventy-five hundred dollars and taking the jewelry.

"Irene Keith knew that I had figured what happened, so she decided to call up and put her cards on the table. She wanted to make a deal and get the whole thing cleaned up."

"What about the murder?" Drake asked.

"From there on we're going to have to rely on surmise because evidently Boles was to get a payoff. He and Merrill quarreled about the amount of money he had coming, and Boles grabbed the gun out of the glove compartment of the car and shot Merrill.

"We don't know just how much pressure was being put on Merrill or by whom. He had mentioned a gambling debt he had to pay and he wanted to make a settlement with Evelyn Bagby. In any event, he had evidently set his mind on a figure of seventy-five hundred dollars and was willing to do almost anything to get it.

"Boles probably had no intention whatever of killing Merrill when they started out. Merrill wanted to drive up to the Crowncrest Tavern, have a talk with Evelyn and make the best settlement he could. Probably he was relying on his powers of persuasion to give her a few hundred dollars, make her a lot of glittering promises and get her to agree not to prosecute him on that old charge.

"Merrill was driving a rented car. He wasn't too familiar with it. It was exactly the same make and model as the car which belonged to Loomis, and, as sometimes happens with cars of a certain make, the ignition keys must have been interchangeable.

"As I deduce what must have happened, Boles and Merrill got to quarreling about how much Boles was to get as his share. Boles probably wanted his cut off the top. Merrill wanted to give Boles a percentage of what was left after he had settled with Evelyn. They quarreled. Merrill had previously shown Boles the gun he had taken from Irene Keith and had put it in the glove compartment, grabbed the gun and threatened Merrill. Merrill tried to grab the gun and Boles pulled the trigger. It was one of those things that happened so suddenly that before Boles fully realized what had happened he found himself with a dead man on his hands.

"Naturally Boles' first thought was to implicate someone else, and Evelyn Bagby was the logical person.

"I am assuming that the murder took place when Merrill was on his way up to talk with Evelyn. The actual killing may not have been too far from the place where the body was found. Boles found an unfrequented side road, drove the car with Merrill's body in there, took the seventy-five hundred dollars from Merrill, cleaned and reloaded the gun, went to the Crowncrest Tavern, found Evelyn was out, deduced that she would be shopping and that when she returned she'd have some clothes to put in the dresser drawers.

"So Boles planted the gun, pulled off one of the pillow slips, hitchhiked his way back to Hollywood, and borrowed Ruby Inwood's car, paying her twenty-five dollars for the use of it.

"That probably was about the time Loomis discovered that his car was gone and reported it as having been stolen. That gave Boles a splendid opportunity to plan an alibi and so he told Loomis that he had seen Merrill driving away only a few minutes before and that there was a possibility Merrill had taken Loomis' car by mistake. Boles said there was some woman in the car with Merrill, that he didn't know who she was. That gave him a further chance to frame the crime on Evelyn and helped give him an alibi because it made it appear Merrill was alive shortly before five o'clock.

"Boles had planted the murder gun in the drawer of Evelyn's dresser. He felt certain she would find it. She would hardly dare report to the police in view of the fact that she had previously found jewelry which had been planted. He therefore felt certain Evelyn would telephone me and that I would instruct her to bring the gun to me at once so that it wouldn't be found in her possession.

"If she didn't walk into that trap then the police would find Merrill's body and would subsequently find the fatal gun in Evelyn's possession.

"However, Evelyn played right into Boles' hands. He was watching her from one of those newly constructed houses with binoculars. He saw her find the gun, then he saw her get into her car and start down the grade.

"From that time on no matter what happened the cards were bound to fall the way Boles wanted them. He tried to crowd Evelyn off the road. If she had gone over the grade and down the hill Boles would have worked his way down to where her car was wrecked, fired a shell from the gun, left it with Evelyn, then slipped the pillow slip over Merrill's head and run the car with Merrill's body in it off the grade at almost the same place.

"It would then appear that Evelyn had shot Merrill, had lost control of her car, gone over the grade and been killed.

"If, on the other hand, she did the most logical thing, grabbed the gun and fired wildly, Boles knew he had her in his power. The only thing that Boles hadn't anticipated was that one of the wild shots she fired would go through the hood or the fender of Ruby Inwood's automobile.

"When that happened Boles was faced with a problem. He returned to where he had left the body of Merrill, punched a hole in the pillow slip, probably with a jack handle, put the pillow slip over Merrill's head, drove the car off the road and—"

"But why didn't he turn the lights on?" Drake asked. "He must have had to have them on in order to see where he was going and—"

"He deliberately turned the lights off," Mason said, "because he wanted Evelyn to tell her story and wanted it to be proven false. He knew that the pillow slip would be identified as having come from her bed, that if the officers looked soon enough they could prove the hole in the pillow slip wasn't a bullet hole. By turning the lights off just before he let the car plunge on down the grade he gave the officers such an obvious clue that he felt certain they would start suspecting Evelyn right away."

"Gosh," Drake said, "can we prove all that?"

"We can prove it," Mason said, "because, unfortunately for Boles, Irene Keith was smart enough to keep the numbers of the bills she withdrew from the bank which she paid to Merrill, and which, in turn, Boles took from Merrill after he had committed the murder. Boles must have used those bills to pay for the new car for Ruby Inwood, and there undoubtedly is a bullet hole in that car of Ruby's which was turned in. That's why Boles invented the story of the traffic accident. It gave him a good excuse to ask Ruby Inwood and Oscar Loomis to furnish him with an alibi and it enabled him to give a good reason for trading in Ruby's car."

"Incidentally," Mason said, "Irene Keith has just made an offer of twenty-thousand dollars for a complete settlement with Evelyn Bagby. I told her I thought that would be all right."

"Twenty . . . thousand . . . dollars!" Evelyn Bagby exclaimed.

"That's right," Mason said. "That will get you a lot of clothes so you can have a good screen test. In view of the publicity you've had I don't think you'll have much trouble getting that screen test now. It will also give Neely a pretty good fee for trying the larceny case, enable me to pay for Paul Drake's services and have a little left over."

"And all you had to go on all this time was faith in me?" Evelyn Bagby asked with tears in her eyes.

"Well," Mason said, "I always have faith in my clients, Evelyn, but after I thought over what you had said about the way that second bullet made a peculiar clicking noise I began to wonder if it hadn't hit the automobile. So when I learned that Ruby Inwood was driving a new automobile the next morning I began to put two and two together."

"You put two and two together and made ten," Drake said.

Mason said, "This case is a very good example of how small, seemingly insignificant facts can be determinative. There were two facts, the new car and the sound of the second bullet striking something that when properly interpreted gave us a key to everything."

Neely took out his handkerchief and wiped his forehead.

"If it's all right by you, Mr. Mason," he said, "I'm going right back to Riverside and build up a law business in the conventional manner. Following you around the last few days has made me so dizzy I don't think I'll ever get back to my normal routine."

"There isn't any normal routine when you're dealing with redheads," Mason told him, grinning.